Revenge Never Dies

MASOCHIST

NADIA AIDAN

Masochist
ISBN # 978-0-85715-980-9
© Copyright Nadia Aidan 2012
Cover Art by Posh Gosh © Copyright March 2012
Interior text design by Claire Siemaszkiewicz
Total-E-Bound Publishing

Published in 2010 by Total-E-Bound Publishing, Think Tank, Ruston Way, Lincoln, LN6 7FL, United Kingdom.

Total-E-Bound Publishing books by Nadia Aidan:

Downing Brothers
Sleeping with the Enemy's Daughter
A Rebound Affair

Heroes and Harlots
A Madam into a Mistress

On a Dare
Every Desire
A Wicked, Wild Three Day Affair
Undercovers
Mating Season
Sex Therapy
On a Whim
Even the Devil Needs Love

MASOCHIST

Dedication

To Melynda P.

Chapter One

La Ville des Dieux...

The city of the gods.

Selena knew better. It was a city full of demons, devils, evil that preyed upon the weak, the vulnerable, the pitiless and the poor.

Mortal men owned the city, controlling the lives of all who lived within its vast borders. They called themselves gods. They weren't. They were just men, with the faces of angels, godlike bearings...but they shared the weaknesses of all men — their sins, their lusts, their desires.

Selena pulled her black silk shawl up higher around her face, slipping through the crowd of patrons who'd come to *La Maison d'Adonis* — the house of Adonis — for the grand opening of the opulent hotel that would bear the owner's name. It was a place of decadence and finery, the gilded golden luxury of the establishment as perfectly and beautifully made as the man himself.

Adonis.

The proprietor of the western district of *La Ville des Dieux* — the most beautiful of the four gods...and the cruellest of them all.

She was dressed in a floor-length, black gown, the sequins twinkling beneath the warm glow of the crystal chandeliers. Her dress was subtle, understated, yet flattering as it raised her full breasts and flared at her rounded hips. The expensive attire had cost her two months' salary, but it was worth it — the expense, the sacrifices would all be worth it, very soon. The dress was necessary. Its opulence gained her entrance — its modesty allowed her to pass through the crowd without notice.

And that was exactly what she wanted — to pass without notice. No one would expect a simple, diminutive beauty who wore the crucifix of His Saviour draped around her neck — the outward symbol of God's handmaiden...a nun by any other name — to do harm to a single person. But her sole purpose for being there *was* to do harm and to reclaim that which had been cruelly taken from her sixteen years ago.

Selena left the crowded ballroom and glided beyond the guest bathrooms into the elevator and rode to the forty-second floor. She then got off, silently disarmed the lock and slipped into the stairwell to climb the last three floors to the penthouse level. A guard awaited her as soon as her heeled feet left the dull grey concrete of the stairwell and sank into the plush, burgundy carpet.

"Excuse me, Sister, but I cannot allow you back here. The chambers in this hallway are private."

The guard was young, handsome...beautiful, as all of the *god's* men were. He favoured beautiful things and beautiful people to mirror the perfect beauty of his own flawless face. That was why he'd taken her, defiled her—her beauty had reputedly surpassed his. But not anymore. Outwardly, maybe, but deep inside she was ugly, the core of her vile and hideous.

She knew what the guard saw when he looked at her—an ethereal angel, a stunning being touched by the divine. She smiled, disarming him with her loveliness before disarming him with her weapon. She raised her hand, trained the gun on his neck and pulled the trigger.

His eyes widened as he clutched his throat and gasped then crumpled at her feet in a heap.

Every movement was muffled, almost silent.

She stepped over the beautiful man and turned the corner. *His* room, she could easily tell, for another two guards stood before the double oak doors.

Selena smiled as she approached and the two men fell under her spell.

Her smile mimicked the pure luminescence of warm sunshine peeking through the dull grey of winter clouds. Before either could react, she shot them both, also in the neck. The mild neurotonic venom seeping through their blood stream would cause immediate paralysis. Unconsciousness would follow in seconds. They would think they were dying. But all would awaken…long after she was gone.

Only one needed to die this night.

She stepped over the prostrate guards and knocked gently on the door. There was no need for pretence. He knew she would come, for she'd told him. Sixteen years ago he'd taken her innocence and destroyed every dream she'd ever had. And sixteen years ago she'd promised him she would do the same to him someday. When he was at the pinnacle of success, she'd promised, she would destroy him as cruelly and carelessly as he'd once destroyed her. She kept every single one of her promises. She'd warned him then. And with a letter just weeks ago, she'd warned him again.

There was no need for pretence for he knew she was there, knew why she was there, just as he knew nothing would stop her.

Adonis.

He bore the face of an angel, and, with a simple touch, a single look, he could inflame the passions of both women *and* men.

His beauty and the desire he ignited with his touch—some said it was his gift, others said it was his curse

As Adonis stood in the doorway to his suite, staring into the ravished eyes of his past, he knew that this woman who had found pleasure beneath his touch was equally cursed by it.

He stepped aside and let her in.

The cobra entering the lion's den. She was small...delicate even. To be disarmed by her diminutive stature was to be foolish. She was dangerous, deadly, and she'd come there to kill.

He closed the door behind her with a soft, ominous thud—the locking of the door sealing his fate...and hers. Tonight would forever change their lives, just as that night sixteen years ago—on this very same date—had irreparably altered their destinies.

There was no turning back—no space for redemption, for forgiveness.

"Selena."

She turned at the deep, husky lilt of her name on his lips. His accent was rich and heady, like potent brandy. Her shawl slipped to her shoulders as she lifted her head and met his gaze.

Piercing amber eyes bore into her, seeing through her, inside her, searing her body, marking her very soul. She shuddered despite herself. He knew the effect he had on women, men...*her*. Yet he did not gloat—he appeared to take no pleasure in the tightening of her nipples against her dress, the slight dilation of her pupils. And for a moment she wondered *why*?

"You know why I am here." Selena spoke softly, deliberately avoiding the use of his name. The last time she'd said it, she'd cried it out in the wake of blinding pleasure. Every time she thought his name, she heard it floating from her lips in the throes of release and it shamed her.

"I do," he said, crossing the room, his back to her. His long strides ate up the distance between him and the bar hidden in a shadowed corner of the expansive suite. It was a long while before he turned to face her again, a small glass of liquor in his hand.

"You are here to kill me," he uttered after swallowing the contents of his glass in a single gulp.

"And, yet, you are relaxed for a man who is about to die." His easy manner was her first clue.

"Am I about to die, Selena?" He set his glass down.

"You know why I am here," she repeated. She should have felt fear...been anxious, wary. He would not simply lie down and allow her to take his life. She knew this—just as surely as she knew, no matter the trap he sprang, she was ready, and she would prevail. Her lust for revenge would accept no less.

"You are here to kill me, but that does not mean I shall die."

Her eyes narrowed.

"You desire revenge, and you shall have it." He stalked across the room towards her, his steps deliberate. He moved with a sensual, practiced grace that demanded attention, that captivated and seduced.

Selena felt the pull of that attraction all the way to the core of her, even as she pushed it to the dark corners of her mind and ignored it. His seductive grace was both sexual and deadly. He was a predator — a killer — trained to take life, to destroy it...just as he was a trained seducer — the bringer of pleasure — trained to inspire lust and fuel it.

"Revenge is a strange thing, Selena. It consumes its owner. It consumes their life." He halted before her, his breath sweet and heavy against her face. The pungent scent of alcohol tickled her nostrils with each breath she drew in.

"I imagine you have killed me a thousand times — swiftly, slowly, painfully, mercilessly..." He smiled, the perfect smile of an angel, a god. "But death, whether painful and slow or swift and merciful, is not what you seek. To deliver death to one such as I would be too kind. I deserve more than death." His breath hovered between them and her heart thudded to the rhythm of his inhalation, his exhalation. She tried to remain unaffected by him — yet she couldn't. With every breath, every smile, every blink of his eyes, she was all too painfully aware until her senses were full of him.

"What would you have me do, then?" She managed to find her voice somewhere between determination and desire. "If not death, then what do you deserve?"

"Revenge, Selena. I deserve your revenge." He transformed before her eyes. The seducer became the killer. His eyes hardened and the perfect beauty of his face darkened.

He slammed her against the wall in a matter of seconds, forcing the air to whoosh from her lungs, his arm pinned to her neck. She didn't move or flinch. Her eyes didn't widen, and she didn't gasp for air.

She nudged the sharp blade of the knife she'd drawn from beneath her dress, strapped to her silken thigh, against his belly, ready to rip through muscle and flesh, bone and entrails with a single, deadly thrust.

"You deserve every measure of my revenge," she breathed out against the pressure along her neck. "That is why I shall kill you." Her eyes became topaz slits. "I could kill you now. With just a simple flick of my wrist, I could end your life."

"But you won't."

His words startled her.

"If you wanted me dead, I would be dead." He leaned in, his liquor-laced, sweet breath warming her face. "You do not want me dead, because you want me to suffer. And I deserve to suffer."

Pain—naked, raw pain—swirled in the depths of his golden eyes. He hurt for her. He suffered for her. She did not care. His pain and his suffering were not enough.

"I deserve your hate. I deserve your revenge." He drew away from her, her neck free so she could breathe. And then she couldn't. She couldn't breathe as she watched him remove his tuxedo jacket, followed by his black cummerbund. Then the long, tanned length of his fingers began to undo the buttons of his white dress shirt.

"What are you doing?"

"I am giving you your revenge."

"What? By stripping naked? How is that my revenge?" she spat.

His eyes held hers, and she saw herself, sixteen years ago to the day. A nineteen year-old girl on the cusp of womanhood—full of innocence and blind naiveté.

He'd taken her innocence, taken her youth…her virtue. She'd never been the same after that. After that night, she'd been broken, crippled, irreparably and irrevocably damaged.

His shirt hung open, revealing the golden planes of his hard muscled torso. Hair a darker hue than the silver blond locks that hung to his shoulders wove a straight path across the centre of his ridged abdomen, disappearing into the waistband of his trousers.

He was beautiful, as perfect as an angel, a god…

He was the devil himself.

"You cannot have your revenge if I am fully clothed. That would be less than I deserve. Just as the peacefulness of death would be less than I deserve."

"And what is it that you deserve?" she asked softly, almost breathless.

"I deserve to suffer as you did." His full sensual mouth dipped, and even his frown was seductive. "I deserve to experience the pain you experienced, the loss you felt. I deserve your revenge."

She suddenly burned with anger — an emotion she'd thought she'd buried long ago and replaced by cold, calculated hatred. "You can never suffer as I did. You will never know the pain I felt, the loss I experienced. You destroyed my life. Killing you is the only way to destroy yours."

He looked down his nose at her. "If that were true then you would not hesitate."

Her palm throbbed under the weight of the knife in her hand, the braided leather of the hilt heavy in her grasp.

Four paces separated them, maybe less. She'd been trained to hurl a blade from much farther, with deadly accuracy. Her eyes narrowed on his chest. His death would be painful, but it would be quick.

"I deserve to suffer, Selena," he whispered, drawing her attention to his face. His golden eyes practically begged it of her. *I deserve your revenge, your pain. I deserve it all.*

"It is impossible for you to experience what I did," she rasped, her voice suddenly ragged and hoarse.

"Is it?"

His eyes flickered and she followed the direction of his gaze to his bedside table. And that was when she saw it — the hard, sculpted object that lay there, benign for now — an innocent tool for pleasure that could easily wield pain. Nothing shocked her anymore, had not since that day sixteen years ago…until now.

"I will still destroy you in the end," she remarked coldly. "Why endure this humiliation only to die?"

"Because I deserve it. I deserve to know the pain you did."

She glared at him. "I do not believe you will truly suffer. I believe you will enjoy it."

"I might." His lips curled into a knowing grin, and her blood turned to scarlet ice at the male satisfaction blazing in his eyes. "I might enjoy it just as you did."

His head swivelled violently with the impact as she struck his face.

"I did not enjoy what you did to me. I hated it. Every moment of it, I hated."

Fury lashed him, not because of his burning cheek, but because the sweet smell of her desire hovered between them heavy in the air, filling up every crevice inside his lungs, just as it had sixteen years ago.

"You're a liar," he said coldly. "You cried out my name. Every time I made you come, you screamed my name in pleasure — none of it pain."

"There was no pleasure in what you did to me. You violated me."

He stilled. "I did." His hands curled into fists. "I had no choice."

"There is always a choice."

If she believed that then she was still the naive, foolish girl she'd been. He knew better...just as he knew it was easier for her to hate him—blame him—than to blame the one responsible or to admit that she was ashamed of her body's response. He'd been as much the victim as she, but she'd never believe that. And that was why he would allow her to have her revenge.

There was some measure of truth to her words. There was *always* a choice.

He could have let her die.

With her knife still firmly in her grasp, she circled him, a caged tiger assessing its prey. He held perfectly still, his gaze trained on the framed picture of a sallow, white orchid hanging along the grey wall of his suite.

She stopped before him, blocking out the image of the flower, trapping him with her swirling topaz eyes. She was so close he could touch her, nearly taste her on his lips and tongue. He drew in shallow breaths so the rich, heady scent of her wouldn't overwhelm his senses as it had only moments before.

"I have not been with a man since you."

Ice. Cold, frigid, unyielding ice hardened his insides, froze the blood in his veins. Her revelation was blurted out, as though wrenched from her, while her gaze danced back and forth between him and the object on his table.

"Why not?" His voice was ragged and raw, straining through the glacial barrier of his lungs.

Before she even spoke he glimpsed the pain, the damage he'd done. He tightened his fists so he wouldn't reach out and stroke her cheek...or slam one into the wall beside him.

"I could not trust anyone after you."

"You need not trust to give your body to another."

"I disagree." She cocked her head to the side, her ink-black hair slipping over one sequined shoulder. "To make love to a man, you must trust him implicitly with your body, your wants, your needs—"

"What we did was not making love," he lashed out and she reared back as if he'd struck her. He would never describe what they'd shared as making love. To even say it was to dishonour her, to disregard what she'd endured. "You should have taken a lover," he said, his voice softer this time.

"Why?"

To ease the pain of our time together...to fill you with new memories, happier memories.

"Why not?" was what he said instead as he stepped closer, but stopped when she shrank away.

She shrugged, but there was nothing casual about the raw emotion blazing across her face. "Soon after, I was shipped off to a convent. I never had the opportunity or the desire."

"You had the desire," he whispered, his expression daring her to say otherwise.

She didn't contradict him, at least not aloud. She remained silent but he heard what she did not say. He had been her only lover. He'd given her pleasure but he'd ravished her soul. With every thrust inside her body, he'd taken a piece of her beauty, her joy...the essence of her. She feared the inharmonious dichotomy of her body and mind. That was why she'd never taken a lover. She could not be certain of her body's response, that it wouldn't betray her as it had done once before...*with him.*

She feared the consequences of the intimacy that would come with making love. She'd once trusted him, once loved him, only to have been destroyed by him. She'd never recovered from what he'd done to her, but she longed to. That was truly why she was there. That was why she had yet to kill him. She didn't even realise it, but he did.

"I cannot promise you I have the power to fix this," he said finally, acknowledging what remained unspoken between them. "I have no idea how you will feel when this is over…"

"But?"

"I want you to feel again. I want you to trust again, to know true desire and revel in it."

"I don't know if I can do that."

He reached for the button that held his trousers together. Her nostrils flared as she watched him, and with achingly slow movements he unzipped his pants then slid them down his legs before kicking the discarded garment aside. He could almost feel her desire, her arousal, hovering between them.

She may not trust, but she wanted. She still desired.

He stood fully naked before her, his skin bare beneath the warm lights

"What would you have me do next?"

She glanced over to his table for the third time.

"This does not change anything," she said finally after a long silence. "I will still kill you in the end."

He nodded in understanding. She would exact her revenge upon his body then do what she'd ultimately come there to do.

"That is your choice."

There was *always* a choice.

The air in Selena's chest remained trapped there, suspended in her lungs. Sixteen years ago she'd been helpless, at his mercy. He'd stripped her of her power and control. Now he wished to return it.

It was too late.

She would have her revenge, and then she would take his life. She just hoped it did not cost her what was left of her soul.

"You can put the knife down. I will not take it from you, nor will I stop you when you decide to use it. But you won't need it for what comes next."

That raised her eyebrows. "You do not care that after I use you I plan to kill you?"

Her words raised *his* eyebrows. "I resigned myself to death long ago." He turned his back to her. "And if anyone deserves to die by your hands, it is me."

She registered his declaration with silence as she wordlessly studied the ridges along his back. His flesh was puckered and welted, and the red scars stared angrily at her. They had not been there before. He'd been burned, whipped...

His entire back had been marred with fire and lashes. The perfect beauty of his muscled frame, a sculpted Adonis... It was *flawed. He* was flawed— imperfect.

"What happened to your back?"

He looked at her from over his shoulder, his golden hair gently caressing his sun-bronzed skin.

"I was punished."

She sheathed her knife. He was right—she did not need it for what would come next. Whatever demons haunted Adonis, they were the reason why he would not stop her when she sought his death. Gazing upon him, looking into his eyes, she saw the truth of his words—he would not try to escape his death when the time came. Which made her wonder...why? Why did he *seek* death? What crime had he committed that was so heinous he'd deserved to have his perfect beauty marred?

"Why were you punished?" she asked quietly.

He held her gaze, intensely, intently for several seconds, before he looked away.

"Why are any of us punished? I did something wrong."

She believed him even as she doubted his sincerity. That he'd done something wrong, there was no doubt. But Adonis was too meticulous, too thorough, to ever be caught...unless he wanted to be. Unless he'd *wanted* to be punished.

"You will not tell me what you did." It wasn't a question, and his stoic silence was his only response.

He faced her again and his probing stare bore into her. Under the weight of his gilded gaze, her heart thumped louder, her blood pumped faster. He stood before her, bare of clothing. His skin was taut across chiselled muscles, while his manhood jutted out from its nest of tawny curls.

Anticipation, not fear, aroused him.

It was the opposite for her.

She had not touched a man intimately since him. She'd not kissed one, made love to one, felt his skin bare and slick with sweat against hers. She ached to experience such intimacy.

She feared it.

He offered memories—fresh, new ones to chase away the old—because those of the past were as painful as they were tragic. Endless days and unending nights she'd spent alone in her modest room at the convent with the image of him as her only companion.

Adonis had destroyed her life. This had all begun with him, would end with him, and only he could make this right again.

That was what she had told herself, but what if it was a lie?

What if she did to him what he'd done to her? What if she killed him after? Would his pain, his death fill the emptiness inside her, the void? What would become of her if Adonis suffered and died and nothing changed? What then?

"I want you to bathe."

He looked at her curiously, as though he were amused. When he spoke, she knew that he was. "I did not know it was necessary for me to be clean in order to experience pain and die."

"You smelled of sandalwood and masculinity when you took me. You smell of it now. I do not wish to be reminded of my vulnerability, especially not on this evening."

He understood, so he nodded and she watched the taut, tight muscles of his backside cross the room until he disappeared into the adjoining bathroom.

Once inside, he did not close the door.

Metal twisted against metal as he turned the knobs, followed by the faint thud of his bare feet as he entered the tub.

Water pelted his skin and the porcelain basin. She heard every sound wafting from the bathroom.

She entered moments later, hovering just beyond the doorway.

Trimmed in gold, the glass of the shower door sparkled in the muted light as steam rose up, filling the room. It fogged the glass, obscuring her view of him, but not completely.

Her breasts grew heavy within the confines of her dress, her nipples tight as she followed him with her gaze. His movements were efficient and precise as he ran the cloth across his skin, cleansing the scents of the past from his body.

Her heart pumped violently, wildly—as fast as a runaway train, spiralling out of control.

Adonis.

His name was only ever spoken in the deep recesses of her mind. He'd stripped her of her virginity and ushered her into womanhood. The act had been tender, when it could have been violent. His motivations had been less noble, just as they were shrouded in mystery.

And so much of this man was a mystery. His past, his life before her…since her. Why she'd been the one he'd chosen to ruin. There were others far more beautiful—why her? Why her, when she'd loved him—so fully and so deeply that she would have eagerly given him her body, her very soul? He needn't have taken it only to so cruelly discard her.

She hated him for what he'd done and hated him more for concealing the truth.

He was mistaken about the main reason for her presence here tonight. She was here to kill him—that had not changed. But, before she did, she wanted the truth. She wanted to know *why*.

Selena had only wanted him to give her the truth before she took his life. She'd never expected that he'd offer her the gift of revenge.

But she would take it…all of it.

The absence of sound was what drew her attention back to him, just as he slid the door open and stepped from the tub.

He pulled a towel from one of the marble hanging rails and began to dry himself. The soft material of the cloth wiped away the spray of droplets and—for the briefest of moments, buried deep in a forbidden place inside her—she imagined she stood in place of that towel, licking every bead of water and sweat from his naked flesh.

She shivered—partially from desire, the rest from shame.

"You still want me," he said—his statement a declaration, not a question. His face revealed neither arrogance nor pleasure at the notion. If anything, his eyes were tinged with sadness.

"I do," she admitted. He would soon die—there was no need to conceal the truth, even if it shamed her.

"Did you think of me all those years inside the convent?"

"Every day," she whispered. "And every night."

His eyes probed her. "Tell me. When you thought of me, what did you imagine?"

He seemed almost desperate to hear what she would say, and she stepped closer, the moisture-laden air clinging to her skin. "I imagined I killed you a thousand times." His eyes darkened. "I imagined I fucked you a thousand more." His amber gaze was almost as dark as her own rosewood eyes.

"Why?"

"Why what?" She cocked her head slightly. "Why did I think of you? Why did I imagine killing you, fucking you—?"

"The last one. Why did you think of fucking me? Why would you ever imagine me touching you? After everything I did to you? After all the pain I caused you..."

"Because you stirred me." Her stare sharpened on his face. "You're the only man who has ever hurt me. You're the only man who has ever brought me pleasure—"

"Because you've never found another—"

"Because I've never wanted to."

He studied her for a long while before he spoke again. "To still desire my touch would make you a masochist, Selena."

Sadness and amusement reverberated in his deep voice, and, for the first time in a long time, she felt the hint of a smile. He could be right. To desire the touch of the man who'd destroyed her life was masochistic, indeed. But, then, what did that make him? A man who begged for his death, begged her to avenge herself upon his body.

"I imagine we are both masochistic," she said finally.

He draped the towel over the shower wall and brushed past her to enter the bedroom. "You will find everything you need inside the closet," he called from behind her.

She glanced at him briefly, before turning her attention to the doors of his closet, which were carved from cherry oak. She crossed the room towards it. Flinging the double doors open, a gasp unwittingly tumbled from her lips at what she found inside.

She whipped around to meet his impassive stare.

"You know my profession." He shrugged. "Besides, I knew you were coming."

His voice was soft and seductive even though she knew he did not intend to seduce. He simply could not help it. Everything about Adonis was designed to engender pleasure.

She did not realise he'd closed the distance between them until she was forced to tilt her head back, dragging in the clean, flowery scent of him.

She stilled. He smelt of honey and vanilla.

She smelt of honey and vanilla.

"Do you often use feminine soap to bathe yourself?"

"Yes."

Her eyes narrowed. "Is it coincidence that we bathe in the same fragrance?"

"No."

He reached out then with blinding speed, but not so fast that she did not guess his intent and drew away before he could grasp her chin or cup her cheek.

His arm fell soundlessly back to his naked side.

"Every day I think of you, Selena. And every night." He turned so that she could see the ravaged scars that marred his back.

"And when you think of me, what do you imagine?" she asked, though she did not know why. She was certain she didn't want to know, but her curiosity overrode logic.

He didn't look at her when he spoke. "I imagine making love to you. Truly making love to you as I did not before. I imagine myself having been with you these past sixteen years, protecting you, healing you, easing you of the pain I caused you."

He turned this time, his gaze slamming into her from over his shoulder and she swore he stole her breath with that single look.

"It is not a coincidence that we bathe in the same soap. I know everything about you, Selena. I have made it my entire life's purpose to know of yours. Your wants, your needs, your deepest fears—I know them all."

"Why?"

Molten fire swirled in the depths of his golden eyes, blazing hot and intense. "How long has it been since you've been with a man?"

She started to demand to know what that had to do with anything, especially when she'd already told him, but the look in his eyes forced her to say it again. "Sixteen years."

He broke their connection and looked away. When he spoke, she almost didn't hear him, his voice was so low, the emotion in it so raw.

"Sixteen years, Selena. Sixteen years, to this day." He glanced at the clock hanging over his bed. "And seven hours. That is how long it has been for me since I've been with a woman — since I've been with *you*."

She shook her head, though she knew he couldn't see it with his gaze averted. "Why?" she demanded.

"The same reason as you."

No. She refused to accept the truth of his words and what they meant, as tears scorched her eyes.

"You broke my heart." She bit back a sob, clinging to everything she believed about him.

He was cruel.

He was heartless.

What he'd just revealed said otherwise.

"I know." He hung his head. "And, when I broke yours, I broke mine. Then, I wanted no other woman but you. And I've wanted no other woman since."

Her anger flared, somewhere between despair and desire…somewhere between hope and need.

Damn him.

Damn him.

This changed nothing.

This changed everything.

She didn't know what to say. Didn't have the words to voice the discordant emotions bombarding her.

She didn't need to.

Before she could part her lips, the double oak doors to the suite splintered open, the ravaged wood crashing against the walls.

Chapter Two

A dozen guards poured into the room, their weapons trained upon her.

Her knife was across the room. The gun that had been tucked inside her dress was already firmly in her palm.

She pointed it at Adonis, who stood calmly, his attention fixed solely on her, seemingly unnerved by his naked state. She remembered he'd once made his living as a consort, a whore. He'd probably spent more of his life nude than clothed.

"I will kill him," she threatened, her voice as hard and cold as the ice storms that plagued the northern plains just beyond the city.

The threat stilled them, the coldness in her voice made them wary. They glanced between their employer — the man whose life they'd sworn to protect — and her, the woman who sought to take it.

"One bullet from your gun *might* kill me, but twelve from theirs would *certainly* kill you."

Selena didn't flinch, nor did she take her eyes off the guards before her. "I *would* kill you. With my last breath I would see to it."

"I am not afraid of death."

This time she did look at him, briefly. "And neither am I."

A golden ember flared in his eyes then quickly disappeared.

He nodded to his guards. "The lady and I require privacy."

"But sir…" The beautiful one—the first guard she'd shot—darted his eyes between her and Adonis. What was left unspoken was nonetheless heard by all. Selena was dangerous, not to be trusted. Adonis could not be left alone with her.

"That is an order, Cassius. Leave us."

The beautiful one was called Cassius. She wondered if he was so named because he'd been born beautiful and his parents had thought his beauty would one day make him vain.

It did not matter, she decided. He left—albeit reluctantly—with the rest of the guards trailing behind him.

She lowered her gun when the much-abused door shut. She was surprised it could even close securely, but it did, with a smart thud.

"We cannot stay here much longer."

"Because the door is broken?" She slipped the gun between her breasts as she glanced over at him. "You own this hotel. I am sure you can find another suite for yourself."

She had figured it was a matter of finding another room, but she sensed it was something more when he began dragging on his clothing.

"Twelve of my guards already know that you are here with me. Soon my brothers will learn of your presence, then others. A day may pass, maybe even two, before *he* learns you are no longer at the convent."

"*He?*"

Adonis did not answer her, and the way he hurried around the room, gathering his things, unsettled her.

"Come. We must go."

He tried to seize her arm, but she shrugged away from his grasp. "Go where? Why?"

"You are in danger, Selena. As am I," he stated flatly. "The moment you came here you put us both in danger."

Danger? What danger? From whom? She raked his dishevelled appearance with her sceptical gaze. "Why should I go anywhere with you? Why should I believe a word from your lips?"

He inched closer, crowding out the air surrounding her. In the span of moments, everything between them changed. He was no longer the willing submissive to her revenge, and she was no longer the deadly assassin. He wielded power and authority, and she would heed him. His expression hinted that he was protecting her, or at least trying to. "If you wanted me dead, you would have killed me at first sight. But you came here for something more and we both know it." His face was flushed with impatience. "I know you want the truth just as desperately as you desire revenge, yet you will forfeit both if you do not come with me."

She could easily kill him now and end this, but he was right. She'd come here for more than revenge, and she craved the truth just as much as she craved his destruction. But what if he was lying? What if this was a trap—

"If I wanted you dead, I would have had you killed only moments ago." His discerning statement jarred her. "You may not *want* to trust me, Selena, but you have always known that you can."

He spoke the truth. She hated that he did. But her hate did not make his words any less true. Adonis was many things, but untrustworthy was not one of them. No...that was *her.*

This time when he reached for her arm, she let him grab it. His fingers were gentle against her skin, almost daring her to pull away. She didn't, and she let him usher her towards his private elevator, nestled in the shadowed corner of the room.

After inputting his code, they rode the car to the ground floor in silence. The metal doors opened to a private garage with space for three vehicles. Only one spot was taken.

The sleek design of the silver sporty automobile held her enthralled—its cool, metallic finish reflecting the harsh fluorescent light that lit the small space.

He helped her into the passenger side of the vehicle, the cream leather seat smooth beneath her fingertips. He slipped in beside her, behind the wheel. Within minutes they were tearing out of the garage and plunging into the oppressive blackness of the shadowed night.

The western district of *La Ville des Dieux* was Adonis' territory.

The east belonged to Apollo, the north and south to Eros and Ares. Their domains were expansive—each district a living, breathing testament to its regent.

Hence, the west was the epitome of luxury and beauty.

During the day, golden statues reflected the light of the sun as they stood beyond the Doric columns and arched gateways of alabaster marble buildings. Orchids and lilies, snow white and flourishing in abundance, burst with purity across the landscape of the city, bringing peace and serenity to its occupants.

Those who called the western district their home were drawn to beauty, revelled in splendour and relished the majestic brilliance of Adonis' creation.

She sensed, however, that its beauty was not appreciated by its creator, nor was the peace and serenity it brought to others felt by Adonis.

"Where are we going?"

As if the car had answered her, it lunged to the right on to a vacant street, disappearing up a winding road that climbed towards the highest peak.

"A place where he will expect me to take you, but a place where you will also be safe."

"*He?* He *who?*" she asked again.

Adonis looked at her. "Your father."

"My father?" She was so stunned she could not say another word. She'd not seen her father, had not once spoken to him, in sixteen years. He'd all but disowned her after Adonis had ruined her. What would he want of her now? And, of all people, why did she need to be safe from *him*? Surely, Adonis had misspoken.

"You are mistaken. I am in no danger from Woodward. My father would never hurt me." *Because I do not even exist to him.*

But Adonis' glare suggested otherwise.

"If you believe that then you are just as naive and foolish now as you were then."

The vehemence of his words was like a slap to her face and she gasped as fury trembled though her entire frame. "How dare you—"

"Save your outrage and anger for the one who deserves it."

"*You* deserve it. Every measure of my anger, you deserve."

His eyes softened and she looked away, staring with unseeing eyes straight ahead. Many things she wanted from this man, but pity was not one of them.

"You are wrong. I deserve your pain and suffering, even your revenge. But not your anger. Your father deserves that."

"Why? My father is not responsible for what you did to me."

His hands knuckling white against the steering wheel was her first clue. The ice hovering in the air between them the second. That he would not meet her probing stare told her what he refused to. She swallowed the hard lump forming in her throat, not knowing where to begin or what to ask.

"Do not ask this of me, Selena," he said firmly, as if reading her mind, "because I will not tell you."

"And what did you think I was going to ask you?"

"How your father was involved...is *still* involved." He glanced at her, fleetingly. "I have kept this secret for sixteen years. I won't have to for much longer. You will learn the truth soon enough. I'd rather you learn it from him. I'd rather you see him for who he truly is."

His statement stunned her.

Her father? He was a stranger. Even before he'd disowned her, he'd been distant and cold. She hadn't hated him, but neither had she loved him, not the way a daughter should. Growing up, he may have ignored her, but he'd never been cruel or done her harm. Why would Adonis think or say such things, knowing them to be a lie and that she ultimately *would* discover the truth. Selena wanted to ask more, but she knew Adonis was determined to keep his silence.

Whatever secrets he guarded, whatever sins her father had committed against her, Adonis would not reveal until he deemed it time to do so. It was all just as well, for they arrived at his home moments later, going straight from one garage into another. She didn't even see his estate as they neared it, but she didn't have to. It stood atop the highest point in the city, a beacon to its inhabitants and to outsiders.

Echoing the flourish and embellishments of the city's architecture, Adonis' residence was beautifully designed, but modest in stature. One would have expected a palatial mansion, but the man's home was simple, understated. Adorned with unique antiques, and boasting classic Greco-Roman decor, his house was a reserved two-storey structure fashioned out of marble and granite.

It was a place of beauty and refinement, its location aloof, much like the man who owned it.

After stepping into his elevator, they rode together in silence as it carried them to the second floor of his house.

"My chambers take up this floor," he mentioned almost casually as he pulled out a key to open the first door they came to. "I will have guards posted at every entrance while you are here."

She still did not share his belief that she was in danger...from her father, no less. She was certain that she did not require protection, nor was she a prisoner in his home, so Selena did not acknowledge his comment about the guards. Instead, she silently stepped into his apartments and he closed the door behind them with a gentle thud.

It struck her immediately that his inner sanctuary was at odds with the outer trappings of his domain, the veneer of his house.

Light and brilliance radiated from the exterior, while his private quarters reflected a deep, brooding darkness. Rich walnut furnishings adorned his living room, blending into walls of maple brown.

Adonis—a man of perfect, almost angelic beauty. The core of him was less pristine, layered with darkness, reaching to the depths of his very soul.

He stood in the centre of the spacious living room, staring silently at her while she perused his collection of books and the artwork decorating his walls. She sought to gain an understanding of the man he'd become.

The light glinted off a tiny object atop his bookshelf and she crossed the room to get a closer glimpse. Recognising the object almost immediately, Selena's heart thrummed a faster beat as she lightly skimmed her fingers across the figurine.

"You kept it," she choked out, emotion clogging her throat. "Why?" she demanded, whirling around, her next breath lodging in her chest when her hair brushed across his torso. He was so close and her body responded instantly to the heat of him, recalling the memory of his naked flesh against hers, inside her, his hips pistoning between her thighs as he claimed her with his lips, his hands, his cock.

She didn't realise she was holding the small, sculpted figurine of a golden angel in her hand until he gently prised it from her fingers and set it back in its place.

"We were to be married," he said simply, his expression stoic. His answer revealed nothing. He'd kept the small, insignificant gift she'd given him on his twentieth birthday. She wouldn't have thought he would have wanted to be reminded of her, of the life they'd shared before that fateful night, or the promise of what could have been. She'd wanted no reminders, no memories, but Adonis did not seem to share her desire for ignorance.

"After that night I destroyed everything. I did not wish to remember," she whispered. She had not meant to wound, but when he winced, even as it was virtually imperceptible, she knew her words had pierced him.

"I kept everything" he said solemnly. "I did not wish to forget."

He had not sought to wound, but his revelation made her heart ache. He'd mourned the loss of an innocent young woman, the life that could have been, while she'd festered in anger, nurturing her hate. A tenderness she had not felt in sixteen years filled her, a tenderness she would have to quell when the time came to set her plan in motion.

There was a humble knock against the door and Adonis crossed the room to answer it.

"Your brothers are here, sir," she heard his guard say.

"All of them?"

"Yes sir."

Adonis emitted a harsh, ragged sigh and there was a long silence before he said, "Send them up."

With a nod, the guard disappeared and Adonis closed the door. When he turned to face her, she knew what he would say from the look within his eyes.

"You do not want me here when they arrive," she offered before he could speak.

"They know you're here. That is why they have come." His features were drawn. "But it would be best if they believed you to be bathing or asleep."

"Why?"

"Because to see you would only remind them of what you represent."

"And what is that?"

"My destruction, my weakness." His smile was wry. "My downfall."

She could not argue that.

"I will bathe then if you would show me the way."

He did, and, just as she began to unzip her gown within the privacy of his master bathroom, she heard the doors to his penthouse open and knew his brothers, the three other gods — all beautiful, all cruel, all powerful — had joined him.

Apollo, Ares and Eros — his brothers, if not by blood and birth, then by the bond they'd formed as they'd grown from boys into manhood together. First in the slums of *Le Domaine du Roi*, then in the brothels of the slums, before becoming the most sought-after consorts to the wealthy. They'd witnessed depravity and darkness together, experienced things no child ever should, and survived what many never could. Their desolate childhoods had brought them together, but a dark secret now bonded them for life.

Adonis closed the door behind his three brothers — the core of them the same, even if their outward appearances could not be more different. Where Adonis was golden light, Ares was obsidian darkness. While Adonis was brooding and inscrutable, Eros was placid and amenable. Apollo was the closest in temperament to Adonis if not in looks, as he shared the same dark beauty as Ares. But despite their similarities, differences still remained between him and Apollo, for Adonis could still feel emotion and experience humour, where Apollo felt neither.

Their lives, all of them so similar, had manipulated them in such vastly different ways.

"You never made an appearance at the grand opening of your hotel," Apollo said from his perch against the empty fireplace. "And then a rumour made its way to those who *did* attend that you had not only left your establishment, but with a woman." Apollo's gaze sharpened on him. "A woman from your past, no less."

"She is here," Adonis said simply, offering nothing else. There was no need, for they all knew the truth.

Ares stood closest to him, in a corner just beyond the door. That was the direction Adonis turned when his brother spoke. "If she is here, then he will come." His lips thinned into a firm line. "Neither of you are safe."

"I can protect her."

"As you did before?"

Rage—pure, molten rage—exploded in his chest as he fixed his glare on Eros who sat with a rigid back in the chair beside the sofa. He was the only brother who sought to recline. He was also the only one to dare in a long time to acknowledge what Adonis refused to. He'd fallen in love only once, sworn to protect her…then failed. In his failure to protect her, he'd done far worse—he'd harmed her. Eros might as well have cleaved out his heart, the wrenching agony of being reminded of his impotency as a man to protect his woman was so painful.

Adonis was halfway across the room to snatch Eros from his seat when Ares stopped him, blocking his path.

"Out of my way."

"Fighting Eros will not change a thing," stated Ares. "Besides, he is right."

Adonis stilled, his hands curling into fists, the words his brothers wielded cutting him deep.

"But it was not your fault," Ares continued. "It was an impossible situation you and Apollo were forced into. You could have ruined her, or you could have seen her dead. Any man in your place would have done the same. No one blames you."

Ares was wrong. "She blames me."

"That is because she chooses to remain ignorant," Apollo said.

He and Apollo, they had shared the same fate.

Destroy Serena—Selena's twin sister—he had been told, and Apollo had.

They both had ruined the lives of the women they'd loved. Apollo had not been the same since then—neither one of them had, but the darkness Apollo carried inside him was so oppressive that Adonis had often feared for his brother's sanity.

"Can you blame her for choosing to remain ignorant? The truth would have destroyed her," Adonis defended Selena.

"It could still destroy her. And she will take you with her." Ares sighed. "Why did you have to pick today of all days to open your hotel? Why did you have to taunt her into seeking you out?"

"Because it was time," he said, but that was a lie. He had yet to tell his brothers the entire truth. He'd had no choice but to draw her to him.

He'd received a letter—actually two. One from *her* revealing she would come for him on what promised to be the greatest day of his life. The second letter had been marked anonymous, though he suspected it was from *him*. It was a warning and a threat. Selena would die, and Adonis knew of only one way to protect her.

"Time for who?" demanded Ares. "You? Her? Him?"

"All of us. It was time she learned the truth, time for me to stop carrying it around alone, time for him to finally face his daughters and pay for what he did to them."

Apollo shook his head as if he thought Adonis a fool...and maybe he was right. What his brother did not say, he read plainly across his face. Out of weakness, Adonis had grown weary of the secret he carried. When Selena learned the truth, she would finally place the blame where it belonged. But no one had asked Selena or her sister if that was what they wanted. What if they preferred ignorance? What if the truth *did* destroy them? Adonis glimpsed this in the depths of Apollo's shadowed expression, along with another truth that burned brighter than all the others.

"You hope that once she learns the truth she will forgive you, that she will love you again." Apollo's eyes filled with anguish, a unique pain shared only by the two of them. "She won't forgive you. What you did is beyond forgiveness. Just as she will never love you. She simply cannot."

Adonis did not want to hear it. Apollo's words rang true, but he refused to acknowledge them aloud. To give voice to such a revelation in the light of day was to speak it into existence and he refused to. There was always hope—foolish, blind hope—but hope, nonetheless.

"I need your help," Adonis said finally. "I cannot protect her alone. Now that he knows Selena is with me, he will assume I've broken my vow. He will come for both of us." He glanced over at Apollo. "Serena will need protection as well."

"That is why we are here," Eros offered from across the room, his voice resolute.

And that was all that needed to be said. Between the brothers there was a bond far stronger than blood or birth.

Adonis' woman. Apollo's woman. They were in danger.

Adonis and Apollo were in danger as well. And Ares and Eros would risk their lives to protect them. Despite their differences and their disagreement over the matter, they were still brothers — bonded by something stronger than blood, stronger than birth.

The secret they shared bound them for life.

* * * *

The four brothers — the four gods.

Shrouded in shadows, Selena had watched silently, peeking just around the corner as, one by one, Adonis' brothers had entered his home.

Equally beautiful, each brother radiated a dark sensuality that was so vivid, so blatant it was tangible in the air.

They were not gods — they were mortal men — born to this world with ordinary lives and pedestrian names. Their beauty was what had distinguished them — their ability to incite lust, fulfil desires and create fantasies was what had made them gods among men.

She barely followed their conversation, skulking in the shadows, snooping to learn what Adonis refused to tell her. From where she stood, she could scarcely hear a thing. She garnered so little it could be considered nothing. Only the cryptic knowledge she already possessed—she was in danger, Adonis was in danger, and somehow her father was involved. Her sister was, too.

Her thoughts strayed to her sister—Serena. Their lives had seen them embark upon vastly opposite journeys. Once as close as identical twins could be, they were practically strangers now.

She started at the sound of footsteps.

The brothers were leaving and, as soon as they were gone, Adonis would seek her out.

She rushed from her hiding place, down the narrow hallway and into the bathroom. Within moments she'd stripped out of her dress and was underneath the spray of the shower.

She was just towelling dry when there was a gentle knock against the door.

"There is a change of clothes for you on the bed."

She mumbled something, possibly a thank you. She could not be sure. She half expected him to be waiting there in the bedroom when she stepped out of the bathroom, but he wasn't. She was alone.

A tray laden with a pitcher of wine, fruit and cheese, and a loaf of bread sat atop his dresser, and her stomach growled at the sight.

Selena would eat after she had dressed. As if on cue, she spotted the fresh, clean garments laid out on his bed. Black slacks and a white silk shirt. She donned them, only mildly surprised that they fit her perfectly.

Adonis knew things about her, things she probably did not even know herself.

Once she was fully clothed, she took a seat on his bed and ate her fill, before washing it down with a cup of wine.

When she was done, she noticed his home was strangely silent. Throwing open the door, Selena stepped into the hallway before making her way into the sitting room. She found Adonis stretched out across his dark leather couch, his eyes closed.

For the second time that evening, her heart gave a small tug. He was boyishly handsome in the serenity of sleep. A small lock of hair fell across his brow, and she balled her hand at her side to keep from reaching out and smoothing it from his face.

He was peaceful in repose. His eyes did not burn with intensity, and the pain that ravaged his soul was not present across the chiselled planes of his handsome face. In his sleep, he was calm, tranquil – as if he truly found quiet solace when he closed his eyes.

She did not want to wake him, not just yet, so she was silent as she watched him. She had come to kill him. How easy it would be to do so now. She'd left her knife in his room along with her gun, both of which were on his dresser beneath her gown. She could try to strangle him with her bare hands but feared he would simply overpower her.

She had come to kill him and she could do so now, but she was without her weapons, which made her question – how badly did she want to see him dead?

An hour ago, she would have said with every breath that entered and left her chest. But now...now she was not so certain or confident.

Secrets.

It was because he harboured secrets – about her, her sister, her father.

The only thing she could have ever wanted more than his death was the truth. The truth about why he'd done what he had. She still did not have that answer. If anything, she was plagued with more questions, new questions. Questions she'd never imagined she'd have.

In the space of an hour, her desire to see him dead had been crowded out by her desire to discover the truth.

And what if you learn something that you don't wish to learn? What if you discover he is not the monster you've made him out to be?

She'd lived with her hatred for so long, Selena had no idea what would anchor her if Adonis was no longer her enemy. She refused to even consider it.

Even if he wasn't the person she'd convinced herself he was, even if there were others responsible for what had happened to her, there was no changing the fact that Adonis had been the one to use her, to ruin her. It had been his cock that had breached her hymen as he'd taken her virginity, his shaft that he'd buried deep inside her tender body until nothing separated them.

As if he knew her thoughts were of him, his eyelids snapped open and she found herself drowning in a pool of swirling golden beauty.

"Are you tired?"

She shook her head. "Are you?"

"No."

"But you were just sleeping."

His lips crooked into what would have been considered a half smile on any other man. On him it appeared almost forced. "I was not asleep. I rarely sleep."

He stood and that was when Selena saw he was bare from the waist up. How had she not noticed the wide expanse of perfectly defined muscle when she'd come upon him, when now it was all she could do not to stare openly at the sculpted sinew and muscle rippling across his torso?

His eyes flickered and his attention slipped to her hip, where a small object peeked out from her pocket.

The air in her lungs stilled.

The air in the room chilled.

"I found it in your closet," she said by way of explanation, inflecting a confidence in her voice she was far from feeling.

"And you desire to use it upon me."

It was not a question.

"A lot has changed since we left your suite."

"Has it?" His eyebrow arched. "It would seem you still clamour for revenge."

"And yet, when I arrived, I *only* wanted your death."

His nostrils flared, but she could not tell if he was angry, hurt, or disappointed. His face was once again a carefully constructed beautiful mask of imperviousness.

"And do you still wish me dead?"

"Yes."

"Even though, deep down, you know I was not the only one responsible for what happened to you."

"No matter what other factors were at play, no matter who else was involved, it was *you* who did the deed, no one else."

He nodded, his expression resigned. Without a word he brushed past her and headed down the hall into his bedroom, leaving Selena with no other choice but to follow him.

Adonis was already fully nude when she entered the room. Closing the door behind them, she locked it.

Her heart pounded harder as she reached for the buttons of her shirt. She wanted this, needed this. Her fingers trembled. He wanted this, too. The shattered pieces of their souls made what would transpire next as inevitable as it was necessary.

She hoped this wasn't a mistake.

She hoped when this was all over that she could still walk away unscathed, that the intimacy they were about to share wouldn't damage her further. She wasn't certain, but that was the chance she was willing to take.

This was her choice.

When she started to remove her shirt, he stilled, every inch of his body radiating tension.

"What are you doing?"

Her eyes sparkled. "That much should be obvious," she said softly as she stripped off her shirt, then her slacks. Selena's heart beat a wild, drumming beat beneath her lungs in anticipation.

She still desired his death.

She still wanted her revenge.

But she wanted something else as well, something she only admitted to herself on the darkest of nights when she was huddled beneath the woollen covers of her convent bed.

She wanted to experience pleasure again. She wanted to once again know lust.

Yes, she wanted to make him beg as she had once begged. She'd begged for him to stop, then she'd begged him not to. She would do the same to him.

Yes, she wanted to shame him. She wanted him to experience the shame of having his body betray him, and to know that the one who'd caused it was there to witness it. She wanted his humiliation at being used and taken, then discarded and ridiculed.

She would have all those things. She would have more.

She would have him worship every inch of her. She would have him yielding to her every command. She would have his surrender, his complete and utter capitulation.

She would have him fulfil the fantasies she'd never wanted to acknowledge and ease the desires she'd long denied.

"I will not make love to you," he said defiantly, the menace in his voice breaking through her thoughts, which he seemed to so easily read.

"You will have no choice."

"I will accept your pain and your punishment, but I will not make love to you."

"And what if that is what I want? What if I *want* you to make love to me?"

His eyes darkened, and she glimpsed the war raging inside him. He wanted to suffer at her hands, but he refused to accept her pleasure. He'd given her pleasure that night, even as he'd taken his. She would accept nothing less *this* night.

"Try to make love to me, Selena, and I will kill you."

His words startled her, but she managed to remain equally stoical. "We will see about that."

He growled out her name in warning, but she shook her head, silencing him. He was a liar. He would sacrifice his life to protect her, only to take it? She would be a fool to believe that. She wasn't a fool. He was comfortable accepting her pain, but not her pleasure.

Just as she'd gifted him with her pleasure and her pain sixteen years ago this very night, before she was done with him, she would have him do the same.

Chapter Three

Selena crossed the room, her nude body illuminated by the silver light of the moon filtering through the sheer, satin curtains draping the window.

His eyes followed her every move—every sway of her hips, the delicate rise and fall of her breasts, the gentle caress of her fingers atop the down comforter.

Under the weight of his stare, the pulsing vein in her neck throbbed.

With his attention riveted on her, her breath rasped.

His bed was soft, his blankets warm as she stretched out across them, her back resting against an array of pillows along the ornate brass headboard.

So many times on so many nights, she'd lain in her humble bed, tucked beneath starched white sheets, her thighs spread, her hand between them stroking the soft bud at the apex of her sex, imagining him, dreaming of him, fantasising only of him.

Maybe she *was* a masochist—to desire the man who'd caused her such pain.

Or did it even matter? Would it matter when he was dead, when she'd killed him? She shook her head. She did not want to think of that—not now.

Right now she only wanted to think of pleasure.

Tonight, her hands found the swollen nub of her desire and with her slender fingers she touched herself, gently at first until warmth burst inside her chest, fanning across her entire body and she thrummed her clit faster, harder.

He stood at the end of the bed, his glare piercing her, the wide slash of his handsome mouth twisted with fury. She held his dark glower, sharing with him her pleasure, the intensity of her desire that must have blazed like a naked fire in her eyes.

He hated her because he hated himself...because he'd wielded pain only to gain her pleasure.

She hated him because she hated herself, and yet she'd accepted the pain he'd wielded, and then begged for her pleasure.

Tonight, he did not want to experience pleasure, yet she desired more than his pain.

"Tonight I shall not call you by your name." In all these years she'd never uttered his name aloud. The memories it evoked were too vivid—the myriad emotions it conjured were too intricate to discern. "Tonight you shall only be known as my *slave*. Come here, slave," she commanded.

She would never know if his increased anger was due to the moniker she'd gifted him with or to the fact that she'd issued him a command, but embers of fury leapt in his golden eyes and he remained rooted to his spot.

"Slave, I said come here." This time her voice was sharper and he must have noticed because he walked with rigid efficiency around the bed until he stood beside her.

"I want you on this bed, on your knees, with your tongue inside me."

His nostrils flared, his brow creased into a deep, hard frown.

This was not what he desired — his face said what his lips did not.

He wanted pain.

She wanted pleasure.

"Did you not put my lips on your cock and beg me to suck you dry?" Her statement registered. She knew it would. She knew reminding him of the mutual pleasure they'd experienced was the only way he would permit himself to know pleasure now.

Her voice was softer when she spoke again. "I want you to bury your face against my cunt and I want you to eat from me until I command you to stop."

Lust flared in his eyes.

Such language from a woman who'd made her home in a convent for the past sixteen years. She felt no shame.

The bed dipped beneath the weight of one knee, then the other. Her next breath became a prisoner inside her lungs as he snared her with his gaze.

When he touched her thigh, her skin burned in the very spot.

She gasped.

He stilled.

"Do not stop," she commanded.

He hesitated a moment, before his rough, callused fingers slid up the inside of her leg. His other hand found her thigh, stroking her skin, pushing her legs farther apart.

Her sex wept with hot liquid and she shivered when he lowered his head and closed his eyes, dragging her scent deep into his lungs.

He had been the only man to touch her body...and it ached for him.

Her fingers against her clit were a pale substitute to the wet fire his tongue ignited the moment it stroked across her sensitive skin.

She fought the urge to cry out as she arched into him, her eyes clenching shut. Her hands wrapped around the brass bars of the bed while he held her, spread before him, his tongue spearing her hot, tight hole.

His tongue retreated, then plunged deep, over and over again, dragging breathy sighs from her lips, dragging a gush of molten heat from her body.

He replaced his tongue with a finger, then another, stretching her, stroking her.

She called his name — *slave*. Her *slave*.

Selena's hips instinctively lifted, but he held fast, trapping her to the bed, keeping her splayed wide as he devoured her with his mouth. She was mindless, helpless as she trembled against him and his full lips wrapped around her aching bud, suckling gently while his fingers pumped harder, thrust deeper.

She quivered beneath his skilled touch, heat uncoiling in her belly to rake its way through her body until the evidence of her desire and pleasure poured forth. Adonis worked a third finger inside her, brushing against the roof of her tunnel, stroking that sensitive place that brought a woman endless pleasure.

She screamed — a hoarse, ragged cry. She screamed her pleasure as her climax swept her away, desperately gripping the brass bars. Shudders racked her, while hot, sticky juice flooded her pussy. She panted as her orgasm began to wane and her body grew soft and pliable.

She had not commanded him to stop, so he didn't.

He remained rooted between her thighs, his face buried in the heat of her sex, still feasting from her wet slit. Selena released the bars to tangle her hands in his golden hair, raking her fingers through the soft strands.

She cupped the back of his head gently, holding him there, though she needn't have. He did not move, did not even seem to want to.

He ate from her, drank from her until she was once again writhing in pleasure. He fucked her with his fingers, four of them now, stretching her more than she'd ever been stretched before.

It felt as if he was invading her body. She clamped one hand against his shoulder, drawing his attention.

He looked up, his eyes shimmering with need and desire, his mouth glistening wet with her essence.

"Do you desire for me to stop?"

She shuddered at his obedience, his obsequence.

Selena shook her head. "Do not stop."

In that moment, a sizzle of scorching energy passed between them. There was acceptance, an understanding.

He probed inside her tight depths with his fingers, still holding her gaze, his golden eyes riveted upon her. She felt so full, so stuffed. Even with her passage slick, his fingers were rough, hard and unyielding.

It made her needy for another part of him — his cock.

To have it stretching her, her flesh yielding as it tunnelled deep, hard, rough inside her.

She gasped.

He fucked her deeper.

It was not yet time for him to experience pleasure. When he was done seeing to her needs, when she was satiated and fulfilled, that was when she would desire his pain.

His pleasure would not come until afterward.

A groan was wrenched from her lips when he dipped his head to take her clit within his mouth again. It was as if he waged a war upon her body, the onslaught of pleasure was so intense, so mind numbing.

The room was cool, but sweat dotted her skin as the musk of her arousal and climax hovered in the air, heavy and thick. She drew it in, savouring it. Her pleasure—a testament to Adonis' mastery.

Adonis sucked her harder, and the pressure sent a spike of heat racing down her spine. A hot blush crept over her and she closed her eyes and parted her lips, but no intelligible sound came out. Only a whispery, ragged moan of completion as an explosion of blinding pleasure went off inside her.

Fireworks exploded behind her lids as she came again and again, one orgasm blending into the next, until she was spent and boneless.

Only then did she command him to *stop.*

Adonis lifted his head from between Selena's thighs, his eyes trained on her.

She was beautiful—ethereal.

Spread before him, revelling in her pleasure, ensnared by the trappings of her lust. No other man had touched her since him, and yet she'd blossomed into her sexuality, awakened into full womanhood.

She was exquisite.

He knelt before her and remained there as she climbed off the bed and crossed the room. She bent down and plucked something from the floor, and his heart stuttered when the moonlight reflected off the object in her hand.

Hard, black and unyielding, fashioned out of pure marble and stained a rich onyx.

His cock hardened despite himself.

The object in her hand was smaller than the nine inches he wielded, but it would bring pleasure just as easily as it could engender pain.

He did not speak as he watched her open a jar atop his dresser and dip the full length of the dildo into the liquid, coating it fully. She'd found the dildo in his closet. She'd apparently found the lubricant as well. There were many objects of pleasure and tools of pain locked within its confines. They were from a time long ago when he'd been a legend among both men and women—a master of pleasure and seduction, his prowess in bed bringing him untold wealth. The riches he still possessed, but he was none of those other things anymore—only a broken man still tormented by his past, still tormented by what he'd done to *her*.

Adonis had not used any of the sexual toys in his closet in a very long time, yet he'd kept them as a reminder of what he'd once been. In his arrogance, he'd been full of himself, full of pride at the fantasies he could so easily fulfil with just the crook of his finger, the slip of his tongue, the whisper of his breath against warm skin. Now he was repulsed by it all. It had been because of who he was and what he did that he'd been chosen to violate Selena—and he never wanted to forget.

He was so deeply lost in his memories of the past that he did not realise Selena now stood within a hair's breadth of him until he felt the soft, wet kiss of her lips against his neck, his shoulder, his scarred back.

He jerked away.

"Do not," he warned. But his warning was futile. Her hands tangled in his hair, urging him close.

"This is my revenge, *slave*. And I desire to kiss you."

He gritted his teeth, biting back his protest along with a vile curse.

She was seducing him, before she inflicted pain — just as he'd once done. She'd begged him not to strip her of her virginity, but her cries had fallen on deaf ears as he'd kissed every inch of her silken skin until she was pliable, biddable, begging him *not* to stop.

Tonight she would coax his body until he welcomed the pain she was determined to inflict, until he begged for the pleasure only she could give him.

Despite that knowledge, his body relaxed beneath her lips and tongue, as she kissed his flesh, damaged by lash and fire. She kissed his back as if it was not hideously scarred and he stretched out flat across the bed, a sigh escaping him.

His eyes slipped shut as she kissed a wet trail across his ass, down the backs of his thighs to the crevices behind his knees. She even licked his ankles and the arches of his feet.

He fisted his hands into the bed covers, his eyes clenched shut. A warm ball of need burst in the pit of his stomach, a mixture of agony and longing. With his burgeoning cock trapped between the weight of his body and the mattress beneath him, he experienced a twinge of discomfort.

Adonis welcomed it. He welcomed the pain, along with the pleasure of her hands, her lips, even the slight tickling of her breath against his skin.

Sixteen years…and now nine hours…since he'd last been with a woman—*her*. His body ached for whatever succour she chose to bestow upon his ravaged flesh, whatever pleasure she chose to appease his raw need.

A groan threatened to escape, but he held it back, trapping it in his chest when her finger, tentative at first, pushed against the puckered hole of his anus. His heart pounded faster. His swelling cock pulsed.

Her finger was wet, as if she'd sucked it into her mouth before probing his hole. She pushed it deeper, to the knuckle, and this time he could not hold back his pleasure as he gasped.

His hips jerked against the bed, then lifted, sending her finger tunnelling deeper. She fingered him with her digit, stretching his unyielding flesh. He stiffened when her lips kissed his buttocks, her finger setting a lazy rhythm. Adonis soon relaxed, savouring the pleasure worming its way through him, the heat stirring in his belly.

She worked her finger inside him harder and faster, going deeper as her tongue teased his flesh. He called her name in desire, in desperation. "Selena…"

The wet slide of her tongue against his hole stilled him and he twisted around, his hand wrapping around her neck. "What are you doing?" he demanded, his chest heaving, his voice harsh.

She did not flinch. Fear did not darken her eyes. Instead, she narrowed her gaze, studying him, searching deep. For the first time that night, she began to peel away the layers he'd buried himself under, the shield he'd hidden behind to protect himself from *her*.

"What are you so afraid of? I have barely begun and yet at the first flare of desire you recoil from me." Her hands were gentle against his arm, coaxing him to relax his hold until he released her neck.

She held his stare, her fingers delicately tracing a path up and down his arm, across his chest, the length of his abdomen. When her fist curled around his cock, pumping slowly, he groaned, a strangled sound even to his own ears.

He did not want to experience pleasure, but she was determined that he would—he could see that now. She was determined to make him enjoy this, as he'd made her enjoy it. She was determined to make him cry out, as he'd made her cry out in pleasure, fulfilment...completion.

He turned back over onto his stomach and this time, when she parted the cheeks of his ass and probed his anus with her tongue, he did not resist. He welcomed the pulsing, throbbing desire that inched its way through his body, making him rock hard with need.

So many years he'd pleasured others, attending to their needs, their wants and desires, but none had attended to him as she was doing now. None had ever sought to give *him* pleasure, even as they'd gifted him with their own. He was weak beneath her roaming hands and her probing tongue. The only woman who'd ever had the power to hurt him threatened to shatter him with her tenderness.

She licked and tongued him until he was on the verge of exploding. He did not believe his pleasure could become more intense...yet it did.

"Roll over," she breathed. "I want to taste you."

His eyes snapped open, and he shook his head, but she ignored the protest forming on his lips as she nudged him onto his back.

A tiny droplet of pre-cum beaded at the tip, and she swiped it with her tongue. Before he could stop her, she took his cock into her hands, before taking it inside her warm, wet mouth.

"Selena," he rasped, gripping the blankets of the bed so that he would not grip her hair or the back of her head, forcing her mouth to take him deeper...or push her away and force her to stop.

Her head bobbed up and down, his shaft disappearing inside her mouth over and over again as she took him down her throat, deep and hard.

The blood in his veins ran hot and molten. His toes curled from the pleasure of her lips around him, sucking him. He thought he would die, maybe even blackout from the myriad intense sensations she invoked within him when she took him deeper than he'd ever been inside another's mouth before. All the way to the back of her throat, she swallowed his cock and that's when he felt it.

Pain. Just a tiny twinge arced through him like a small lightning bolt—from his stretching rectum all the way up his spine to the base of his skull.

She sucked his cock deeper into her mouth.

Pleasure.

His body hovered somewhere between pain and pleasure as she deep-throated his cock in one moment while she stretched his rectum with the dildo in the next.

The dual sensations—at war with one another, blending into one another—raked through him. His insides were on fire, his body throbbing with hot, pulsing pleasure.

She pumped the fake cock inside him slowly at first, gently, until his body relaxed around the invading object. Then she went deeper, harder, faster. Her mouth echoed the same drumming rhythm—taking him deeper, harder, faster.

Frissons of fire and ice raced up his spine. Every cell within his body sizzled. The wave cresting within him threatened to drown him with its intensity. The hurling force of his impending climax was impossible to stop.

He called her name in warning, his hands pushing against her shoulders.

She held fast, her lips clamping around him hard as she shoved the solid dildo all the way inside him on one violent thrust.

Pain raked through him, clawing at his chest.

Pleasure raked through him, clawing at his belly.

He came, his voice a hoarse, tight shout as he shot stream after stream of his milky white seed into her mouth, down her throat. The heavy sacs beneath his cock drew tight against his body as if they were emptying every drop of semen into her, inside the velvety warmth of her waiting mouth.

It had been so long, too long, since he'd experienced pleasure in another's arms. His orgasm seemed endless, the pleasure of his climax practically wrenched from his body until he was boneless, satiated and forced to beg her to *stop.*

Selena tasted the essence of Adonis on her lips, her tongue. Leaning back on her haunches, she rested her hands atop his thighs, her body still within the spread V of his legs.

His cock was soft once again, his golden skin flushed red. His eyes were hooded as he stared up at her. His brow furrowed into a frown. She was not certain if he was unhappy because he'd begged her to stop, because she'd done just that, or because she'd driven him to such a mindless state of pleasure that every vestige of control he'd possessed had been lost beneath her touch. She suspected it was all of those things.

With blinding speed, he shot up off the bed and was across the room within the blink of an eye.

His hand curled around her gun, and she stood slowly, carefully, her gaze wary. He returned to where she stood, facing her, and pressed the cold metal of the gun into her palm, with the barrel to his chest.

"You came here to kill me," he said in answer to the question in her eyes. "So do it."

She jerked her hand away, forcing him to hold the gun. His eyes were wild, desperate, and she sensed that what they'd just shared had ignited something within him, something long buried and long denied.

There was genuine fear in his amber gaze. He was afraid—not of any physical threat, but of an emotional one. In his eyes she saw it, what he feared.

She'd touched a part of him that he'd wanted to remain untouched. She'd opened a wound he'd thought long healed.

"When I am ready to use that gun, I will, but I am not ready." Selena inched towards him, but stopped when he backed away. "What is it? What has changed between us that has made you so wary, so afraid?"

She'd hoped to placate him, but, if anything, her words had ignited his anger. Before she could take her next breath, her gun was once again in her hand, her back against the wall with his hand clamped around her throat.

"Now you shall use your gun."

She would have laughed at the blatant provocation that was no more threatening than the gentle breeze just beyond the window, but the fear in his eyes truly made her ache for him.

"Why should I use my gun? Because your hand is at my throat?" A hand that gripped her so loosely, she needed to only turn her head to be free. "Because you have my back against a wall?" He did not even hold her securely.

"You're a fool if you do not fear me."

"Then I'm a fool," Selena shot back.

Anger stole across his face, along with despair and pain. His eyes closed as he leaned his forehead against hers.

"I will not survive this night if you continue to treat me as you do."

Selena curled her hand around his, the one that still held her throat. One by one, she pulled his fingers away as she palmed his cheek with her other hand.

"And how is it that I treat you?"

"With care, with tenderness." He opened his eyes. "I hurt you."

"You did."

"And yet you nurture my desires, you seek to please me as no other has done before."

He spoke of not surviving this night, but she was worried about her own survival. She despaired that her heart, her very soul, would not remain intact when they were done. As she stared into his eyes, she did not see the man she'd hated and blamed all these years. Instead, she saw one whose body had been used and brutalised, whose heart had been battered, his soul stripped from him when he'd been far too young.

Adonis.

His face, his beauty, his body had made him a legend. The pleasure he wielded, the desire he ignited had made him a god.

And yet, no one had ever sought to please him, to fulfil *his* desires. Not once had he ever abandoned himself to the pleasure of his lover's arms. She'd met Adonis when she'd been too young to love, and they'd been set to marry. In her arms, he would have abandoned himself. But he'd hurt her. On the day they were to announce their engagement, he'd ruined her and for all these years she could see he'd been tormented by it—by what he'd done and what he'd lost.

She cupped his face between her hands, but he resisted when she tried to pull him close.

"No."

"Kiss me," she whispered.

"I do not want this."

She forced back a sob at the despair in his eyes that said he was not worthy of her touch.

"But you need this." She tipped her head back and tugged on him firmly. "Kiss me, *please*," she begged.

The last word had barely left her lips before he crushed his mouth to hers in a desperate, searching kiss, full of pain and need.

Her arms twisted behind his neck.

He set the gun aside then clamped his hands around her hips, his fingers biting into her flesh. She ignored the pain. All she felt was the pleasure of him, his lips, his tongue stroking inside her mouth, twining with hers.

She drew his breath deep into her lungs, inside her body, until every pore, every cell was full of him. He seduced her with hot, deep glides of his tongue, his kiss igniting a toe-curling fire that spread throughout her blood, shaking her entire being.

Her hands found their way into his hair, digging into his scalp, holding him locked to her. In that moment, imprisoned within his embrace, she accepted that if he was desperate to abandon himself to the pleasurable arms of a lover, then so was she. As their tongues twisted together, their bodies melding and meshing, something shifted between them— something small, almost imperceptible, but their need for physical companionship brought them together, bonding them.

Adonis — the man, the god.

Could she still hate him when this was all over? That question reverberated to her very core.

From a distance, locked away in the convent — when he'd been the seemingly immortal, impenetrable, untouchable godlike being — she'd loathed him.

But locked in his arms, experiencing his passion, his raw need, his soul-stirring pain...

When she touched him — he was simply a man.

A mortal man just as desperate for love as she.

A knock at the door forced them apart, and they released one another, their eyes wide, their chests heaving.

Shocked silence hovered between them as if neither one could discern what had just transpired.

Adonis was the first to recover.

"What is it?" he bit out, his voice deep and gravelly and not at all steady.

"It's Ares," boomed a deep voice full of authority from the other side of the door. "I need to speak with you and the woman. There has been a fire at _Épicurien_."

Selena froze, ice water settling in her veins.

Serena.

Her sister.

She was in danger.

Chapter Four

Selena entered the living room with Adonis at her side to greet Ares — the dark god — whose countenance was stark against the smooth, white marble of the fireplace. As the flames in the fireplace leapt behind him, he seemed every bit as darkly sensual as his reputation proclaimed.

Darkly sensual *and* dangerous.

"You said there has been a fire at my sister's bordello. Has she been harmed?"

"No," Ares said flatly. He raked his gaze over her and her back stiffened beneath the weight of his probing stare. *He knew.* Though she wore fresh, clean clothes, and every hair on her head was in place, she might as well have been dishevelled from the knowing glimmer in his eyes. He knew she and Adonis had made love, and he did not approve. She lifted her chin, her eyes defiant, and the gesture did not go unnoticed by him, but she refused to cower, or feel shame. Ares may not approve, but he did not have to.

"Serena has not been harmed, but I have not been able to discern the magnitude of damage that her establishment has sustained."

She glanced at Adonis. "I need to check on my sister."

"I do not think that is wise."

Selena turned at Ares' stern voice.

"Exposing yourself will only put you both in greater danger," Ares continued. "My brothers are there as well as several guards. They will see to your sister's safety."

"That is all very well that you have her safety well in hand." She glowered at him. "But I would like to know how my sister fares."

"Why?" His eyes narrowed. "You have not spoken to her in over a decade. Why do you care how she fares now when you never have before—?"

"*Ares*," Adonis warned, but Selena barely heard him. Her attention was riveted on the dark god before her.

His words sliced her like a knife, and she drew in a deep, jagged breath. "No matter our differences, Serena is still my sister and I love her."

"Really? My brothers, we have our differences, but we do not abandon one another. You claim you love your sister, but you certainly have an odd way of showing it."

"That is *enough*, Ares."

Selena placed a gentle hand against Adonis' sleeve when he moved as though to cross the room towards his brother.

"It is fine," she said to Adonis.

To Ares, she asked, "What is it to you?" Why did he care that she and Serena shared a strained relationship—a strained relationship for which they *both* were to blame, not just her.

"It is everything to me." Ares left his perch against the mantle above the fireplace and walked towards her, darkness and danger radiating from him. "My brothers will be destroyed by you and your sister. I would see that doesn't happen."

Anger poured through her then. "I refuse to stand here and let you blame me and Serena for what happened to us. We were innocent victims—"

"Just as Apollo and Adonis were innocent tools of manipulation. Your family has brought nothing but pain to my brothers." Ares' black eyes grew harder—darker, if that were even possible—and Selena fought back a gasp at the intensity raging in his gaze. "When will it end?"

She flinched in shock at the vehemence in his eyes, the conviction in his words. Adonis had destroyed her life, but it would seem that Ares believed she'd destroyed *his*.

"That is enough, brother," Adonis interjected. "We should go."

"Leave her here," Ares snapped, looking straight at Adonis—*only* at Adonis, as though the very object of his anger did not exist.

But she would not be ignored as she spoke up. "I go with you or on my own. Either way, I will see that my sister is safe this night."

Ares glared at her, his expression one of fury. He hated her. It was there in his eyes. He blamed her. It was all over his face. But he could not be rid of her, because, by some twist of fate, his brother still cared for her. He resented that fact—his eyes said that as well.

With a sensual elegance that one could only be born with, he twisted around and stalked out of the living room, out of Adonis' home, leaving them no other choice but to follow him.

* * * *

Selena had arrived at the grand opening of Adonis' hotel nearly five hours ago with the sole purpose of ending his life.

Now she sat beside him, in the passenger seat of his car, trailing behind Ares' vehicle to her sister's bordello. Death had been crowded out by desire, replaced by thoughts of succumbing to his desires, of fulfilling hers.

Selena had not understood then, as she'd stood before him and he'd told her baldly that to have his death and to have her revenge were *not* the same. She understood now.

Yet, what still eluded her was just how important his death was to her. Twenty-four hours ago, it had been the only thing of importance to her. Tonight, as she'd held him in her arms, as she'd touched his soul with a kiss, his death was no longer foremost in her mind.

So much had changed in the small space of a few hours. More secrets had been followed with little truths. That was why she longed to see Serena — maybe talking with her sister would reveal some of the answers to the questions that now brewed inside her head.

She glanced over at Adonis. His hands were tense as they gripped the steering wheel, his eyes haunted.

She wondered then, what if she took her revenge upon his body and made him suffer, then afterwards she did not want his death? What if she let him live? Would either of them be free of the pain that night long ago had wrought? Would either of them be free to love again, to experience happiness and joy?

"Why does your brother feel such hatred towards me and my sister?"

The interior of the car, which had been plunged into silence, now reverberated with unspoken accusations and silent guilt.

Adonis sighed wearily, as if he dreaded answering her. "After what happened, Apollo and I were never the same. Ares is the oldest of us all. He feels responsible for us, which is why he mourns the loss of the men we were, and that he could do nothing to stop it."

"But he blames Serena and me, as if we had something to do with it all." Fury began to vibrate through her at the very thought. "It's as if he blames us for what we suffered, as if we wanted any of it."

"It is not you and your sister, so much, as what you represent."

"And what is that?" she asked, though she already suspected, and when he remained silent she knew her suspicions to be true. *Her father.* Whatever role her father had played in all of this, Ares blamed him, and thusly he blamed her—her *and* Serena.

She understood the rationale, even if it all did not make sense. The worst her father had done was to disown her and Serena and send them away to the convent. He'd not been the one to take their innocence, to publicly ridicule them and shame them. Adonis and his brother had done that, and all for what? Money? Prestige? Adonis had promised to marry her, but instead he'd taken her, made it known to all then abandoned her. The skill with which he'd taken her virginity had been heralded. He'd become an even greater legend after that. And she'd been ruined. No man would have her. She'd had no choice but to enter the convent.

Her sister had disagreed.

It was as if Serena had been liberated by what had transpired, while she'd been imprisoned by it.

The path her sister had taken had so diverged from her own that Selena had not even recognised her.

She'd blamed Adonis and his brother for that, as well. What they'd done had forced a wedge deep and wide between her and Serena until the closeness they'd once shared had become a memory of the past.

The car slowed then came to a stop outside Serena's bordello.

Épicurien – the pursuit of pleasure.

That is exactly what patrons of Serena's establishment found when they came to her — pleasure. The fulfilment of every wanton, hidden desire.

Selena had not visited her sister since she'd opened these doors, but she'd heard rumours of this place, of the decadence that could be found within these walls.

Located in the eastern district — Apollo's domain — *Épicurien* eschewed all the values for which he stood — truth and purity, a virtue of body that was above the temptations of the flesh.

He'd tried to have her bordello closed, but Serena had stood against him, preying upon his guilt.

He'd owed her this. Eventually, Apollo had given in.

Selena stepped out of the car, greeted by black granite columns and a white marble façade. Three storeys, *Épicurien* was an elaborate building with statues of lovers twisted together in every imaginable position displayed within the lush, green gardens of the entryway.

With Adonis beside her, and Ares to the right of him, they walked along the cobbled stones, past the fountain in the centre of the garden, and up the steps.

Tonight, *Épicurien* was empty of patrons and, as soon as Selena stepped inside, she understood why. From the exterior, one could not see the damage, but, once inside, she saw the fire that had blackened the walls along with the ceiling and the floor of the greeting room. Charred paint and wallpaper were peeling and the acrid burning smell of smoke still choked the air.

From the corner of her eye, Selena caught a flash of crimson and her gaze easily found her sister, a beacon of scarlet light among the darkness. Like her own, Serena's skin glowed a shimmering bronze, her raven hair hanging in wild abandon to her waist, framing her perfectly sculpted face of pure beauty. Serena's wide topaz eyes registered surprise, then pleasure, even as they hinted at the anxiety the fire had caused. What was *not* present was pain or suffering. What was *not* present was anger or even the desperate need for revenge.

Selena envied her sister. She always had.

Serena had not blamed Apollo as Selena had blamed Adonis, so her sister did not labour under the weight of bitterness. Freed of her virginity, Serena had felt free to pursue the pleasures of the flesh, to indulge in the carnal desires that had been buried deep inside her.

Serena had not felt ruined. She'd felt liberated.

Selena had hated her because of that...and envied her.

She'd wanted to feel liberated, to be free. She'd tried desperately to feel those things, but she couldn't.

"Selena." The whispery soft voice was as genuine as it was lovely, as pure as it was seductive.

Her sister moved towards her as if to embrace her, but at the last moment she stopped, as if the years and recriminations that had torn them apart still stood between them, separating them.

"Where are my brothers?" Ares asked, his brusque tone breaking through the awkward moment.

"They are outside trying to determine the source of the fire."

Ares nodded and started in the direction Serena had pointed.

"I will go with him," Adonis said from beside her. Selena looked up at him, her eyes saying what her lips would not—*please do not leave me alone with her.* She'd all but demanded to come along to see her sister, but, now that she'd seen her, Selena did not want to remain in her presence any longer. It was awkward and strained.

His eyes replied what his lips would not—*you need to speak with her.*

He followed after his brother, taking with him his warmth and the security of his presence. Selena had not realised how much she'd needed it, how comforting his nearness had been, until he was gone.

She stared at his retreating back until he'd disappeared outside. Once Adonis was gone, she had no choice but to turn her attention upon her sister.

"Serena."

A smile, identical to her own, flashed across her sister's face. "I am surprised to see you, but I am glad you are here." Her smile dimmed somewhat. "Why *are* you here? With Adonis, no less?"

"I was with him when I learned of the fire," she said truthfully. "I wanted to be sure you were all right." Another truth.

A host of emotions shimmered across her sister's face—all of them pained Selena. Her sister had always been more sensitive than she. Selena could tell the absence of their closeness had hurt Serena deeply. It had hurt Selena too, but she was more adept at burying pain, hiding it.

"I've missed you," Serena said finally, quietly.

Silence.

Nothing but silence hovered between them until Selena relented. It was not Serena's fault that she had not been as broken by what had happened. She'd blamed her sister, felt betrayed that Serena had rejected living in a convent to seek out a life so different from her own. It was not Serena's fault that she still openly experienced passion, while Selena had been torn apart by it, shamed by the very thought of it.

None of this was Serena's fault.

"I've missed you, too."

That admission surprised her sister, which was why she probably felt at liberty to be more candid with her.

"Does that mean you've forgiven me?"

"I've never sought your forgiveness, because there was nothing to forgive. You've never wronged me, Serena."

"But I let you down."

Selena acknowledged that, but only to herself. Much had happened in the years that separated them. She'd finally understood that her lust for revenge would have eventually strangled Serena. It would have crippled her vibrant and loving sister until she was as hollow and empty as she.

Yes, she'd felt let down, but Serena had had to remain true to herself and to her needs. It would not have been fair to force her to carry the weight that only Selena seemed to be burdened by.

She understood that now.

"You had an obligation to yourself. I cannot find fault with that."

Serena's smile was serene, which was probably why she'd been so named. Though she was the younger twin, her sister had always possessed an intuitiveness that seemed to give her peace, whereas Selena could find none.

"Does that mean you've forgiven Adonis then?"

Her belly clenched at Serena's question. *Forgiven Adonis?* She'd touched him intimately, kissed him and allowed him to do the same to her. And they were not yet done. At some point she would take him inside her body, and take his pleasure, his desire, his essence.

She wanted him…fiercely.

But forgiven him? She had not.

"I do not think I will ever be able to forgive him."

"And yet, you've allowed him to make love to you."

Selena gasped.

"I am a courtesan," Serena offered in answer to the question that must have blazed in her eyes. "The moment you walked in I knew. He stood close to you, a gesture of protection, but also one that spoke of possessiveness. And your eyes—they glow with fulfilled desire, as do his. Even had I been blind, the scent of him is all over you, so strong it is, as if you've bathed in his essence."

Serena—her innocent, naive, guileless sister. That's how she'd remembered her. The woman before her was none of those things.

There was a confidence in her words, a knowing that spoke of sophistication and experience.

Her sister was an infamous madam, a legendary courtesan. Lovemaking was her profession and her passion.

Serena turned from her and sauntered over to the bar where she poured herself a glass of wine. Selena shook her head when she lifted an empty glass, offering her one as well.

After taking a sip of the rich, red liquid, Serena turned her attention upon her once again — the gaze of a wizened, mature woman.

"You still blame Adonis for what happened to you, but you shouldn't."

Selena's eyes became hard slits. "Just because you've forgiven Apollo does not mean I should do the same."

Serena took another sip from her glass, the grace with which she drew the wine into her mouth and down her throat giving Selena a brief glimpse of why her sister was the legend that she was. The simple act, thoughtless and casual, had exuded pure seduction.

"You *should* do as I've done because, like Apollo, Adonis was just as victimised by all of this as we were. That you do not acknowledge this, that you do not accept this, will only continue to prevent you from finding happiness. This bitterness you carry inside you will only destroy you in the end."

"Happiness?" She sneered. "Is that what you've found in this whorehouse of yours?"

Serena set her glass down, harder than necessary. That was the only indication of her anger, which she masked well.

"Hurl names at me all you like, but I've found freedom here. I've built a place of my own, a life of my own. What have you found, dear sister, locked away in that convent—yielding beneath the dictates of others, nurturing nothing but guilt and shame for something that was never your fault?"

Serena might as well have struck her, the truth of her words stung so painfully. Growing up, they'd rarely argued. Selena was not prepared for such an exchange. She gathered herself, putting aside the years of resentment and envy she harboured towards her sister for being brave enough to forge a life for herself. Selena focused instead on the question that had plagued her on the drive all the way there.

"What do you know of Father's involvement in what happened to us?"

"Father?" Serena's eyes rounded, her cheeks paled. "What does he have to do with any of this?" Her lips twisted into a bitter smile. "Besides the obvious, like disowning his only daughters and secreting them off to a convent." Serena shook her head then, her brow creased as if she'd just mulled over the question in greater depth and had come to a resounding conclusion. "Why would you believe he had anything to do with all of this? He was not even in the city at the time."

"I know," was all she said.

Her sister appeared as ignorant as she, which made her wonder about another question that had plagued her for some time.

"The brothers seem to believe that Father was involved somehow. I did not believe them—I still don't. But, on the way over here, I wondered if you knew something that I didn't." Selena speared her sister with identical brown eyes. "I wondered if the reason why you were able to forgive Apollo was because you knew someone else was at fault."

"That is the very reason why I forgave Apollo."

Selena's eyes rounded. "But you just said—"

"That I have no knowledge of Father being involved, and I don't. What I do believe, however, is that Apollo hurt me because he was compelled to do so. Did you not wonder what their motivations were, what had prompted them to go from loving fiancés to cruel and distant strangers?"

Of course she'd wondered—many nights that was all she'd ever thought about.

When she shook her head, Serena continued, "Well, Father owed a debt and *Dieu* forced us to pay it. That is all I know. All I've ever known."

Selena started at her sister's revelation. *Dieu* – the man who'd taken in the four men who would later share his legend, who would later share his namesake. He'd given the four brothers a home and a way of life. And that life had corrupted them, tainted their souls.

They owed *Dieu* everything and would have done anything for him, even destroyed the lives of the women they'd loved.

"Adonis and Apollo were just as manipulated by him as we were."

"And Apollo told you this?"

The light seemed to dim in Serena's eyes. "Apollo tells me nothing."

Then how is it you know these things? Selena wanted to demand, but before she could, they were interrupted by the presence of Ares and Adonis. She let the subject drop, determined to probe deeper elsewhere.

She wondered then what other truths still lingered out there, unknown and unspoken. If there had been a debt owed by her father, what had he taken—from the man everyone called a god because he was so feared—that had been worth the very lives of his only daughters?

"You did not tell us the fire began in your private chambers," Ares said as soon as he stood before them.

"Because you did not ask." Serena shrugged. "Besides, you still have not told me why you're here. This is Apollo's district. I understand why he came to investigate, but not why the rest of you have joined him."

Ares' lips thinned into a firm line, and Selena wondered if he ever smiled, the slash of his mouth was so tight. That mouth did not seem forthcoming with answers, either.

"The fire was started in the sitting room just beyond your bedroom," Adonis offered even as he shot his brother a quelling glare. "It was made to appear as if one of your candles fell over accidentally, but there are distinct footprints that lead from your bedroom outside, and disappear into tyre tracks. This was no accident, and whoever did this certainly thought you would be inside your bedroom."

"And usually I would be at this time of night."

"So why weren't you?"

They all turned at the deep, masculine voice that was a rich, throaty baritone.

Apollo.

His gaze was riveted on Serena, both accusatory and haunted, as if he wished she'd been in that room, though he knew it was wrong to.

Serena glimpsed the look and acknowledged it by the fire flickering in her eyes in answer to his dark stare.

"As you well know, Apollo, I retire around ten o'clock to entertain guests, but tonight I was to present a new girl so I remained downstairs." She levelled her gaze at him. "And that is why, when the fire began, I was *not* in my chambers."

The look that passed between Apollo and Serena, the veiled meaning beneath their seemingly innocuous words, hinted at deeper animosity, unspoken guilt, and a desperate longing that had never been fulfilled. Selena knew this was so because she felt it...and shared the same feelings with the man who stood beside her.

"Why would someone want to harm Serena?"

"The same reason why someone wants to harm you." Eros, who'd remained outside to further investigate, drew their attention as he entered the main dining area. "There has been a fire at the Convent of Her Lady Francis."

"What?" Selena gasped.

"Another fire at your hotel, Adonis."

Selena's blood ran hot then cold. Someone was after Adonis, her sister, and apparently now her. No one had even known she was leaving the convent tonight, so everyone would expect her to still be there, tucked away in her bed, fast asleep.

Just as Serena should have been in her bedroom with a guest.

Just as Adonis should have still been in the midst of his grand opening.

A nun and a whore—it was laughable. Selena and her sister were not important enough to harm. Adonis?

Now *he* was different, but why threaten him now? Why all of them on this night?

It made no sense—none of it. But, to glimpse the faces of the four brothers, one would think it made sense to *them*.

"What do you know that you're not telling us?"

"What I've been trying to tell you all night," Adonis said to her, his voice quiet but not so low that the others could not hear him. "That the moment you came to me, you became a target, as did everyone who had anything to do with that night."

"If that is true then why set fire to the convent, knowing I would not be there?"

"I imagine they thought you would have done what you'd set out to do and returned by now," Ares replied. "*Or* there could be someone at that convent who also knows the truth—who knows where you are—which could be why Adonis' hotel was targeted as well."

"The truth? What *is* the truth?" she demanded, her attention settling on each brother. They seemed to know this truth, while she and her sister remained woefully ignorant.

"I thought I knew," Eros said softly and that was when she noticed he held something in his hand. It reflected the light—pure platinum shimmering with diamonds that formed a single letter—D. "But I found this outside. It must have been dropped when whoever set that fire escaped."

"That is impossible," Ares whispered. The steely edge to his voice was like ice creeping down her back.

There was real fear in his voice.

She looked at all of them—the four gods.

There was real fear on their faces.

"What is it?" she asked, but none looked at her—they simply stared at the ring Eros held.

"It cannot be," Adonis said from beside her. "He's dead."

The sheer terror in the eyes of each brother told Selena that whoever they'd thought was dead was probably very much alive—and that their return to the living did not bode well for any of them.

Chapter Five

"Who's dead?" Serena asked.

The four men looked at her as if she was a ghost they could see through — they did not see her, nor did they answer.

Selena decided to remain silent. Adonis was not given to answering her questions in private, and she surmised he'd not answer them now either, but her curiosity burned through her, making her restless.

"Ares, will you take Selena home? I will join you shortly after I've visited my hotel."

Selena moved to protest, but the look in Adonis' eyes stilled her. His expression was more telling than anything, even the tension that radiated from his rigid body revealed much. When they were alone, he would willingly submit to her, but not before his brothers, and not when her life was in danger.

She bit her tongue.

"I will go to the convent, then," said Eros. "Though I imagine the fires were set by the same person — "

"Or several are working together," Ares added.

There was no doubt of a connection between the three fires, just as there was no doubt that, if there were multiple individuals involved, they were connected as well.

All eyes swung to Apollo, the dark beauty of his face shadowed beneath the faint light in the room. Despite the darkness, his scowl was visible, the tension emanating from him palpable.

"I will remain here with Serena," he bit out tightly, harshly. It was apparent that he would have preferred any other task but this, and Selena gathered why.

The entire time, his eyes had flickered with longing—and with hate—whenever they had landed upon her sister. He still wanted her, but loathed himself because of his weakness and his desire.

Selena understood the war that raged across his face, the torment that burned through his body. She was an intimate prisoner of the same burning affection held for one man whom she knew it was wrong to still want.

"Do not do me any favours, Apollo." Serena shot back, her voice cold. "I am more than capable of taking care of myself."

Without so much as a courteous farewell, Serena gathered her billowing skirts in her hands and swept out of the room with all the beauty and grace of the most sought-after courtesan in the city.

Serena's lack of decorum was telling. Her sister had always been a stickler for niceties and politeness. That she'd forgone such courtesies revealed to Selena that her sister was furious—the sole object of her anger embodied in the one man she could not seem to stop loving…*Apollo.*

She started after Serena, the protectiveness she felt instinctive, but, again, Adonis stilled her with the shake of his head, his expression imploring her to let her sister be.

She would be fine, his eyes said, and Selena knew this to be true. Serena was resilient, her inner will even stronger than Selena's.

"We must go." Adonis' voice was quiet, but everyone heard and understood. Whoever was stalking them, setting fire to their homes, had a plan — one they needed to discover, and quickly.

* * * *

Selena did not grasp how weary she was until she entered Adonis' home half an hour later. The door closed behind her, the sharp thud reminding her that Adonis did not stand beside her. That in his place stood his brother, the oldest of them all, the most dangerous and the most feared.

She turned to face him, meeting his black stare. His obsidian eyes were seductive, fathomless and she imagined any woman who stared too deep or too long would become spellbound by their intensity, enraptured by the desire they invoked.

But there was only one pair of eyes that could do the same to her. They were golden, pure and radiant, and they made her burn with need and longing every time they touched upon her.

"You do not like me very much, do you?" Her voice broke through the tense silence, her question seeking confirmation of what she already knew. She did not need his approval — she only needed to know why she didn't have it.

"I have not been acquainted with you long enough or even well enough to make such a sweeping statement of you as a person."

"And, yet, that does not stop you from hating me or blaming me."

His brow furrowed, his eyes as hard and unyielding as the granite they'd seemingly been carved from. "I don't hate you."

What he left unsaid spoke loudly and clearly.

"Your brother used me then ridiculed me before my family and friends." She shook with barely leashed anger. "And yet you stand there, full of impudence, blaming *me*."

He stalked towards her — there was no other way to describe the feline grace of his predatory movements. When he halted before her she was forced to tilt her head back, meeting the full weight of his glare. "Adonis was forced to do what he did —"

"By whom?"

Her question startled him. "He did not tell you?"

When she shook her head, his reaction stunned her. He smiled. A small furling of the corner of his mouth. "All this time I thought you were playing ignorant but you truly do not know." Within the blink of an eye, his mocking smile disappeared. In its place was the cold stare she was becoming accustomed to. "If Adonis has not told you, then I shall not. It is not my place."

"He mentioned my father," she hedged. "He said he had something to do with this all."

"And he did, but that is all I will say."

Something in his voice caused her to study him through narrowed eyes. "I do not believe what your brother and now you have implied about my father. He would never hurt me or my sister."

Fire flashed in his eyes, but his icy expression did not change. "If that is true, then you have no cause to be concerned, now, do you?"

His tone was mocking, challenging, but she did not rise to his bait. She only had one question for him, one he'd not yet answered.

"Why do you blame me for what happened?"

"I do not blame you for what happened, Selena. I know better than anyone what happened to you was not your fault, nor did you bring it upon yourself. You were innocent. I have always acknowledged that..."

"But?" she offered, when it did not appear as if he would continue.

His expression hardened, then turned cold like a freezing wind whipping across her skin. "But... I blame you for what happened after. I blame you for what you did later."

"What I did? After that night, I was disowned by my father and forced into a convent. I did nothing after that—"

"Oh, you did a great deal, Selena." He inched closer, his low voice as seductive as it was dangerous. "You destroyed my brother, ripped out his very soul. With your lies, you slowly tortured him, killed him."

She gasped at the conviction of his words, the vehemence in his eyes. *Lies? What lies?*

"What is it that you *think* I said?"

"Do not pretend ignorance—"

"Does it look as if I am pretending?" she snapped. He'd condemned her and she deserved to know why.

He stood rooted to his spot, studying her closely. She knew the moment he glimpsed the truth buried deep in her gaze. "It would seem that we've all been manipulated by him," he said finally, his eyes flat. "Every single one of us."

"What is it that you think I said?" Selena repeated.

"It does not matter."

"It matters to me," she said quietly. "If it tortured your brother then I want to know."

He regarded her with wary eyes, measuring the weight of his words. When he spoke again, the statement that tumbled from his lips made her blood run cold until her heart seized in her chest.

"Adonis believes you told your family and your friends that he forced himself upon you—"

"*What?*"

"You can imagine what that did to him," he continued past her outburst. "How others looked at him, treated him. He could have denied it, but he didn't. He believed it to be true. It killed him to know you believed him to be such a monster. He's hated himself ever since."

She could not speak. Her throat closed up, her vocal cords raw. Adonis had done many things that night, but forced himself upon her he had not. He'd seduced her, taken her virginity, bragged to others of what he'd done, then ended their engagement. Those were all truths, but that he ever took her by force was a lie.

Bile rose up inside her. It all was painfully clear now. Why he welcomed his death at her hands, why he accepted her revenge, demanded her to make him suffer. She felt sick.

Yes, she wanted his suffering and her revenge—but she wanted those things because with his cruelty he'd destroyed her life, made her body betray her as he'd seduced her, and her weakness still haunted her...still shamed her.

She wanted it for what he'd done, not for what he hadn't.

"I never said such things."

"I realise that now, though Adonis does not."

She closed her eyes then opened them again as if the simple act could somehow blind her to the pain Adonis must have laboured under all this time.

"The rumours say that you are heartless and cold." Ares' statement broke through her thoughts. She did not know what prompted it, but she could not help but smile.

"Rumours say the same of you."

His lips twitched as if he wanted to smile, but the slight flicker in his eyes was the only indication that she'd amused him.

"You care for my brother," he stated flatly, the tone of his voice daring her to say otherwise.

She didn't.

She couldn't.

What he said was true. She did care for Adonis.

"I wish I didn't." That raised one dark eyebrow. "Your brother did not force himself upon me, but he *did* seduce me, ridicule me then humiliate me. No one would have me after that. I went into the convent because I could not face the world afterwards."

"He had no other choice but to do what he did—"

"That is what you keep telling me, but yet you tell me nothing else. The more I talk to you and your brother, the more I realise there is a great deal to the events that prompted that night of which I am ignorant—"

The abrupt sound of the front door opening then closing halted her next words.

"The one who should answer your questions is Adonis, not me."

Heavy footsteps muffled by plush carpet drew closer.

"He refuses to tell me anything."

Ares' eyes flashed dark as a pitch-black night. "I imagine you possess the tools to force him to reveal to you anything your heart desires."

She gasped at the meaning of his words and the provocative glint in his eyes.

It disappeared when a shadow fell over them.

Adonis had returned.

His eyes were haunted and weary. Tonight had taken its toll upon him. She was surprised by the tingling of her fingers that itched to reach out and smooth the lines of exhaustion from his brow. She longed to kiss him until the intense scowl disappeared from his face. Selena forced herself to clench her hands into fists so that she would not succumb to such foolish impressions.

"Did you find anything?"

Ares claimed Adonis' attention. The ring in the palm of Adonis' hand ensnared Ares' gaze in return.

A single letter encrusted in diamonds was set in sparkling platinum, of such a brilliant radiance that it glowed a silver white. It was identical to the one Eros had discovered earlier.

"I found this in the rubble. The damage was minimal. The fire began in my penthouse. My guards put it out soon after it started."

"And where did it start?"

"In my bedroom." Adonis looked at her, his eyes full of accusation. His expression puzzled her until he held out his other hand. "I also found this." He handed the object over to Ares who studied it for maybe a second before his gaze joined Adonis', both pinning her down.

"You think I put that there?" she cried, pointing to the small explosive device in their hands.

Their shared silence said that was exactly what they thought.

"I've lived in a convent for sixteen years with peaceful nuns. You cannot think that—"

"That you what? Don't know how to make a bomb?" Ares' brow arched. "The Order of Her Lady Francis is known to study the Eastern fighting arts, as many monks and sisters of the holy order do. Rumours abound that you've mastered these fighting arts, that you are adept at wielding a number of weapons, that you are equally capable of disarming *others* of a number of weapons." His expression hardened. "While you were locked in that convent, it is obvious you did more than remain on your knees in fervent prayer.

"It is interesting that the one connection between these fires is that *you* seemed to have been at each and every one of the places where they all began. You could have planted those devices and set them to go off long after you would be gone so that no one would ever suspect you."

Her jaw clenched in anger. "I did not start those fires. I did not place explosives there." She looked to Adonis, imploring him. "You cannot possibly believe I would ever harm my sister."

Whatever he saw on her face, glimpsed in her eyes, caused him to waver. "No. I do not believe you would harm her."

Selena did not imagine Ares' snort, especially not when Adonis glared at him.

"She could be lying."

"She could be telling the truth," Adonis retorted. "No device was found at her sister's bordello either."

"Thus far." Ares' eyes sharpened on her, before he glanced at Adonis. "What about Eros? Did he find anything?"

"I have not yet heard from him," Adonis replied.

"He is probably still at the convent. I will join him there."

"Before you do, what do you want me to do with the ring?" Adonis held it out to Ares and Selena was certain it was not her imagination that his brother shrank away from the glittering piece of jewellery.

"Keep it," Ares whispered. "There is obviously a meaning to it we have yet to discover."

Ares crossed the room towards the door. "Once I've met with Eros, I will contact you with what we've learned. In the meantime, I suggest you find somewhere else to stay."

"My home is secure," Adonis assured. "Between my guards and the security system, I will be safe."

Ares glanced at her. The motion was fleeting, the message was not.

But will you be safe from her?

This night, Adonis was safe from her, but she could not promise any other. She looked away, knowing her flickering gaze would further confirm Ares' suspicions, further condemn her in his eyes.

"Be careful, Adonis," Ares said quietly, yet pointedly, then stalked out of the room, every movement as silent and deadly as the man himself.

"He does not trust me," Selena said as soon as the door closed behind Ares.

"Because he senses the reason for your presence and knows you mean to do me harm." Adonis shrugged out of his suit jacket, then peeled off his shirt, discarding each article of clothing as he made his way to his bedroom, seemingly untroubled by what he'd just said, as if her desire to kill him did not cause him a care in the world.

She followed after him. "And that does not bother you—my intent to kill you."

He stared down at her, and she held his gaze so that she would not lose herself in the beauty of his bare chest.

"I have already told you, it has yet to be determined if you will actually carry out this plan of yours."

He cupped her cheek, the gentle touch of his fingers against her face causing a shudder to race through her, singeing her toes.

He smiled—at the desire he'd ignited in her…and at her inability to hide it. She wanted to pull away, but she couldn't. She wanted to feel shame for her traitorous reaction, feel anger at his arrogance, but she didn't.

"Why are you and your brothers afraid of that ring?" He'd left the ring in the other room, seeming almost in a hurry to set it down.

His hand dropped from her face, the absence of its warmth making her want to reach for him and drag his hand back. She restrained herself.

"It's not the ring, but what it represents."

"And what is that?"

He sighed, and she glimpsed the battle raging in his eyes. He wanted to tell her, but was not yet certain if he could.

She waited. He had reason not to trust her. But someone had set fire to her convent believing her to be there. If he was in danger, then so was she. That bonded them, even if it did not warrant complete and unconditional trust.

"It represents my father. The ring represents his omnipotent power."

"*Dieu*?" she asked, before she could stop herself. Now she understood. Their father had been dead for more than a year now. "I take it his seal is somewhere with his personal effects."

"It *should* be in our family safe at our old home."

Their former home, which lay at the centre of the four districts.

"Obviously, someone who saw it has made a replica of it."

That was logical, but the pensive expression on Adonis' face suggested otherwise. "That is possible," he acknowledged.

"But you do not believe it."

"Besides our father, only us four know of it. He never wore that ring in public. I've only seen it inside his safe."

His voice trailed off as if he wanted to say more, as if there was something else to the story.

She didn't press him. Too much had transpired this evening. She was tired. He was tired. All she wanted was to go to bed.

Selena stared up at him, and the shadows beneath his eyes weakened her. What she'd learned from Ares pierced her in her heart, in the very place she'd thought frozen all these years. That it hurt for the man who stood before her said otherwise.

Tonight was not the night to broach the subject, nor was it the night to continue their game of revenge. Tomorrow maybe. In the morning.

If someone did not set fire to his bedroom where they slept. If they were still alive...

"Will you sleep beside me tonight?" she offered, her voice quiet.

So much had changed from the moment she'd entered his penthouse.

Yet so much was still the same.

What Ares had revealed begged her to forgive Adonis...until she remembered how she'd suffered. Then forgiveness was replaced by pain that soon gave way to bitterness.

Adonis may have been a tool of manipulation, but who would use him to hurt her? Why would anyone have cared to ruin a spoilt, pampered heiress? No one. Even if Adonis was not solely guilty, that still did not excuse what he'd done. Nothing ever would.

Despite his protests, he'd had a choice. He'd chosen to destroy her.

She looked into his eyes. He was stretched across the bed, his golden body beneath the white satin sheets. He pulled aside the covers, offering her a place to sleep beside him as she'd just asked.

So much had changed from the moment she'd entered his penthouse. Yet so much was still the same.

A lump clogged her throat as she removed her shirt and slacks and, wearing just her undergarments, slid into the bed beside him.

If what Ares said was true then Adonis had suffered alongside her, and yet he would accept her own suffering in order to heal her, to unburden her of the pain she still carried within.

Before she could think about her actions, before she could stop herself, she palmed his stubbled jaw and leaned in, her lips finding his in a kiss born of need, full of memories from the past.

She poured herself into that kiss, much as she'd done earlier, until they were panting. He wrenched his lips from hers, his hands clutching the sheets, his eyes clenched shut.

He would not make love to her, even as she begged him with her lips, her eyes, her entire being—he still resisted. He'd hurt her. He did not deserve her tenderness, her desire. He only sought to experience her pain, her suffering. But he'd been hurt too, not by *her* exactly, but he'd been caught up in the scandal that had ruined her, that she now realised had ruined him too.

Before they were done, she would have his pleasure, but not this night.

She stroked his cheek.

"Goodnight," she whispered as she lay down and fell asleep beside him.

Chapter Six

The same vision haunted Adonis every night. The image that was branded on his subconscious found its way into his dreams, as it did *every night*.

He awoke with a start, his gaze clashing with deep, topaz eyes, identical to the ones belonging to the woman he saw in his dreams every single night.

She blinked, the fan of long sooty lashes shadowing wide, beautiful eyes.

The vision he'd glimpsed had only been a dream, yet the woman before him was real.

Tiny embers of sunlight brushed over her shoulder, bathing her skin in its golden rays. It was barely dawn. Like so many nights before, he hadn't even slept five hours.

"You called my name in your sleep." Her soft voice broke through his thoughts as he sat up.

He knew what she saw when she looked at him, a face that was as perfectly beautiful as it was eerily cold. Adonis avoided her searching stare. What could he tell her? That he called her name in his sleep every night? That sometimes he awoke clutching the pillow beside him as if he was reaching for her. Many times the image in his dreams was so real that he thought he was going insane. And many times he wished he *would* lose his mind so he wouldn't have to face the bleak existence that was now his life.

He slipped from the bed without a word.

"You did not force yourself upon me," she blurted out, her words cutting like a knife, to the very heart of him. He twisted around, the emotions swirling inside him too conflicting to even begin to sift through.

"You kept saying you were sorry. You begged me to forgive you for forcing me." She sat up, clutching the covers to her chest. "But you never forced me. I wanted you that night. I took you to my bed willingly."

"Because you were naive and foolish," he sneered. "You didn't stand a chance the moment I touched you."

"You're right. I didn't." Her words deflated his anger in an instant. "Your skills were legendary. Of course, I did not stand a chance against you, but that did not mean I did not welcome your touch."

"You begged me to stop." The words came out raw as if ripped from his chest. They might as well have been. He saw her eyes as they'd been—full of fear, tears shimmering in their depths just before he'd pushed his way inside her body.

"I was a virgin. Of course I begged you to stop. That was only because of the physical pain—"

"But I didn't stop."

"Because I begged you not to."

He frowned. "Why are you telling me this now?"

"Because I want you to know it's not what you did that night that I blame you for. It's what came after."

He retreated from her stare. He did not want her pity. He wanted her forgiveness. He didn't deserve it, but he longed for it nonetheless.

She'd never forgive him. Her last statement said as much. Apollo was right. She just couldn't.

"Where are you going?" she asked when he turned to walk away.

"To bathe." He did not stop.

"Can that wait until later?"

He stilled. It was the unspoken need in her voice that halted his steps. "I would have you touch me again," she whispered.

He faced her. The needs of her body were revealed by the yearning shimmering in her eyes, the dark flush of her cheeks.

His body responded to the lust radiating from her, the desire that hovered between them. In an instant his manhood unfurled from its nest of curls and grew ramrod straight.

"And what if I do not wish to touch you? What if I wish for you to touch me?"

Puzzlement gave way to knowing as the flames of desire burned higher in her eyes.

"You want me to hurt you," she stated matter-of-factly.

"I want the pleasure-pain of yielding beneath your touch."

In his teens, he'd become a consort to both men and women. He'd learned the needs of their bodies and he'd fulfilled them. Never had anyone fulfilled his — until Selena. At the naive age of nineteen, she'd looked into his jaded eyes and seen him for the man he was. She'd looked past his arrogance and accepted him, loved him. She'd offered him the gift of her body and in turn he'd been forced to destroy her because she'd dared to love him.

Last night he'd glimpsed the passion they could have shared had fate not torn them apart, and he yearned to experience that again. He longed to lose himself in her. He did not deserve such pleasure, but she was determined to have it. And, if it was even possible, his body grew harder at the notion of him surrendering to her as he'd done last night.

He followed her with his gaze as she swayed across the room, her hips supple, her breasts full. She stood before his closet and opened it. He knew the item she sought and his breath caught in his chest when she pulled it out, along with a small bottle, and closed the doors.

"You will have to help me. I've never worn one of these."

His brows arched as he stalked towards her. "I would think you'd never seen one either or known of its purpose, but apparently I am mistaken."

Her lips curled into a delicate smile and his heart lurched at the simple gesture. He'd amused her with his teasing. How long had it been since he'd laughed, enjoyed banter...even smiled.

"I may have lived in a convent but I was not entirely sheltered. I read things, saw things."

He grinned, even as it was faint and fleeting. "I do not doubt that."

His smile faded then, his eyes pooling dark when he said, "Take off your underwear and bra."

"Why?"

"Because it will be that much more pleasurable for you as the leather pushes against your clitoris."

Her eyes rounded and her cheeks pinked but she did not protest. She set the object down on the floor between them and stripped out of her bra and underwear. When she was done she picked it up again and the bottle she'd set down as well, but, before she could put it on, he stilled her with the touch of his hand.

"Do you trust me?"

The tapestry of emotions that flickered in her eyes told him just how deeply his question affected her.

"I mean, when it comes to sexual matters," he added.

"I trust you in many things," she murmured. The truth of her words was there in her eyes. She may trust him in many things, but not all things—her eyes said that too. Maybe one day that would change.

With gentle hands, he took the items from her and set them atop the bed.

"I would have you lie down and spread your legs."

Her eyes rounded. "But—"

He silenced her with a single finger against her lips. "You said you trusted me in this. So, trust me."

She hesitated only a moment before she stretched out across the bed and parted her legs. He sucked in a breath, drawing in the scent of her, the essence of her arousal that was glistening wet against the lips of her sex.

He plucked the bottle of lubricant from the bed and set it atop his bedside table.

"If I am successful, we will not need this," he said in answer to her question, hooking his arms within the crook of her thighs to splay her wide open.

"But I thought—"

His eyes twinkled, disarming her. "I said trust me."

Before she could say another word or protest, he dipped his head to bury his face against the dripping wet heat of her sex.

Desire lanced through him as he stroked his tongue inside her, the heat of his arousal mingling with hers, coiling in his belly.

Her soft gasp was a seductive whisper stroking over him, as warm and intimate as a kiss. He savoured her pleasure as he devoured her with his tongue and lips, until she poured forth her desire. Her body vibrated around him, her thighs trembling beneath his hands. When he closed his lips around her hard, tight bud, he was rewarded with her wet heat and a deep, stirring shudder that fired his blood. He moaned against the lips of her sex, sending tiny vibrations tingling through her.

She gasped again, then cried out, her hands finding their way to his head to tangle in his unbound hair.

Within minutes, he had Selena writhing beneath him, panting from his touch. He needed her to come, to climax against his mouth, to drench him with her essence. He spread the lips of her pussy with one hand, while he plunged two fingers from the other inside her.

She cried out in pleasure, her back arching off the bed. Her body was tight around his fingers, clenching him like a fist. He bit back a groan, as he resisted the urge to cover her and bury his cock balls deep inside her heat.

Soon.

Soon he would have her desire, her pleasure.

Soon she would fulfil his needs.

Soon they would both yield to the mutual pleasure these long years apart had denied them, but this morning, with the first light of dawn, he wanted only to yield to her.

Tremors raked their way through her as she dug her nails deeply into his scalp. She was close, her body trembling with need and pleasure.

He pumped inside her faster, his fingers curling against the roof of her sheath until she splintered apart around him. He sucked on her nub until she begged him to stop then sat back to watch as waves of pleasure swamped her, leaving her flushed and spent.

While she still lay there, nursing the afterglow of her orgasm, he speared her with two fingers, coating his fingers with her cum. She watched him through hooded eyes as he spread her cream over the rubber cock that bobbed back and forth against the harness.

Understanding darkened her gaze and she stared at him in silence as he coated the long length of the cock with her cum until it was glistening wet.

Without a word, he handed the harness over to her and watched her in rapt fascination, as she'd just watched him.

She slipped it on as if it were a pair of lace panties. But instead of lace, the harness was fashioned out of leather with metal buckles against her hips that she adjusted until it fit her snugly. The rubber shaft was positioned over the mouth of her pussy so that every time she pushed inside him, it would push back against her.

The thick, hard phallus held her attention as it bobbed in the air. When she touched it, stroking it as she'd stroked his shaft last night, he sucked in a breath, desire bubbling in his veins.

His sharp intake of breath drew her attention, her gaze colliding with his.

"How would you like me?" he asked her, even though this had been *his* idea, *his* fantasy.

"I wish to look into your eyes as I fill you, as I give you pleasure. I want to glimpse every moment of your desire. I want to see you at the very moment you come."

Her words caused a knot to coil in his belly and tighten. Without breaking her stare, he lay down across the bed before her, flat on his back.

She hesitated at first as she hooked her arms beneath the crook of his knees as he'd done to her only moments ago.

"Will this hurt you?"

"As it hurt you the first time I took you? Yes."

"But I thought that... I thought..." She blushed a deep red.

"That I've lain with men?" he asked and when she nodded he replied, "I have, but not in a very long time." He did not add that it had not been his choice. That he'd never wished to spend his days and nights pleasing either men *or* women. So little of his life had been his choice. So few things within it he'd chosen.

"But I've never allowed a woman to do this to me, so I imagine it will hurt some."

"If you've never used this, then why do you even have it?" she asked, gesturing down at the harness she now wore.

His smile was gentle, patient. "People own artwork and sculptures that they never use. This is the same for me."

She did not look at him as if that was a strange statement, but he did not know if she truly understood either. He'd lived his life with sexual desire as his constant companion so he'd begun collecting tools of pleasure more out of habit than anything else. As he'd said, just like artwork, he admired such objects, though he did not use them.

"I do not wish to hurt you."

"You are wrong, Selena... You do."

She seemed to want to argue, or to disagree. He did not care. Seizing her hips with both hands, he pulled her forward, a small moan dying in his throat when the slick wet tip of the rubber shaft nudged his hole.

She moaned as she pushed inside him, and he imagined the pleasure she felt. The leather and rubber pushing together to brush against her clit, trapping it, applying a steady, constant pressure as she sank her way inside him.

His cock wept a single drop of pre-cum, and he wrapped his firm hand around his hard staff and stroked himself as she filled him.

Selena watched him closely, her cheeks flushed, her lips slightly parted. He could have drowned in the deep pools of her eyes, could have died from the pleasure of her stretching him.

He experienced a dull, throbbing pain when she was seated fully inside him and her eyes widened with a soft gasp, followed by a gasp of his own.

"Am I hurting you?" she asked, already retreating, but he gripped her hips firmly, sending her ploughing back inside him, eliciting mutual moans that blended together.

"Fuck me," he rasped harshly, directing her hips until she grasped the rhythm, the age-old pace that joined their bodies, that bonded them.

A fresh urgency raked through him with stroke after sensuous stroke and the blood in his veins grew hot, pumping molten lava.

Her desire and sensuality matched his, and he responded to it...welcomed it. With soft murmurs and faint words, he encouraged her until her strokes quickened, her body straining for the release that his sought.

He pumped his cock faster.

He took her thrusts deeper.

He called her name, squeezing his ruddy length in the palm of his hand, fisting it tight until she found that soft sensitive spot deep inside him and he exploded, his semen pouring from his body in thick ropes against his belly as he came on a splintered cry.

Selena watched him, drinking in his passion, her eyes glittering with satisfaction at his release. Only then did she seek completion.

Sweat dotted her naked body, her breasts swaying gently.

"Come for me, Selena," he urged, his hands finding her hips to quicken her thrusts, until she tensed against him, above him. Her hair brushed across her shoulders as she threw her head back and orgasmed on a long ragged scream, her eyes clenched shut.

She collapsed against his body and he wrapped his arms around her, stroking her back, listening to the soulful serenade of her heart beating in time to his.

He wondered if she noticed this herself, if it amazed her as much as him that their breath mingled in harmony and their hearts beat in unison. If she did notice, he wondered if she would think anything of it. Would she understand the complexity of such a thing or dismiss it?

The girl he'd fallen in love with would have been awed and pleased by such a thing. He gathered that the woman he held in his arms would not feel such stirring emotions. If she did, she'd deny them, hide from them, pretend they didn't exist. After all, that's what she'd done for the past sixteen years.

She soon pulled out of him and removed the harness to fall asleep beside him, still nestled in his arms. It was a long while before he moved, but, when the sun inched higher in the sky, he forced himself to leave the bed.

She was still twisted in the white satin sheets of his bed after he'd showered and dressed, and Adonis decided not to wake her. The night before had been a long one, full of mysteries and shrouded in danger.

He knew last night was only the beginning.

He slipped from his chambers and took the stairs to the first floor, where he was surprised to be greeted by a message from one of his guards so early in the morning.

His brothers—they wanted to speak with him. Already, they were on their way.

He grabbed a quick breakfast of fruit, sat down at his dining table and waited.

It did not take them long to arrive. He was surprised to see that Apollo was not with Ares and Eros.

"He is still with Serena," Ares answered him after taking a seat across from Adonis.

He wondered how his brother was managing that— being confined in Serena's presence, labouring under the intensity of his need for the woman, battling against his desire even as he waged his own hellish war with his guilt. Adonis understood perfectly what Apollo was going through.

He worried for him.

"Do not concern yourself with Apollo."

Adonis' inquiring gaze narrowed on Ares.

"I know you well, brother," Ares responded to the question in his eyes. "You do not have to say a word for me to know that Apollo's well-being concerns you, but he can take care of himself, just as he can take care of Serena."

"Besides," Eros interjected, "we have far more pressing problems to concern ourselves with."

His brother's statement raised his eyebrows, while the pictures Eros slid across the table furrowed his temple.

"If the nuns knew I'd taken these they would have confiscated them, but Ares managed to keep them distracted long enough."

"Who is it?" Adonis studied the photograph of a mangled corpse, blackened and charred. The person was unrecognisable.

"We don't know." Ares shrugged. "The nuns believe it to be Selena. We did not see fit to correct them."

Adonis froze. "I take it all of the nuns are accounted for so it cannot be one of them."

"Everyone but Selena has been accounted for. And, since the fire began in her room, everyone believes her to be dead."

Adonis nodded even as he wondered why someone would fake Selena's death when there were others who knew she still lived. That question plagued him as he began to sift through this turn of events, this new puzzle that was now spread before him.

"Did you find anything else when you searched the convent?"

"If you're asking did we find another ring, then yes." Eros brandished a ring fashioned out of the same platinum and boasting the same diamond pattern as the other two rings. "It was near the bed, not far from the body, but obscured from view. We only found it upon closer inspection of the corpse."

Adonis stood from the table. "It's a message." A clear one. A threat to him, to Selena and her sister...to all of them. That their stalker had struck in the holiest of places was a bold statement that said Selena was not yet dead, but soon she would be, and there was nothing any of them could do to protect her, to stop him. There was no place safe or sacred.

Ares joined him on his feet. "A message from whom?"

"*That* I do not know, but it is obvious the message is meant for all of us."

A silence descended upon the room, drawn out and oppressive.

"You think *he* is alive," Eros said finally, breaking through the silence with a hushed voice, as if speaking such a thing too loudly would bring the man they all feared into existence.

Adonis looked at his brother Eros, whose golden beauty was as fair as his own. "I don't know." But that was the only explanation for it all—for any of this. Adonis thought it, but he did not say it. He didn't have to. They knew.

Dieu—their adoptive father. He was alive. He'd come back from the dead to terrorise them, to haunt them, to do what he'd promised he'd do with his dying breath—destroy their lives…destroy them all.

Chapter Seven

Silence—ominous and oppressive, it stretched between the three brothers as they sifted through the prevailing thought.

Silence...soon broken by a gut-wrenching scream that rent the air.

Their adoptive father had plucked four boys from the streets, taken them in and redefined their entire existence. Trained in the incongruent arts of love and war, they'd been courtesans to the wealthy elite...but also spies, as well as assassins. It was the instincts of the latter that propelled them into action.

Adonis took the twisting labyrinth of stairs that led to the second floor two at a time, with his brothers on his heels.

Another scream sliced through the air and it had its intended effect of ripping his heart open.

The entire second floor was a long hallway with mirrors at each end, the staircase and banister to one side, and three doors leading into a different part of his private chambers on the other.

They each tried one door, only to find them all locked. Adonis kicked one of the doors open without much forethought or hesitation and rushed inside. Upon entering his living room, he did not immediately glean the source of Selena's distress but he smelt it—acrid smoke.

He followed the charred scent, letting it lead him into his bedroom where the smoke thickened and a scorching fire blazed with menacing intent just beyond the door to his bathroom.

The fire was steadily encroaching upon him, the smoke making every breath he took harsh and ragged. He covered his mouth and nose with his sleeve as he wove a path through the dancing flames that stretched towards him.

All of a sudden, droplets of water pelted his face from over his shoulder, subduing the fire as he inched closer to the bathroom door. He didn't turn around, though he suspected one or both of his brothers were filling containers with water from the other bathroom and hurling it at the fire in an attempt to aid his journey. And his journey was an arduous one, seemingly taking him forever to cross the small space to the bathroom door.

As he drew closer, the thumping sound he'd heard upon entering the room grew louder. It was Selena, desperately trying to escape the bathroom, which for a brief moment caused a tendril of fear to curl inside his belly as he worried about what was on the other side of the door.

He called out to her.

"Adonis?" The relief in her voice threatened to still him...that she'd called his name nearly buckled his knees. It had not escaped his notice that up until that moment she'd refrained from using his name. He wondered if she'd even realised what she'd just done.

"Are you all right?" he called.

"No, I am not all right!" She sounded indignant as if she thought he was being absurd. He almost smiled. "Your bathroom is on fire and I cannot seem to put it out. And the door is locked."

"Stand back," he shouted, deciding not to tell her that there was also a fire in his bedroom.

"I've already tried kicking the door open..."

Her voice trailed off when the door crashed in upon itself, yielding beneath the force of Adonis' booted foot.

He didn't waste a moment to gloat as he swept her into his arms, tucked her within the folds of his suit jacket and barrelled out of the room into the living area.

Despite his brothers' attempts at quashing the blaze, tiny flames flickered on the shoulder and arms of his jacket as he rushed from the room. After setting Selena down, he snuffed them out before they could burn through.

There was a flurry of activity within the living room as half a dozen of his guards rushed inside with extinguishers in their hands, and without a moment's hesitation proceeded to put out the blazing inferno in his personal quarters.

With the fire now subdued, his guards returned to him, awaiting further instructions. Having none, Adonis nodded to his men, dismissing them. He waited until the door closed behind the last of them to check on Selena.

She sat in the chair closest to him. Her hair was in disarray, her skin flushed red, but — with the exception that she was only wearing a towel wrapped around her body, and Ares' dark suit jacket now draped over her bare legs—she did not appear unduly distraught, as if she faced near death experiences every day. He gave a mental shrug. In a convent? He doubted. But, with Selena, one never knew.

"It is as I feared," Ares said. "Selena is not safe here."

"She is not safe anywhere," Eros responded.

Adonis shot them both disapproving looks. With one hand he stroked Selena's thigh through the jacket separating skin from skin. That she welcomed his touch with soft eyes did not go unnoticed by his brothers, but only one was overly troubled by the bond that had begun to form between them.

"I promised I would protect you and I meant it." Adonis spoke quietly to Selena, although, with the unnatural stillness of the room, his brothers heard every word. He was grateful they remained quiet—Ares especially, who was of the opinion that, no matter what any of them did, Selena's death was inevitable.

She looked at each of them. "Who would want me dead? The truth," she demanded. "If you believe it is my father then do not spare me. I need to understand why."

Her eyes implored them to tell her the truth, but the events from last evening to this morning had revealed to them two things—what they'd thought was the truth was no longer certain...which meant they did not, in fact, know who was terrorising them.

"To be honest, we don't know what is true any longer," Adonis replied.

"Well then, tell me what you thought before and what you believe now."

"Later," Ares interrupted. "When we are somewhere safe, somewhere secure."

"I thought you said I would not be safe anywhere," Selena challenged.

"And you will not be, but there is one place where only *one* person would dare to harm you and, if he comes there, then we will all know the truth, just as we will all be prepared for him."

Adonis shook his head, Eros joined him, but Ares was resolute.

"There is no safer place," Ares insisted, and the sharp assertion in his voice brooked no argument. Both Eros and Adonis knew that tone well, and, if Selena didn't, she was still wise enough to follow suit and remain silent.

It took Selena and Adonis only minutes to gather what few things they possessed before they departed his home to the one place he'd sworn he'd never return to. A place that ironically now offered him a safe haven, when it had once been his prison of hell. A place that haunted his nightmares and even now stirred the contents within his belly.

He'd sworn to never return, but for the love of one woman he would brave even his darkest fears.

* * * *

La Ville des Dieux had once been *La Ville de Dieu* — the city of God, one god, known only as *Dieu*.

His arrogance had been astounding, his beauty spellbinding. He'd taken the most beautiful of boys and turned them into men. He'd taken the strongest of boys and made them gods.

They were not gods, none of them, not even *Dieu*, but the people who lived within his territory had treated him as such. He'd been feared by all. His word was the law, and everyone who chose to make their home or livelihood within *La Ville de Dieu* had understood that and respected it.

Dieu's home pierced the very heart of the city, its looming towers and fortified buttresses of grey stone were as ominous and imposing as the man himself. *Le Siège d'un Dieu*, as it was known, gave the appearance of a medieval castle overlooking its territory. As if it was the very *seat of God*, which it proclaimed itself to be, it sat upon a natural plateau in the centre of the city, buffeted on one side by a small natural lake and a series of jagged hilltops on the other.

Though it had never needed the fortifications of its natural position, *Dieu's* home was a strategic feat for anyone who dared to enter. At least that's what Adonis was counting on. Whoever sought to do them harm would certainly take a moment to reflect on the wisdom of waging an attack upon them while they were in residence.

The security his adoptive father's home offered was the only reason why he'd agreed to come back. He glanced down at the woman who was curled up within the covers of the bed that had once been his. The security this place offered *her* was the *only* reason.

Their father had been dead for over a year. Except for the guards who patrolled the grounds and the inner sanctum as if it was a sacred museum, and the weekly cleaning staff who kept the place free of dust and vermin, *Dieu's* home had been vacant ever since.

It was vacant no more.

Adonis closed the door to his old chambers and joined his brothers in the main den. Though it had been many years since he'd set foot in his father's home, the ornate furnishings were the same as he remembered. A large portrait hung above the black marble fireplace of a perfectly handsome man with blue obsidian eyes, so dark they appeared violet. *Dieu.* Adonis felt a chill along his spine. Even in death, even though he knew the portrait was still and lifeless, he could not shake the feeling of being watched, of being stalked by the very man who'd both saved his soul and destroyed it on a careless whim.

"Selena is asleep," Adonis said as soon as his brothers' eyes lit upon him.

"That is good," rejoined Ares. "Hopefully she will still be asleep when we return—"

"I will not leave her."

Adonis did not miss the scowl that crossed his eldest brother's face. His brother thought him foolish in his love for this woman who would only cause him pain. Adonis thought Ares foolish for thinking such a thing when he'd never known love. Yet, if he ever did, Ares would finally understand that love was both reckless and foolish and it was the greatest gift a man could ever receive.

"There are guards posted just beyond the lake, and more who are monitoring the exterior walls. No one will enter without our knowledge."

Adonis would have still protested but Eros interceded. "I will stay with her until you both return." His lips twitched into a semi-smile. "Since I was the only one out combing the city *all* night, I did not manage to get much sleep. I will take a nap in the sitting area, just outside her bedroom. She will be safe and I can finally get some rest."

Adonis still did not want to leave her, but he trusted Selena's welfare to only three men and one of them would be with her.

He gave his youngest brother a curt nod, then followed after Ares, who led him beyond the safety of the fortress that had once been his home. Together they plunged into the bustling city that was alive and vibrant during mid-afternoon.

* * * *

La Ville des Dieux was a thriving, modern metropolis. The financial district, military headquarters as well as the epicentre of contemporary sports could be found in Ares' domain. The arts was Adonis', along with the frivolity of being the shopping hub. Apollo's boasted the dualities of sin and salvation—brothels and religious institutions clamoured for supremacy within his territory. Meanwhile, Eros paid homage to any and all pursuits of knowledge within his domain.

To navigate the winding maze of thoroughfares, through the meticulously refined and ordered city, one would never garner that the proprietors of such a carefully ordered and peaceful domain were capable of depravity. They could so easily succumb to the violence they'd been born with and had been bred to nurture.

As Ares brought his vehicle to a stop and they gracefully slipped from the automobile, both men fought hard to restrain the brutality that was as much a part of their existence as their shared beauty.

Neither carried a weapon as they approached the four-storey brownstone in the heart of Swan Pointe, one of the wealthiest neighbourhoods within Adonis' district, but the violence radiating from the two men was palpable. As they crossed the sidewalk, the few people milling about saw them, but none dared to speak. In a neighbourhood as exclusive as Swan

Pointe, few people were about. Those who were knew that when any of *Dieu's* progeny came calling, it was best to disappear then later pretend as if they'd witnessed nothing.

A woman with a stroller, and the two gentlemen who'd been walking towards them all found something to draw their attention in the opposite direction and proceeded that way. The two brothers ignored them as they climbed the concrete steps of the looming brownstone.

Adonis stood beside Ares on the small front porch and rang the bell. At the same time he gave his brother a sharp look until Ares set his foot back down on the ground.

"At least let's ring the doorbell *before* we resort to that."

Ares' only response was a shrug, but at least he complied. Adonis was grateful. He'd learned throughout the course of his life that aggressive tactics only made it more difficult to obtain information. And information was what they sought on this day.

There was the soft patter of footsteps, a brief pause, followed by a gasp and another pause until the door was finally opened—just a small crack—to reveal a petite woman with wide frightened eyes and frizzy ringlets that framed her cherubic face.

"May I help you?"

"We are here to see your employer," Ares answered, not waiting for an invitation as he pushed past the woman into the foyer. With a sigh, Adonis followed him. *So much for not using aggressive tactics.*

The maid gave the impression of a fish out of water as she floundered and blustered helplessly, trailing behind the two men who seemed intent upon ignoring her as they began searching her employer's home.

"What are you looking for?"

"Your boss," Ares replied, not stopping his efficient perusal of first the living room, then the dining room. When the kitchen and finally the closets turned up empty, he focused his ferocious gaze on the poor woman.

"Woodward Gowen—where is he?"

The girl looked as if she was about to disintegrate into a puddle right there in the middle of the dining room. Adonis, who'd been on his way up the stairs to the second floor, intervened.

"We don't intend any harm. We just need to speak with him."

He ignored Ares' measured glare, not once batting an eye at his twist upon words. They did only want to speak with him, and they did not intend to harm him *unless* he said something that confirmed what they already suspected. Only *then* would they harm him.

"He—he is not here," the frizzy-haired girl stammered.

"Well then, where is he?" Ares snapped impatiently.

She visibly flinched. "I don't know and he did not say, but he hasn't been here in over a month."

He exchanged a quick, telling glance with his brother.

"Who else lives here besides you?" Adonis asked.

"Just myself and Earl." She gulped. "Earl tends the yard and does regular maintenance, while I serve as the cook and housekeeper."

Adonis studied the woman. "How long have you been employed here?"

She gulped again. "Two years, sir—"

"And in all that time it has just been you and this Earl?"

"Oh no." She shook her head vigorously. "There was Mr Gowen and then his son, Jarrod."

His son?

Adonis and Ares exchanged a longer look this time.

"You said Mr Gowen left about a month ago. What about his son, Jarrod?" Adonis probed.

She cast furtive glances between both men, as if she knew it was in her best interests to tell them, just as she knew it was in her best interests not. Adonis moved to continue up the stairs as if to say that she could provide the answers he sought, or he could rummage through the entire house, leaving a mess in his wake, to find them on his own. Her eyes were wide and guileless, but apparently she was smarter than she looked.

"Jarrod Gowen does not live here, but he visits." Adonis noticed she had begun to wring her hands. "About once a week he comes in and spends about an hour locked in his father's study. He does not wish for us to bother him, so we don't. Then he leaves."

Adonis made his way back down the stairs. He needed to get inside that study and discover what secrets it held. However, he was certain that, despite who they were and that the woman was terrified of them, to let them into her employer's private study would be out of the question.

"Around what time does Jarrod Gowen visit?"

The woman's wringing grew more pronounced and Adonis knew he would only be able to get maybe two more answers out of her before she would be compelled to ask them to leave.

"On Mondays, sir, around noon."

It was Friday.

He could not wait three days for answers. He might not be alive that long.

"So he was here this past Monday?" Adonis wasn't sure why he asked that question, but something demanded him to probe deeper. He was glad that he did.

If the frizzy-haired girl wrung her hands any more he was convinced she would begin to rub away her skin. "Well, it is odd that you would ask. He *didn't* come this past Monday. He didn't manage to get around here until Wednesday and when he did he stayed a very long time, far longer than unusual. I thought nothing of it." She stopped, her gaze sweeping over them.

"Well, I thought nothing of it until *now*."

* * * *

Selena awoke sometime in the middle of the afternoon to find Eros asleep on the couch in the sitting area just beyond her bedroom. He'd been left behind to guard her, while Ares and Adonis had gone on some secret mission they'd refused to share with her.

Faced with just a few hours of sleep, and after battling a fire that had been deliberately set to claim her life, she hadn't protested all that much when Ares and Adonis had departed. She'd decided that sleeping was her best strategy at the moment, and that once she'd woken she could ply Adonis with questions then. That Eros still slept outside her bedroom told her Adonis had not yet returned, which left her to her own devices to explore his childhood home until he did.

With the practiced grace of one who'd studied the Eastern fighting arts for more than a decade, she crept out of the room, her footsteps silent.

As soon as she closed the door, she found herself in a cold, draughty hallway with harsh fluorescent light spilling from the lamps that hung along the walls. Her feet were bare, the cool stone slabs beneath them chilling her to the bone as she made her way down the hall.

Adonis — the man — intrigued her. The home he'd been reared in, even more so. Years ago, she'd been set to marry a man she did not know but had longed to. Adonis, even then, had always been both a blank canvas and a stone wall — hard to read, difficult to know. He'd been impenetrable, but she'd loved him anyway. Her belly twisted into a fierce knot. Deep down in that secret part of herself that was not tainted by revenge, she *still* loved him.

She'd come to realise that, had come to accept it as she'd desperately called out his name when she'd thought she would die.

To still love a man who had hurt her so deeply was torture. To love a man who sought to take that hurt inside his body, to ease her of her burden, tortured her more. But to not love him — to somehow stop — would be death itself, worse than torture.

Making her way through the winding halls of the sprawling home, she allowed a small smile to cross her face. Adonis had been right. She *was* a masochist — they both were.

Every corner she turned seemed to lead her into a hallway darker than the last. She had no idea what she was searching for, what propelled her forward, only that this place — Adonis' former home, a place he hadn't wanted to return to, the memories of which still haunted him — held the answers to a man who was still as much an enigma to her as he had been the day they'd been introduced at the Winter Cotillion.

She cautiously approached a stairwell. The winding staircase was shrouded in darkness and shadows, the dim fluorescent lamps straining to bring light to the oppressive darkness. Selena wasn't certain of what urged her upstairs, but she continued along her journey until she was three floors higher.

She stepped into the hallway, which stood in firm opposition to the floor she'd just left, even the stairwell. Brightness assaulted her immediately. The carpet was a fiery red, the tapestries along the walls a vibrant gold with splashes of deep rose.

The soft plush carpet was heavenly against her bare feet and she wriggled her toes, her feet sinking deeper. The entire corridor was immaculate and well maintained, the brilliant strokes of rich colour alluding to a woman's touch. And not just any woman, but a vivacious, decidedly feminine one with a penchant for outrageousness.

Selena tried the nearest door, surprised to find it locked. She tried the next one, and then the next. She went down the entire hallway, only to find every door locked. Her elation at finding such an oasis of colour among the drabness of the rest of the home soon dissipated.

She turned to leave, but, as she did, she was struck with alarm when she swore she saw a shadow disappear into the stairwell as if its owner had been on its way towards her. She crept closer to the dark stairwell, cautious and alert. She heard nothing, not the hurried pitter-patter of footsteps along stone, not hands sliding across a brass rail. She heard nothing, so she relaxed.

As the tension eased from her body, she glanced over her right shoulder, as if her gaze was being drawn in that direction, independent of its master, and that's when she glimpsed it.

A portrait, done in the classic, wistful pastels that had been popular over two decades ago. A beautiful woman with smiling eyes stared down at her from the golden framed portrait, as if she had a secret to tell, as if she possessed not a care in the world.

Selena knew the era of the painting because a portrait of her mother had been done in a similar motif and her mother had died more than twenty years ago.

Selena knew the *woman* in the painting because it *was* her mother.

"She was beautiful, wasn't she?"

Selena whipped around, her gaze clashing with Adonis'.

"Where did you come from?" she exclaimed. Startled, her heart hammered in her chest. "When did you return?"

She thought of the dark shadow she'd glimpsed earlier and wondered if it had been him, deciding it must have been.

He nodded to a door over his shoulder, at the other end of the hallway.

"There are two entrances, one at each end. I came up that way. I cleared my throat as I approached so as not to startle you, but you must have been so engrossed in the painting that you didn't hear."

The painting. She glanced at it again, her eyes riveted upon it.

"Why is there a picture of my mother in your childhood home?"

"Your mother?" He looked between her and the portrait with astonishment, then with what she could only describe as a measure of acceptance when he

121

glimpsed the obvious similarities. Same topaz eyes, dark sienna complexion and ink-black hair. Rosalind Gowen's cheekbones were higher, her lips fuller, her eyes slanted at the ends, but the stark resemblance was still there.

"Answer me," she demanded, when Adonis simply stood there staring between her and the portrait in stunned silence.

His gaze finally settled upon her. "I have no answer."

"What do you mean, you —"

"I think we should return to my chambers and talk."

"No," she protested. She would not let him derail her on this point as he seemed adept at doing with all the others. "Tell me why my mother's picture is here and I will go downstairs with you. It's that simple."

His eyes, golden and fathomless, became cold, hard gems, anger and frustration swirling in their depths.

"It is not that simple, Selena —"

"Why not? For once, just tell me the truth."

"That's just it. The truth I know is that the woman you *think* is your mother is mine as well."

Chapter Eight

Selena was nauseous and disoriented all of a sudden. She reached for Adonis, then thought better of it and shrank away, but her world would not stop spinning. Everything that anchored her, every truth in her fragile, sad life was revealing itself to be a lie.

"Oh, dear God. That's impossible." Her stomach lurched. "That would make us...us..."

She couldn't say the words.

But obviously Adonis could. "Half-siblings?" He frowned. "Highly doubtful. My mother was a drug-addicted whore, my father a petty thief. They both died when I was nine." He glanced at the painting above them. "Rosalina was my *adoptive* mother."

"That is what you called her? Rosalina?"

He nodded. "Rosalina d'une Dieux."

She bit back a snort, full of contempt and disdain. *God's Rosalina.* As if she'd belonged to the man? How arrogant.

"My mother's name was Rosalind Gowen. She died when I was fourteen." Selena spoke to Adonis as if somehow *her* facts of her mother's life would reveal that this woman, who he claimed to be his mother, was in fact not.

"My brothers and I came to live here when I was eleven. Rosalina died when I was thirteen." His eyes sobered. "After that everything changed. She was the light that anchored my father's darkness. He'd only adopted us to make her happy because she could not bear children. With her gone, he had no use for us — so he found a new one — *several*."

She knew of the cruelties of the man known only as *Dieu* and she ached for the man before her, who'd once been a boy who lost not only the woman he'd loved as a mother, but also the man he'd called his father.

Her empathy for Adonis did not prevent her from working through the deductions that plagued her, all of which suggested such a thing was an improbability. She sifted through her memories. There'd been no funeral. Only a memorial service and her father imparting to her and Serena that their mother had been cremated. She'd never questioned the location of her mother's ashes. It had never seemed important until now.

She looked up at the portrait, staring, but not seeing. *I watched my mother die — she died in my arms...*

It was as if Adonis knew the moment she'd pieced together the puzzle inside her head because he reached for her, only to curl his hand back at his side when yet again she drew away from him.

"That woman in that painting cannot be my mother," she began, surprised by how steady her voice was, given her inner turmoil. "The timing of her death and the death of your adoptive mother is off."

"It would seem that way. But then that would make the anomaly that we apparently shared the same mother a coincidence and we both know it is not."

Anger infused her skin. "What are you suggesting? That my mother lived some double life?" She swept her hand to encompass the portrait. "Yes, Rosalind and Rosalina are similar names but that means nothing." she insisted.

"Selena—"

"That picture could be a fake. It means nothing as well."

His expression was incredulous, furious that she was adamant in ignoring the truth that was so plainly staring them in the face. "I know this must be difficult, but you know none of this is just a coincidence."

"I never said it was." She spoke quietly, even as anger and helplessness roiled through her. She was desperate to understand, to make sense of this but she just couldn't. Just as she could not accept that it was possible her mother was not the woman she'd believed her to be—how else would that portrait be in this home, when one identical to it had also hung in her own for many years. "This may not be a coincidence, but I refuse to jump to conclusions when I do not know the truth.

"Let's say Rosalind was your mother," she continued desperately, doggedly. "And Rosalina was a woman surgically altered to look like her." Her eyes bored into him. "Or maybe it was the other way around—"

"Or maybe it's the most obvious answer of them all," he whispered inching closer, his movements as seductive as his throaty voice. "Like you and your sister, your mother may have had a twin."

Selena was already shaking her head. Plausible, but still impossible. "If my mother had a twin, I would think I would know about it."

The relentlessness in his eyes was joined by ruthlessness and she concluded that his next words would be the worst she'd heard all night. She was right.

"Like you knew about your brother?"

"My brother?" Her eyes rounded. "I do not have a brother—"

"You do, Selena," Adonis said harshly. "Your father did a spectacular job of hiding his birth records, but everything can be found with the right price, especially when one owns the whole damn city.

"In his old age it would seem your father became sloppy or he just didn't fucking care anymore. Jarrod Andrews Gowen—born to some unknown woman your father had an affair with while still married to your mother. Your father paid handsomely to have another couple raise him, and only recently claimed him as his son and heir a year ago."

Selena could not breathe, the air dragging through her lungs frozen. For the second time this night, she found that everything she'd known, everything she'd believed...none of it was true, all of it lies.

She shook her head vehemently. "My father would never do such a thing. That cannot be tr—"

"If you say that cannot be true, I swear to God I will shake you, Selena," Adonis thundered. "When will you wake up and see your father for what he is? He sold you and Serena to my father to pay off his debts. He does not care about you, he does not love you. Everything Woodward has ever done has been to benefit him. He is selfish and cruel and the only reason why he did not threaten your life sooner was because he could not obtain full control of your mother's estate until your thirty-fifth birthday."

He stopped, his chest heaving, his eyes a mixture of sadness, pity and frustration. She wondered if he'd stopped because he was simply done, or was it owing to the look in her eyes that revealed so clearly that he'd crushed her soul and ripped out her heart?

"Serena and I turned thirty-five yesterday," she said absently, mindlessly. The attacks had begun last night—on the sixteen-year anniversary of that fateful night, on the sixteen-year anniversary of what would have been their engagement announcement, on what had been her thirty-fifth birthday. She did not want to believe him…she did not want any of it to be true. Yet, when she stared deep and long into his eyes, she knew every suspicion, every dark thought that had needled her all these years. She knew he was telling the truth, although her mind had never wanted to accept it.

She did something then that she hadn't done in years.

She began to cry—gut-wrenching, bone-numbing sobs. She cried for so long, and so hard that she did not realise she'd slipped to the floor and Adonis held her to him, rocking her slowly as if she were a child.

She cried for the mother she hadn't known well, but may not have known at all.

She cried for the man who was her father, who she'd never known.

She cried for her sister whom she'd once known but didn't anymore.

She cried for her brother whom she hadn't known at all, but now desperately wanted to.

She even cried for herself, the woman who had built her existence upon a family that was as alien to her as a group of strangers on the street.

Ironically, the only constant seemed to be Adonis. He'd betrayed her with his body, but his eyes had promised to love her forever. He'd kept that promise. Even as she'd sought to end his life, even as she'd vowed to cause him pain—he'd still loved her in spite of it all, in spite of herself.

She wasn't certain of when she'd stopped crying or when Adonis had carried her down the three flights of stairs back to his bedroom. She only became aware of her surroundings when her back sank into a soft, feather mattress.

Adonis undressed her in silence, then himself, and, when he joined her on the bed, she found her way into the warm circle of his arms.

He held her gently, tenderly, as if she would break or fly away, as if she were a precious gift too fragile to open.

Adonis' gift.

That night sixteen years ago, that was how *Dieu* had presented her to him—'*Adonis' gift*', he'd sneered.

She closed her eyes then, shutting out the memories of the past, as sleep began to steal over her.

* * * *

Selena awoke with the feeling of eyes upon her. She sat up with a start, clutching the sheet to her chest. The sun yawned in the sky, peeking through the heavy-paned window to battle the shadows of the gothic room for supremacy. Beside the window was where she found him. His long legs were stretched out, his arm draped lazily over the twisted oak of the chair.

His eyes were riveted upon her.

She wasn't certain of what made her do it, but beneath his piercing stare she self-consciously tightened her hold on the sheet to her chest.

The almost imperceptible motion did not go unnoticed, and his eyes shimmered beneath arched brows.

"You still do not quite trust me."

It wasn't a question. It wasn't a lie. She still did not entirely trust him, so no words to the contrary were necessary.

He stood, crossing the room to where some of his things from his home were scattered atop an intricately carved dressing table. He gathered his belongings to shower, but with his back to her she was reminded of his scars.

She hesitated for only a second.

"What happened to your back?"

He turned at the sound of her whispery quiet voice, his eyes meeting hers from over his shoulder. He held her attention for a second, then released her from the spellbinding intensity of his gaze when he twisted his head back around.

She slid from the bed, taking the bed sheet with her and securing it around her body. On bare feet, she padded over to him, knowing she was daring a lot.

"How is it you are upset that I do not trust you completely, when you will not even trust me with your secrets, with a past that caused you so much pain?"

He faced her so quickly, she did not even breathe in that single moment. His hands shot out to grip her by the hips, and he pulled her close. She was overcome by the heat of him, scorching her through the garments that separated them, his hands heating the flesh at her sides. Every part of her seemed to ignite, every cell stretching to fill itself with the warm and golden radiance that was Adonis.

"Why do you refuse to call me by my name?"

She blinked in surprise. His question caught her off guard, but that had been his intent. She tried to move away, but he held fast, pulling her closer, deeper into the warmth of him.

She would not be deterred.

"Answer my question first," she demanded.

His eyes flickered, revealing what she already knew.

So much had changed between them. So much still remained the same.

"You hesitate because you still feel it," she said finally. "You still feel what stands between us. You do not trust me any more than I trust you, because you are uncertain of my motivations, just as I am uncertain of yours."

"I know your motivations, Selena."

She tilted her head to the side, raking him with questioning eyes, but remained quiet.

"You're motivated to kill me out of revenge and retribution," he answered her probing stare. "You're motivated to keep me alive because of your physical desires, but also because you desire the truth."

She could not deny his words, not any of them—every word he uttered was true. She should not have been surprised—Adonis knew her, he knew the hidden yearnings etched within her soul. He knew her as intimately as one could. It shouldn't have surprised her. But it did.

He set her away from him and with his belongings in hand headed towards the bathroom. She stared after him, her eyes digging into his retreating back.

"I know your motivations as well, *Adonis*." He stilled, the sound of his name on her lips freezing him in place. He waited, his back to her, his entire body rigid.

"You're motivated to protect me out of fear." She crept closer as she spoke. "You're motivated to take my pain away out of guilt, but, just like me, you desire the truth." She touched him then, her fingers tracing the uneven skin of his back. He flinched beneath her touch, but he did not pull away. "And, just like me, you are motivated by your own physical desires. But you were wrong on one point. I am not certain that I am still motivated to kill you."

She came around to face him. His expression was hard, unreadable. The only indication he gave that he was angry was the small tick of the muscle along his jaw.

"Why are you angry? Because I would touch your scars?" She ran her hand across his torso, through the fine sprinkling of hair that tickled her palm. "Because I have now decided to call you by your name?" In hushed tones she said his name again. "Adonis…"

He seized her hand within his, halting any further perusal of his naked chest. "You say you are no longer certain of your motivation to kill me." His gaze did not waver upon her. "I would be sure of my position if I were you."

Adonis released her hand and with long strides stalked into the bathroom, closing the door firmly behind him. She waited until she heard the sound of water rushing from the shower.

He heard Selena twist the knob and open the door. The slight creaking of metal against wood hinted at her presence. The perfumed scent of her skin and the soft fragrance of her hair floating on the current of warm steam enveloping him was what ultimately gave her away.

He sensed her hesitation, in that she dared push him after he'd already retreated from her. She knew he was angry, but even he wasn't certain *why* he was upset. Was it because she had touched his scars? Or used his name after all this time? Because she'd demanded he trust her when she still did not quite trust him? Or was it because she still wavered on the decision of whether he deserved to live or die? It was all of those things…none of them…something more.

She was bold. Brazenly undaunted by his silence, she faced his anger as she stepped into the tub, yet he did not turn around.

He did not turn around when she began to wash his back with warm soap and a soft towel. He did not turn around, not even when she spoke.

"Why did it take you so long to tell me about my father? My brother?"

Weary and exhausted last night, they'd fallen asleep before they could discuss this subject, but he'd known these questions would not be far from her lips, because they were not far from *his* mind.

"I only found out about your brother yesterday," he answered truthfully. "Your father's deceit I discovered last year." That was not entirely true. He'd long known of her father's role in that night their lives had been shattered, but he hadn't understood the enormity of Woodward's involvement until a year ago. Many secrets had come to light with the death of his father — while many had been buried with *Dieu* where they promised to stay.

"I don't know anything about my mother's estate, or even what is entitled to me. I stopped caring after my father cast me out and disowned me. But if what you say is true, then I understand why he would want me and Serena dead. What I don't understand is why he would want *you* dead? Why would he attack your hotel?"

"Because you were there. Because he thought you were still there. The only reason he set that fire at my private residence is because he discovered you'd left my hotel and were there instead."

And only a few people had known of his departure with Selena. Woodward had an accomplice. Someone on Adonis' staff, one of his guards, perhaps, was a snitch and a traitor, at the least. At the worst, someone in his employ, someone Adonis trusted, was the one who'd set those fires in his home and at his penthouse within the hotel.

Her hands stilled against his back, and he turned around to finally face her. Selena's eyes were hooded, but he knew her too well. She was far too smart not to put the pieces together, far too intelligent not to know.

"You deliberately opened your hotel on the anniversary of that night, which you knew was also my birthday, in order to orchestrate my return."

"If I visited you at the convent and told you that you were in danger and needed to leave, you would have refused. I reasoned the only way to draw you out and bring you to me was to provoke you.

"Your last words to me that night were a promise. I knew, if nothing else, you would honour them. *'This was supposed to be the happiest night of my life, and you have destroyed it, you have destroyed me. Be warned, I shall pay you back in kind'.*"

Her eyes registered the words she'd hurled at him right after he'd ridiculed her and then ended their relationship all those years ago.

"And when I sent you that note, you realised you had me."

He touched her cheek, to reassure her that she'd not been manipulated, despite that that was exactly what he'd done. "I knew you would come to me. And having you near is the only way I know how to keep you safe."

The water turned cold against his back, and he reached around to turn the knob again until it blasted warm water.

"When I arrived at your penthouse... How did you know I wouldn't kill you?"

"I didn't."

She flattened her palms against his chest and drew closer. The steam and mist swirling around them thickened. His body, which had been alert to her nearness, responded to the subtle change in the small space between them.

"So you did not anticipate what came after."

What came after...that he would allow her to take him as he'd taken her, take her pain and pleasure and give her his.

"No, I didn't anticipate that."

"But you suggested it." She curved one hand around the nape of his neck. "So you must have thought about it." His breath grew ragged. Hers joined his in its arduous rhythm.

"Many nights."

Her other hand slipped down his body to curl around his turgid flesh, and the skin of her palm was satiny smooth against his rigid length as she pumped him gently.

"What else did you think about?"

Her question gave him pause, the images it conjured stealing what was left of his breath.

"When you did not dream of suffering at my hands, what other fantasies gave you pleasure?" She stroked his cock faster, harder. Her pace was relentless, her words more so. "Sixteen years is a long time not to warm the thighs of a woman, not to feel the hair roughened skin of a man against your back. When you were alone in your bed, stroking your cock just like this, what were the fantasies that gave you pleasure, that made you come in your hand?"

He bit back a groan, his eyes shadowed with lust, his pupils dark with desire. In a single, fluid motion he twisted her around and fixed her palms against the solid marble tiles.

Her back was arched, her legs spread. She looked at him from over one shoulder, her coal-black hair wet and slick against her back. She was mesmerising in her beauty. She was perfect.

Adonis settled behind her, covering her body with his own. His erection nudged the folds of her buttocks, and they both drew in a sharp gasp. He cupped one breast from around her body, while the other hand rested over her hand against the tiles.

"You play a dangerous game, Selena." His breath warmed the wet skin along her neck, and she shivered. "You know nothing of what it's like to love a man in one moment, only to take his life in the next."

Her gaze imprisoned his. "And you do?" she challenged.

"I do."

Her gaze did not yet set him free. It was unwavering in its intensity. "I do not want to talk of love and death. I want only to know of your fantasies."

A deep chuckle rose out of him, and he kissed her lips gently as he pushed his way between the folds of her sex, nudged at her opening then slowly pressed inside her body. "I would not have us talk at all. I would rather do to you what I could only imagine, when I was alone in my bed, with my cock in my hand and my thoughts only of you."

He drove home then, filling her with his hard erection until he was buried to the hilt. Her sheath washed him with heat and desire and the pulsing electricity of his passion throbbed in his veins, pumping through the organ between his legs. She clenched around him, yielding to him, surrendering to the deep, plunging thrusts he gave her.

Adonis was riding the thin edge of control, his lusts unabated and unchecked threatening to claim him. He was not certain of when the game had changed between them. He sought to take away her pain, to suffer beneath her touch. Yet she'd refused. She would only have his pain if it also meant his pleasure. She was relentless. Even now, as her body yielded beneath his, she mastered him — even now she still controlled him. He'd set out to heal her with his touch, but it would seem she would heal him with hers.

"Even now you are brooding, when I would have you fuck me," she said, as if she could hear his thoughts.

She linked her fingers with his against the wall of the shower. The tender gesture was oddly intimate. It made his heart clench.

"Sometimes the greatest revenge is the sweetest."

Her words broke through his thoughts — words that hit their mark so eerily as if she truly *could* read his mind, words he was not convinced he entirely believed.

Revenge *could* be sweet, but this was no longer about revenge.

With their fingers still linked, he released the warm, full flesh of her breast to bury his other hand in her tangled, wet locks. Gripping her hair, he gently dragged her head backwards, tilting her face to snare her lips in a deep, demanding kiss that made the slow burn of desire curl through him until it seared his blood.

His strokes quickened inside her and he went deeper, deeper than he'd ever been before. With his body he claimed her. With his lips he branded her. With his entire being he marked her soul. In that moment he made it clear — she could take his life if her bitterness drove her to it, but there would be no way for her to escape the memories of him. He would haunt her forever.

Their bodies came together in twisted limbs, slick with water, and he clung to her, the wet heat of her pussy clenching tight around him with every thrust. It was heaven inside her, to lose himself within her wanton body. He'd only ever abandoned himself to the pleasures of the flesh once. Only with Selena, only in her arms.

She moaned against his lips, and he swallowed the throaty sound deep inside him, their breath becoming one as their bodies tightly fused together. When she rocked back against him, sending him tunnelling deeper, all pretence of control disappeared.

He wrenched his lips from hers to bury his face in the hollow of her throat where he could drink in her scent. His cock pummelled inside her, through the taut muscles of her tender flesh. The tingling at the base of his spine warned him of his impending release and he unfurled his hand from her wet hair to snake it between the slick, wet lips of her cunt. He thrummed her clit in time to the punishing rhythm of his strokes.

Their bodies slapped together, wet flesh against wet flesh. Tiny flutters feathered across his cock. She was close. He was close.

She cried out his name on the verge of her climax. He wanted…no, he *needed* to hear his name on her lips again in the throes of passion, as desperately as he needed to breathe.

"Say it again," he rasped. "Call my name again. I want to hear my name on your lips when you come."

"*Adonis…*"

She cried his name, then she screamed it as she splintered apart in his arms.

"*Adonis!*" It came unbidden from her lips on a ragged, panting moan.

In all his years pleasing others, *no one* had ever called his name as he'd made love to them, as he'd fucked them. He'd specifically instructed them not to. Not until Selena had he allowed another to call his name in the midst of climax. No one else but her.

Selena's orgasm ripped through her, at the same time his own roared through him — his name stealing from her soft, sweet lips shattering him.

He clung to her, his fingers gripping hers tighter as he continued to spurt his seed deep inside her on a harsh, jagged groan.

"Selena." Her name was wrenched from him, tortured and needy as he poured his fluids into her waiting flesh, as he filled her with his warm essence until he was spent and had nothing left of himself to give.

It was a long while before he noticed the water was freezing against his back — longer still before he found the strength to leave the warm, safe haven of her body and pull out of her.

When he did, they both felt the loss of contact as if their joined bodies had anchored them.

He turned off the water and, with her in his arms, he stepped from the shower. Silence stretched between them as he towel-dried her body and then his own. Neither one wanted to speak for fear of breaking the tenuous, fragile bond that now connected them, the truce their bodies had brokered.

When he finally did speak, his statement was perfunctory. "I will leave you to dress. When you are done, you can join me for breakfast if you wish. Otherwise, we can get an early start."

"An early start?"

He nodded. "You said you know little of your mother's estate. I say it is time we change that."

* * * *

Ares' domain was the very antithesis to Adonis', yet it epitomised the man who governed it. Towering skyscrapers of dark-paned glass dominated the skyline, while the threat of death and violence was ever present in the air. There were few residences in the southern district—few could ignore the cold, harsh landscape of the architecture. Business was conducted in the southern district, and many came to enjoy the fleeting pastimes the sports teams offered, but, when night fell, most returned to their homes in the other districts where shadows did not encroach upon the light.

During the day, Ares' domain was tolerable, despite the army of buildings that blocked out the sunlight and the routine fire crack of bullets, reminding all of the military's presence as they trained daily.

Woodward Gowen's attorney kept his office in the heart of the southern district, so that was where Selena and Adonis found themselves just before noon. McGurie and Associates was located in a small suite on the bottom floor of an eleven-storey, nondescript black building, which, Selena decided, was not quite as oppressive as the others.

As Selena stepped inside his office, she did not question Adonis as to how he'd discovered the identity of her father's lawyer or if they even had an appointment. Adonis was a man of vast resources. Information he wanted, he got. As to whether they had an appointment, it did not matter. Adonis was a man for whom appointments were unnecessary. Rutherford McGurie would simply *make* one for them.

They were greeted by a pleasant-looking secretary, whose cheery face clouded with confusion then dismay when Adonis brushed past her desk. Selena had no choice but to follow.

"Sir, you cannot go back there—"

"Do not worry," Adonis said to the fretful woman. "He's expecting us."

"But, sir—"

Adonis' booted foot sent the door crashing inward. Again, Selena had no choice but to rush inside behind him. He slammed the door in the woman's face.

"What is the meaning of—"

"Sit down, Rutherford."

Rutherford McGurie was a jolly-faced, portly man. His expensive suit was too tight, the fat from his neck spilling over his designer shirt. His ruddy face reddened some more as he sputtered, but in the end he sat back down in his seat.

An imposing man in both stature and bearing, Adonis was even more so as he towered over the quaking attorney and Selena felt sorry for Rutherford, but she did nothing to ease his discomfort as she stood beside Adonis.

"Wh-who are you?" Rutherford questioned. "And wh-what do you want?"

"My name is Adonis. You may not know me, but I am certain you've heard of my father." That got the man's attention. Everyone had heard of Adonis, just as there was no one who resided in *La Ville des Dieux* who had not heard of *Dieu.*

Rutherford's fear was palpable, the terror in his eyes unmistakable. His jowls wriggled as he gulped. "H-how may I help you, sir?"

"I need to see whatever documents you have on the estate of Selena and Serena Gowen, and their father Woodward."

The man's ruddy face turned pale white. "H-he is a client. I am not at liberty to disclose—"

The feral smile Adonis gave him made Selena's blood run cold. She could only imagine what it did to the simpering attorney. "I am sure you will make an exception." He glanced at her. "Besides, this woman is Selena Gowen. If I am correct, you are in possession of specific stipulations regarding her estate, which she is entitled to see."

Rutherford's attention snapped to her, and he plucked his glasses from the table, set them on his portly face to study her closer.

"Miss Gowen?"

She nodded.

All of a sudden he began rummaging through papers on his desk. Not finding what he searched for, he took his search to the file cabinets behind him. All the while, she could still smell his agitation in the air. She wondered what had him so riled, but soon found out.

He brandished a folder from the cabinet as if he was upon a stage performing magic. After several seconds of flipping through the large folder, he pushed it across his desk towards them.

What she read ignited the dark fire of rage inside her, setting her blood to boil. When the words began to swim before her eyes, she looked up, treating the man to the full weight of her angry glare.

"I am Selena Gowen, and I assure you I am very much alive."

The blustering, blubbering attorney tugged at his tight collar as if he wished he was anywhere else. It wasn't his fault, but that did not ease her fury.

"I am sorry. I was presented with a signed and triple sealed death certificate two days ago. In accordance with your mother's will, your estate was transferred to your father."

An estate worth millions—of which she knew nothing, and she was certain Serena was just as ignorant. When Woodward had kicked them out, he'd disowned them, so they'd believed nothing of his was theirs.

The tragic events of her life began to fit themselves together in her mind as she skimmed through the documents before her, growing angrier with each piece of paper she read.

With Rosalind Gowen's death, Woodward had retained guardianship of his daughters' portion of their mother's estate. Yet, Rosalind had made certain their apparently shiftless father could not touch a single dime of what was theirs, even as he was the guardian of their holdings. On her thirty-fifth birthday she would retain full control of her estate *unless* she was dead. With her dead, everything would become his.

Selena wasn't dead, but Woodward had made it appear as such. Contained within the file were the pictures of the corpse found at the convent. There was no one to deny her death...*except her.*

"You said someone presented you with a death certificate. Who was it?" she demanded to know.

He hesitated. "I-it was your brother. Jarrod."

She pursed her lips into a thin, tight line. *Jarrod.* The brother she didn't know. The brother she'd never met. She was starting to understand some of his role in this treachery, but she wondered if he was an equal player or an innocent victim.

"How do we correct this?" It wasn't about money. Selena didn't need it, she didn't even care. It was that her mother, who'd loved them, had left something to her only daughters, her only children, that her father had taken away, a man who'd never once shown them a measure of love, a man she was starting to realise didn't love her or her sister at all.

Rutherford's face was as helpless as it was hapless. "You could show me your birth certificate to prove your identity, but it is already too late. I transferred the money into the account I was given."

Selena curled her hand into a fist and prayed she did not lose herself and slam it into his desk or worse.

"What about Serena's portion?" Adonis asked, and she was grateful for his question because it reined in her fury, for a moment at least, and allowed her to focus on something else.

The attorney shuffled through a few papers. "As far as I can tell, it is still here. And it will be here until she is ready to claim it."

She exchanged a brief look with Adonis that required no words for either of them to understand.

Serena's portion was still there, but not for long. Either Serena would die, or someone else. It did not matter.

They needed to warn Serena to be on the alert. If someone could enter Adonis' home, trap her within his bathroom and set it on fire, they could do the same to her sister. She turned to leave. There was nothing else Rutherford could do or say to help them.

Adonis apparently disagreed.

With almost superhuman speed, he was across the room, behind the large oak desk and dragging the wide-eyed man to his feet. Adonis pinned him against the wall, his fists curling into Rutherford's already strained neckline.

"I am not entirely certain you are not protecting Woodward's interests, or even that of his son's, so before I leave I will need you to do two things."

As much as Rutherford could, with two fists pressed to his neck, he shook his head.

"First, you will assure me that if anyone besides Serena Gowen walks into this office to claim her portion of her mother's inheritance, you will turn that person away, and then you will contact me with his identity. Will you do that for me?"

"Y-yes. Of c-course," he squeezed out.

"And second, you will reverse the fraudulent transaction that was made and return Selena Gowen's inheritance to her —"

Selena protested. "Adonis, that is not necess —"

"I-I cannot do that," Rutherford sputtered.

Adonis' expression was lethal, deadly. "You cannot do it, or you *won't*?"

"I do not have that authority —"

Adonis flung the attorney away from him as if he disgusted him. "Fine. I will see that my brother strips you of your licence, and then denies your lease until your practice is closed. I imagine that will take...oh...about a week? Only a negligent or incompetent attorney would allow something like this to happen. And which are you, Mr McGurie?" Adonis' glare did not falter. "I suspect you are both."

"No, no, there is no need to be so rash." Rutherford McGurie chased after Adonis who was already headed for the door. He stopped to peer down at the bumbling man. Once McGurie had his attention, he poured forth a wealth of knowledge. "*I* cannot reverse such a transaction personally, but I am sure, if I give you a letter stating that I was just as much a victim of this fraud as Ms Gowen, and you take it to your brother, it will be well within his purview to see to this matter."

Adonis did not hesitate in marching back to the attorney's desk. He pulled something out of his suit jacket that caught a glimmer of light. She didn't realise what it was until he placed it firmly into Rutherford's fleshy hand.

"Then by all means please get started on typing this letter, and here is my pen for you to sign it."

* * * *

Adonis made two calls as he left Rutherford McGurie's office with an official, *signed* letter in his hand. The first was to Apollo — warning him that Serena was in even greater danger than they'd first suspected, and their homes were no longer safe.

"Take her somewhere even we wouldn't suspect you to take her and have Eros go with you. Ares can stay with us. Only contact us if there is an emergency. I do not trust our cell phones."

Selena did not realise until much later that Adonis meant for Apollo to disappear with Serena so that none of them would be able to track them, find them, or communicate with them.

His second call was to Ares and consisted of telling him to locate the transfer of money, and redirect it into his account. By the time they pulled away from Rutherford McGurie's office, Adonis was pocketing his phone.

"What now?" she asked once they'd merged into traffic.

He glanced at her, a faint smile playing at the corners of his mouth. Adonis rarely smiled, if ever. It was disarming in a breath-stealing way.

"I am hungry. I would like to stop to eat. You?"

She was incredulous. "We just stole money back from whoever took it—"

"We know who took it."

That wasn't the point. "And he is going to want it back. You just told Apollo to take Serena and *hide*. Meanwhile, you want us to go *out* for lunch?"

"Yes, because he is already searching for Serena. He won't be expecting us to reclaim the funds. We have maybe one day, even two, before either your father, Jarrod or both double back—"

"And then what? All hell breaks loose?"

His smile was grim. "I assure you, it will probably feel like worse. I believe money is just the foil. What has driven your brother and your father to seek your death is something far deeper."

She scowled at him. "That is not comforting." Selena looked away to stare out at the passing landscape.

She turned back around when he sighed. "Fifteen minutes. I only mean to stop at a restaurant to pick up something to eat. It will give you and I a break from being closeted in my father's home, and all of us a welcome reprieve from Eros' cooking."

She didn't want to smile, but she couldn't stop the small grin from inching its way across her face. Eros' culinary skills *were* lacking.

"Tell me the real reason why you want to stop for a while," she said after she'd sobered.

He did not look at her, he didn't have to. Selena knew what demons plagued him. She simply wanted to hear it from his lips.

"After I left, I swore I'd never return. My father's home holds nothing but painful memories."

"They were not *all* painful. There was a softness in your voice when you spoke of your mother."

He glanced at her. "I wondered if you would mention that again." Thankfully he turned his attention back to the road ahead of them. She *hadn't* wanted to mention it, but they could not avoid the subject forever. "I have not told my brothers. I wouldn't even know what to tell them."

"There is nothing to tell. We shared what *appears* to be the same mother, but we do not know that for certain. How would telling them at this point change anything, when there are still so many unanswered questions?"

"I take it you have no intention of telling Serena then?"

She shook her head. "I have no doubt there is more to this story, but until we know it—as I said before—there is nothing to tell."

He seemed to accept her decision with silent affirmation. For now, this would be their secret.

Adonis eased his foot off the brake when the stoplight turned neon green, but no sooner had he pressed the gas than he jerked the car to an abrupt halt. A shadow fell over them followed by a series of heavy thuds, as something pounded against the top of the car to the windshield then the hood until it stopped there.

Bile stuck in Selena's throat at what she saw. She was too sick to scream.

But the pedestrians lining the sidewalks did it for her.

Chapter Nine

It had been Rutherford McGurie's body on the hood of Adonis' car. His portly frame had been stretched out on his stomach with his head twisted towards the windshield so his empty, unfocused eyes looked through them, seeing nothing. Blood had seeped out from under him, pooling around his body. They discovered he'd been shot, three times in the chest.

After contacting the proper authorities and having Rutherford's body removed, she and Adonis drove home in a car haunted by silence with a dead man's blood stained across it.

They were greeted by more silence when they returned to the empty estate. Presumably, Eros was now with Serena and Apollo, while Ares, who had not answered his phone in the past two hours, was nowhere to be found.

With the events of that afternoon, Selena and Adonis had not stopped for food, but she found she had no appetite as she made her way upstairs and collapsed atop the bed. Adonis followed after her, but he did not join her there.

Instead, he sat across from Selena in the armchair that was tucked in the corner. He brooded quietly, his glare alternating between nothing at all and the phone in his hand.

"Your brother will call as soon as he can."

"I am not worried about my brother. He is known for these unexpected absences."

Selena had no doubt such was the case. Ares struck her as a man of his own mind and purpose, one who was impossible to make demands upon unless he wished it.

"I thought you said we would have a day, maybe even two?" Selena queried.

"There has not been enough time for them to alter their plans. They are still after Serena."

"Then who is after us?" What she left unasked was—who had killed Rutherford, who knew they'd even visited him or what he'd told them about rewiring the money, within just *minutes* of them leaving his office?

The dark scowl across Adonis' face filled her with dread and a sense of foreboding she'd managed to evade, until now.

His next words did not improve her feelings of unease when he said quietly, "I don't know."

* * * *

Ares sat in his nondescript black car with its tinted windows, his eyes on the home of Woodward Gowen. He continued to sit as the beaming, blazing afternoon sun yielded to the burnished rays of dusk until twilight settled over the affluent neighbourhood. He waited, his eyes stalking.

He did not relish keeping secrets from his brothers, but this would not be the first time. Ares had many secrets. His soul was burdened by every one of them. Compared to the secrets he carried inside him, this one troubled him the least.

Dieu had glimpsed a darkness inside Ares that he'd nurtured then unleashed upon his enemies. Ares was adept at the art of subterfuge...and the art of murder. That was why he was quick to spot amateurs in the game he'd been born to play and trained to master.

Woodward Gowen was still missing, and that concerned Ares somewhat. His son, however, was very much present and alive, as Ares soon spotted him walking up the steps into his father's home.

Ares had been born and bred to play the game of intrigue and murder well. He wondered if Jarrod Gowen could say the same. He was never one to dismiss or underestimate any opponent, but on this point, he doubted if Jarrod Gowen had played this game before. If he had, he would have known to disguise himself or to only walk around under the cover of night.

With Rutherford's death and the blatant manner in which his body had been disposed of, Jarrod Gowen had to know he was being watched. Ares would have gone into hiding, but Jarrod Gowen was walking around as if nothing was amiss. Either he was arrogant or foolish — Ares suspected both. He also suspected that Jarrod Gowen was purposely baiting him.

When the entire street was plunged into darkness and the moon hovered high in the sky, Ares slipped from his car. It did not matter whether Jarrod Gowen was arrogant, foolish or an unrivalled master in this game. Even if he was baiting Ares, drawing him into a trap...well, then, he'd let himself be caught. The man had answers and Ares needed them—desperately and quickly... before another body was found. Before one of his brothers was caught up in this game Ares had unintentionally set into motion, and died because of the one secret that still burdened his soul.

Ares found the small window the young maid had left unlocked and slightly ajar. She did not want to lose her job, but, when Ares had returned alone to question her, she'd stared into his black, empty eyes and had quickly concluded there was more to lose than one's job. Ares was obscured by the darkness of the night and black clothing as he pushed the window open and crawled inside, landing on his feet with not so much as a sound. He moved like a silent panther stalking through the jungle as he made his way to the main level of the house.

The stairwell led up to the dining room, and from his earlier visit he knew the study was just off to the left. He turned the corner and was greeted by the door to the private office. He tested the knob. That it was locked was neither a surprise nor an obstacle for him. With practiced skill, he pulled out a small metal rod—curved at the ends, no longer than his index finger and no thicker than a hairpin—slipped it into the keyhole and slowly twisted it until there was a faint click. This time when he tried the knob, it turned in a clockwise motion and he was able to slip quietly into the study.

He pocketed the metal rod and pulled out a small flashlight, which he used to guide his footsteps to the desk. Papers were scattered atop the desk and Ares rummaged through them.

Bills, correspondences...nothing of note.

The drawers to the desk were unlocked and one by one he pulled them open, searching for anything that would yield the answers he sought. He got to the last drawer, which was locked, but he made quick work of it. Only then, as he opened it and learned what was inside, was he faced with answers to questions he'd never had. The shock of what he found was probably what made him careless. He didn't sense the other presence in the room until it was almost too late.

He reached for the gun, holstered beneath his arm at the same time that he heard the click of a gun being cocked.

"I wouldn't do that if I were you."

Ares slowly pulled his hand away from his weapon and raised his hands high into the air.

In one moment he was staring into the darkness, listening to a disembodied voice. The next the room was awash in light and he was staring into hard, walnut brown eyes.

The man before him could have easily been one of his brothers. His hair was a reddish, golden brown and curled about his shoulders, his eyes were of the same hue, his skin a smooth copper. He was the male embodiment of the woman who now slept in his father's home—Selena and Serena's brother—Jarrod Gowen.

Jarrod was ethereal in his beauty, his handsomeness. His very presence was magnetic and seductive. If he didn't know better, he'd think Jarrod Gowen had been born of *Dieu's* seed.

"I will put this gun down if you promise not to reach for yours."

That surprised him, but Ares nodded, relaxing when Jarrod lowered the gun, and he in turn lowered his hands to his sides.

"You could have killed me," said Ares, "but instead you trust me enough to lower your weapon with the assurance that I will not reach for mine. Why?"

He shrugged. "I know well of your reputation. I might shoot you, but I have a feeling you would not die. If anything, you'd rise from the dead to kill me."

Ares bit back a smug grin because Jarrod's words were not far from the truth. Ares' life had been threatened many times before, and, yet, here he stood.

"Besides, killing you would only hamper my agenda," Jarrod added, his statement raising Ares' eyebrows.

"And what *is* your agenda?"

"I just caught you rummaging through my personal files, so why don't you tell me?"

Ares considered how much he was prepared to reveal and what he still wanted to keep to himself. He decided to proceed with caution.

"I must say I did not expect this turn of events. It seems you both have us all fooled."

Jarrod surprised him again by smiling. His plan had been uncovered, the success of which Ares now threatened, and he stood there wearing a grin as if nothing had changed. Ares wondered if indeed nothing *had* changed as far as Jarrod was concerned.

"And even with the information you have, there is much you still do not know. I realise it is tempting to put an end to our plan, but I assure you this engine cannot be stopped. There are more factors at play and more players involved. I suggest you return home and get a good night's sleep and simply accept that you cannot stop what must happen."

"I cannot do that." Ares face was grim. "Your plan has dragged my brothers into this and placed them in danger."

"That is where you're wrong. *You* placed them in danger. You thought your actions would save them, but you only ensured their deaths. If you do not stand in our way, there is a chance we can all survive this."

Ares didn't ask how, for to ask *how* would be an admission to the act he'd committed a year ago—an act only four people knew of...or so he'd thought.

"I will see you out now," Jarrod said after a long silence stretched between them.

Ares had no choice but to walk before Jarrod Gowen as he escorted him to the front door.

"I am sure our paths will cross again," Jarrod assured him before he closed the door. Ares stood on the doorstep for only a moment before he marched down the steps and got into his car.

Very few could boast that they'd outmanoeuvred him. Ares had no doubt he would be seeing Jarrod Gowen again—it was a certainty.

* * * *

Adonis watched Selena until she fell asleep across his bed. Hours later, when the darkness of night began to creep through the shuttered windows, she still slept, while Ares still had not returned.

His brother's phone was turned off, his outgoing message revealing nothing of his whereabouts, but that was just like Ares, the eldest of them all.

Dieu had often used his oldest son to do his dirty work. When they walked into a room, down the street, whispers followed in Ares' wake, and people unconsciously took a step or two away from him.

Out of all of them, Ares was the most feared, for he'd seen and done things no man should ever have to.

Adonis did not fear for his brother, for whom killing was as natural as breathing. Adonis feared for the person Ares would unleash his fury upon.

With his brothers gone and Selena asleep, he was restless, the home of his childhood eerily quiet. He dreaded getting up, walking the empty corridors alone, but he could no longer sit beside Selena's bed — his mind and body could no longer weather the stillness.

This was what he'd feared, why he'd resisted returning to his father's estate. When the house was empty and the rooms silent, Adonis swore he could feel his father's presence, as though his ghost haunted the space.

Since that night, over a year ago, the four brothers had never mentioned what had happened in these halls, nor the dark secret that now bound them together for life.

His bare feet were silent as they padded across the cold, marble floor. Everything about *Dieu's* home epitomised the man himself. Lavishness, opulence, extravagance. *Dieu* had thought himself a god and no one had dared to correct him. To know the man *was* to know a god. *Dieu's* beauty had been unrivalled, even by his sons. He could seduce with a single look — he could destroy with a single touch. That was why Adonis had been chosen along with Ares, Eros and Apollo. Each brother embodied the qualities of *Dieu*. Both the darkness of cruelty, and the pure light of ethereal beauty — each man possessed a godliness that one could only be born with. *Dieu* had glimpsed that in each one of them, and then he'd nurtured it, manipulated it...corrupted it.

Adonis strode through the corridors, aimlessly wandering down the stairs to the chambers below.

The demons that still haunted him and the ghosts that lurked in the shadows of his mind — their presence surrounded him as he plunged deeper into the bowels of his father's home.

He knew what awaited him below, and it had been many years since he'd returned to the chambers where he'd been stripped of both his boyish innocence and his manhood. The stairway came to an end as he entered a narrow corridor. He walked through darkness that was only pierced by the occasional light from a wall sconce. Adonis did not need to see what surrounded him. He could have closed his eyes and the vision would have been as vivid as ever.

Even now — though it had been sixteen years since he'd been trapped within these walls, his usefulness to his father found only in these chambers — he could still smell the heavy cologne and perfume that clung to those who visited this place, those who'd visited him. Soft music had always played, filtering through the rooms to mute the sounds of sex and sin. But even music could not completely drown out the ever-present sounds of a brothel. There was nothing that could do that.

Overhead, a light flickered, casting shadows on the closed doors that led into opulent bedrooms. He stilled when the flickering stopped but a shadow continued to darken the hallway. He peered into the blackness, moving towards it, then stopped at the sound of footsteps behind him.

He whirled around, his hand already curled into a fist. In the last instant, he froze before his hand could strike its mark.

Wide topaz eyes stared at him in shock, and two delicate hands hovered in the air, poised to deflect his attack.

"Why did you sneak up on me without warning? I could have hurt you," Adonis bellowed, trying to ignore the furious hammering of his heart in his chest.

"I thought you heard me. I even called your name." Selena looked over his shoulder, then back at him. "What were you staring at? What had you so absorbed that you did not even notice my presence?"

He glanced in the direction she'd just looked, but the corridor was empty. "Nothing." His brows knitted together. "What are you doing down here? I thought you were asleep."

His cryptic response to her question did not go unnoticed and she frowned, but he was grateful she did not probe deeper. "I was, but then I missed your presence. When I awoke I came searching for you." She brushed past him, glancing about. "What is this place?"

He did not answer her immediately, so when she tried a door and found it unlocked, he had no choice but to follow after her. Adonis knew what she saw as soon as she stepped into the room. It was as if he stared through her eyes.

Dieu had always believed in the irony of things. He enjoyed paradoxes. While the other bordellos and brothels in the city were fashioned in rich, decadent hues of sable and scarlet, the walls of *this* room, as with all the others in this secret place, were a pure, radiant white. The furnishings, the bed covers—a beautiful tapestry of shimmering gold and bone white. Only a man who thought himself a god would portray the baser sins of the flesh as the purest of virtues.

Selena studied the room much like one would the finest art in a museum—with awe and amazement and a quiet reverence.

"Why is this painting hidden behind a curtain?" she asked, pushing aside the heavy brocade drapery to reveal a portrait depicting a bouquet of white orchids in a simple crystal vase.

He came up behind her, pulling the curtain closed, his hand lightly brushing hers in the process.

"The painting actually functions as a window of sorts. Behind it sits a camera. The curtain stayed closed when there were guests, and open when there weren't."

"Did the guests know there was a camera behind the painting?"

"Yes."

Her brow furrowed. "Then why even have a curtain? If it was closed when you had guests, and open when you didn't, what would be the point of even having a camera?"

"To provide the illusion of privacy. The camera possesses infrared X-ray technology. It can see through these draperies, just as easily as it can see in the dark. The guests believed they weren't being viewed, but every moment they spent within these walls they were being watched."

"It was for security, then, to make sure you and your brothers were safe?"

Adonis recalled all of the cruelties he'd suffered at the hands of one guest after another — the brutal violence, the pain...all in the pursuit of pleasure. His smile was humourless as he grasped her arm, led her from the room, and closed the door firmly behind him and the memories of his past. "It was so that one man could feel he had unlimited control and omnipotent power over everyone who came here." He thought of guests who'd later been blackmailed by *Dieu*.

That was the problem with sins of the flesh — the high cost one had to pay for one's perversions.

"Did you ever enjoy being a consort?"

He glanced down at her — her question an odd one and wholly unexpected — but he did not stop as he propelled her upstairs, far away from the chambers below.

"No."

"But you were good at it."

"One of the best."

His statement silenced her — out of shock, revulsion or both, he wasn't sure. But she did not speak until they were once again upstairs in the outer chambers of his bedroom.

"Serena is also one of the best."

He looked closely at her, trying to discern the direction of her thoughts, the direction of this conversation even. Her face, which was normally so expressive, stared at him in contemplation.

"She is," he responded, giving voice to the rumours that abounded that indeed she was, mainly because he did not know what else to say. Selena stared at him expectantly as if she desired an answer to a question she had not posed.

"All these years, I wondered why Serena sought such a life, how she endured it." Selena's eyes snared him with their subtle intensity. "But when I spoke to her, I could tell that she'd sought such a life because it appealed to her. Her life as a courtesan has freed her, it has liberated her."

"It is that way for some." Adonis thought of Eros. Of the four of them, he was the only one to revel in such a lifestyle. Even now he still entertained those who would pay *well* for pleasure.

"I thought something was wrong with me, that I would choose to live in a convent, while my sister chose the life of a courtesan. I could not bear the thought of so many men touching me after what happened. And I didn't understand how she *could.*"

"There is nothing wrong with you," he said harshly, rougher than was necessary. Some of that was owing to the conviction he felt…but most of it was because of the guilt. "We are all made differently. You may be twins, but your needs are not intertwined with your sister's. After what was done to you, you both sought solace in your own ways. That does not mean anything is wrong with either of you."

She seemed to consider his words with the tilt of her head to one side, her unbound locks caressing her shoulder. He followed the tendrils of hair as they came to rest just beneath the curve of her breast. His heartbeat quickened and a steady pulse of heat drummed through him.

After what had transpired in the bathroom, he'd vowed not to touch her intimately again. He couldn't, because every time he did, he lost another piece of himself to her, another part of his soul.

His heart had always belonged to her, but his soul… He'd convinced himself he'd lost it to sin and depravity long ago. But, every time she touched him, she healed him and he swore he could feel his soul mending.

He didn't deserve it—to have his ravaged soul healed. He didn't deserve any of it. Not her touch, not her salvation. His life had been an endless wheel of suffering. He wasn't even certain if he knew how to exist in the space of happiness. And that was what she offered. In the stolen moments when he was inside her body, she offered him salvation and happiness—

neither of which he deserved. Neither of which he'd ever had. Both of which he would die without when she took them away.

His resolve was strong inside his head, but now she stood before him removing her clothes and he was weak once again.

"Selena..." He backed away from her, calling her name in warning, but she did not stop her advance upon him until his back was flush against the wall, and even then she didn't stop until a mere inch separated them.

"Why do you fear touching me now, when you have not before?"

That was not true. He'd feared touching her from the very first moment. He'd feared what touching her would do to him. His fear had not been unwarranted.

"Someone is trying to kill us. It is best that we remain alert and vigilant."

"Are we not safe within these walls?"

"We are not safe anywhere."

She continued to remove her clothing until she wore nothing, his warning falling upon deaf ears.

"Do you think we will survive this ordeal?"

"I cannot answer that, Selena, because I do not know."

She touched her palm to his torso, her eyes gentle. His breath stilled in his chest.

"If you died tomorrow, I would mourn you, Adonis, just as I would be grateful to you for showing me true passion. For giving me new memories to wash away the old ones, for taking my pain away and giving me pleasure. Would you deny me such pleasure, when your body desires this too?"

He sucked in a sharp breath when her hand began to wander, but he did not relent. "Three days ago you wanted to kill me. I do not believe that you would mourn my death."

"Much has changed in three days."

He captured her hand when it settled atop his thickening erection. "And much is still the same."

"If I died tomorrow would you mourn me?"

His voice was ragged when he spoke, but he did not lie. "Of course I would."

"I could die tomorrow, we both could, and yet we have tonight to celebrate that we are still alive." She resumed her perusal of his body, and this time he did not stop her. "Do not deny us this, when you so desperately want it, just as desperately as I do."

He closed his eyelids, shutting out her eyes that shimmered with desire, her cheeks that were flushed red, her full lips that glistened beneath the moonlight.

He could not have resisted her if he'd wanted to, been commanded to...even if his life had depended upon it. He'd never been able to deny her anything.

Tangling his hand in her hair, he pulled her close. "You will be the death of me," he rasped just before he crushed his mouth to hers. She would be the death of him for so many reasons and in so many ways.

Adonis urgently kissed her with a fervour that shocked and scared her, but she did not retreat. She clasped his head within her hands and held him close, fusing their lips, melding their bodies together until nothing separated them.

She would be the death of him... That revelation had been wrenched from him, torn from his lips as if it had been ripped from his very soul. She understood such sweet agony, the torture of one's mind and body warring for dominance, because she felt it to the core of her being.

She loved Adonis and hated him in the same breath. She understood why he'd resisted her touch — it was the feelings aroused when they were together like this, making him vulnerable...*to her*. She understood because she was equally vulnerable to him.

When they were together like this, one could almost imagine the past didn't exist, that if they survived there was hope for a future. Such thoughts were foolish, but she was unable to stop them. Selena could not help but wonder — could two people so scarred by their joined past actually heal together and find happiness?

It was futile to think such things when her next breath wasn't even promised and neither was his.

She'd come to him to kill him — the last thing she'd expected was that she'd regret or question her decision, but she did. Her hatred was wasteful and useless and it had consumed so much of her life — a life that could end at any moment.

If she died tomorrow, she would have experienced so few moments of happiness and joy. If she died tomorrow, her life would have been such a waste.

That was why she kissed him with her entire being, why she took his warm breath inside herself and absorbed his entire essence. If she died tomorrow or the next day or the day after, she would always have these stolen moments with the man who'd destroyed her life and had given it back to her in the same breath.

Their kiss seemed to go on for hours, days, though it could not have been for more than a few minutes. Each of them clung to the other, the solace of their bodies providing respite from the turmoil that was now their lives.

She drew away from him, ending their kiss, her chest heaving as she lost herself in swirling amber eyes that stared down at her as if she was the most beautiful, most desirable woman in the world.

Her heart skipped a beat at the look in Adonis' eyes, his feelings so openly revealed in the golden beauty of his tawny gaze.

She wondered what he saw when he looked into her own eyes. The pleasure he invoked, the desires he fulfilled? Or did he see what she so desperately tried to hide from him, from herself — the look of a woman who sought love, and offered it in return. With death hovering all around them, she offered her heart, and demanded his in return. To lose her heart to a man she'd never stopped loving was a small price to pay when she could soon lose her life.

Selena twined her fingers with his and led him to the bed. His chest was bare, and he removed his pants, stepping out of them to kick them aside. No words were exchanged as he lay across the tousled bed, his golden body sparkling beneath the silver moonlight.

She straddled his torso, her hands lightly tracing the contours of his chest, her eyes meeting his. She bent down to kiss him, her lips gentle at first until he cupped the back of her head, deepening the kiss, his mouth searching, his tongue probing.

She abandoned herself to the pleasure he aroused inside her. The heat he awakened in her belly uncoiled to spread throughout her entire being. Her breasts were heavy with desire, her nipples almost painfully tight as the lips of her sex grew wetter, her tunnel slick. She could feel his cock hard and ready, nudging against the swells of her ass, gently teasing her flesh, and she reached behind her back to grasp him, stroking his length with her curled hand.

He groaned against her lips, and she drank in his pleasure and satisfaction. Tightening her hand, she pumped him faster until she felt a slick wetness along her fingers.

Pre-cum.

The metallic scent of his arousal tickled her nostrils, and she absorbed it, filling every part of herself with the essence of him.

His hands gripping her hips startled her, and she wrenched her lips from his, staring down into his flushed face.

"Get on it," he croaked out.

The words came out as a harsh, needy command and her pussy clenched at the image his words conjured before her eyes — their bodies intertwined, her buttocks bouncing against him, her hips rolling as she took his shaft inside her cunt over and over again.

She pushed backwards at the same time he lifted her hips. He settled her atop him, her entrance poised against the tip of his cock.

In one smooth, fluid motion, he released her hips sending her sinking down upon him, inch by torturous inch. Her heat enveloped him. His cock stretched her. Groans poured from their lips in unison, their pleasure mingling, meshing together until their bodies were one and he was buried to the hilt inside her.

She felt so full of him, so stuffed, but even as she struggled to adjust to the thick length of his cock, she braced her palms against his chest and began to move. She rocked against him, slowly at first, her hips undulating in lazy circles until he was panting beneath her, his eyes hooded, his fingers digging into the tender skin along her hips.

His body radiated with unleashed power beneath her, his restraint wavering. Her own body sought the release he offered. She began to move in earnest then, impaling herself on his cock, taking him hard and deep until sweat poured from their skin.

Sin and sex hovered in the air, clinging to their bodies and the walls around them. Their lovemaking was wild and primitive, tinged with desperation. Gone was any hint of tenderness or restraint. The threat of death would do that.

Selena pumped her hips up and down, swallowing his shaft with each thrust. Her nails raked his chest, his nipples, and he gasped in pleasure and pain. Her wildness fuelled his, and he surged up into her, matching her strokes with driving, slamming thrusts of his own.

The sound of flesh slapping together echoed in the room. It was only drowned out by their sighs and groans, and the steady rocking of the headboard ricocheting against the wall. The bed squeaked and protested beneath them but they heard little else over the drumming of their hearts.

A gush of feminine wetness poured from Selena's cunt, drenching his thrusting cock and Adonis sighed then groaned out his pleasure, sexual energy crackling and pulsing all around them.

Selena called his name as she quickened her pace, a toe-curling fire beginning to spread throughout her. Her orgasm hovered inside and all around her. She dug her nails deeper, clenching her sheath tighter until she shattered into tiny pieces, screaming his name in pleasure and sweet agony.

He joined her instantly, his head thrown back as he pushed up inside her, his hands imprisoning her hips as he pumped his seed into her waiting body on a deep, hoarse grunt. Adonis spurted inside her as if he had not come in ages, filling her, scorching her.

The essence of their climaxes came together in a harmonious blending of pleasure until it overflowed her body and trickled from her.

As she settled into the afterglow of her pleasure, her strength seeping from her, she slumped against him, completely boneless. Their breath was stilted, their heartbeats hammering in unison. It was a long time before their bodies recovered and either of them could move.

Still joined, Adonis rolled them over so that they lay face to face, while one of her legs remained draped over his hip and the other trapped beneath him. She ignored the slight discomfort of his weight, holding him close to kiss him gently.

It was an oddly tender moment, given the brutal intensity of their lovemaking that had claimed them only moments ago. She'd thought her heart was frozen—that she could never, would never love again, and certainly not this man—but she felt it beginning to thaw as he steadily chipped away the ice surrounding it, with his tenderness, his compassion...his vulnerability. Adonis the man, the god, he was not who he seemed. He was deeper, far more complex than she ever could have imagined.

Adonis' eyes darkened and the air around them shifted. She gasped when he brought their bodies closer, his manhood stiffening inside her.

Her eyes rounded in surprise, conveying her thought—she could not imagine he had already recovered, that his body craved her again—but when he pulled her head towards him and claimed her lips, she surmised that it did.

The position made his strokes shallow and this time their lovemaking was slow, languorous. He ignited a fire of pleasure inside them, slowly building it, stoking it until sexual heat danced all around her, and she welcomed his thrusts with the gift of her slippery, wet heat.

His shallow thrusts drove her crazy, made her wild until she begged for more. Her body needed more. Adonis rolled her beneath him then, covering her body with his and she gasped in pleasure when he drove home, hot and hard, giving her everything she'd clamoured for.

His strokes were still slow, his pace unhurried. Their bodies, which had just been sated, relished the languid rhythm of his lovemaking. Selena savoured his tender thrusts, the gentle caresses of his chest against hers — brushing her nipples with each stroke — the teasing slide of his fingers against her bare thighs as he ploughed deep inside her.

Her hands took their time exploring his body as well. With her fingertips, she traced every sinew of muscle in his chest, his shoulders, his arms. Every touch drew from him a soft sigh or a sharp gasp. When she twisted the flat nubs of his nipples between her fingers he let out a deep, hoarse groan. She teased him, taunting him with her touch. He did the same with the slow slide of his cock inside her pussy.

It was a long while before the slow burning fire inside her began to leap and rage out of control, and when she felt her orgasm coiling at the core of her sex, she welcomed the dull throb of release. This time her climax came on a furling wave of sensuous pleasure as her tunnel clenched with tiny flutters all around his stroking shaft.

The tight fist of her cunt surrounding him dragged Adonis with her, and he orgasmed on a deep groan, his face buried against the crook of her neck as he shuddered then shot a stream of warmth against the entrance to her womb.

They were both boneless by the time he collapsed atop her — their bodies weary, but pleasantly so. They held each other, their limbs entwined. The intimacy of the moment was not lost on either of them and they clung together in silence, not wanting to sever the fragile bond that was steadily building between them, growing stronger with every gesture of trust and tenderness. Neither wanted to speak for fear of breaking the spell.

But nothing lasts forever — neither pleasure, nor pain.

A door slammed and footsteps echoing against hardwood floors brought a swift end to the intimacy of the moment.

The initial fear that there was an intruder eased upon recognition of the familiar, steady, confident rhythm of booted feet striking the floor.

Ares had finally returned.

Chapter Ten

Selena soon discovered where Ares had disappeared to and to whom he'd spoken when almost as soon as he returned home he began calling her name along with Adonis'.

They exchanged a curious glance as they hurriedly pulled on their clothes. They were just walking into the adjacent sitting area when Ares barrelled into the room.

His eyes locked on her, deadly and intense. She barely had a moment to secure the belt of her robe before he was upon her, his hand imprisoning her neck as he slammed her into the wall.

She struck out with her fists to his face, then her knee into his groin, but he was relentless. In the distance she heard Adonis calling his name, she saw him trying to pull his brother off her, but Ares was ruthless.

"I visited your brother this evening. And do you know what he told me?" Ares snarled at her.

She could barely breathe, let alone talk, so she remained silent, imprisoned within his grip against the wall.

"Let her go!" Adonis boomed, his voice reverberating through the room. It must have registered somewhere in Ares' mind because he did just that, and she could breathe again, but he still crowded her, as if he half expected her to attack him.

"What is wrong with you?" Adonis demanded. "Attacking Selena like that?"

"Tell him why I attacked you, why I trust you even less than I did before."

She looked at Adonis, then at Ares, then back at Adonis. He must have seen it in her eyes...or did he smell it in the air?

Betrayal was a funny thing—it was the only emotion that could wound deeper than heartbreak. He'd broken her heart and now she'd betrayed his trust.

She looked back at Ares because she could no longer bear to look into Adonis' eyes—the eyes of her past. He'd bared his soul to her and she'd done nothing but lie to him.

Selena had underestimated Ares. She had not seen this coming.

With a sigh, she revealed the truth, or at least what she was prepared to reveal...for now. "That you visited my brother, I believe. That he told you anything, I highly doubt. Jarrod has his own agenda, consistent with mine. To reveal it to you would not be in his best interests, which is why I know you must have put the pieces of the puzzle together on your own—or at least what you *think* is the puzzle. What did you find, Ares, that gave me away?"

"Correspondence between the two of you in his office. To your credit, the messages were cryptic and brief, but it contained enough for me to realise that you'd lied about not knowing Jarrod and that he was your accomplice in something. The rest I figured out on my own."

"You think you've figured it out." Her smile was slight. "But I assure you this game is bigger than all of us combined."

Ares' gaze turned menacing. "Tell me your role in this now or I will kill you myself."

"Killing me will change nothing. My death will not stop what must happen. But as to my role in all of this?" She cocked her head to the side, wondering how best to proceed. She could not tell the entire truth, but neither could she keep *all* of her secrets. Ares surely wished her gone because of her deceit, but Selena still needed something from them. And because she still needed them, she needed them to believe she was not a threat, even if they could not trust her. "Well, it is simple," she said finally.

"You were right, Adonis," she admitted, although she did not look at him. She still couldn't. "The money is just a foil. Not even that. It is simply a diversion." She kept her eyes trained on Ares as she spoke. "As you already know, sixteen years ago Woodward orchestrated the events of that night where Adonis was forced to ruin me and then humiliate me. I always knew my father was behind it, from the very beginning. After what happened, he disowned me and petitioned the courts to have me cloistered in that convent where I was a prisoner. I could not leave. For many years I was trapped there under the watchful attention of nuns who thought they were protecting me. I've always known of Woodward's involvement. What you don't know is why he would do such a thing."

That raised Ares' eyebrows but he remained silent, waiting for her to finish speaking.

"My mother died when I was just fourteen. But she did not simply die of natural causes as everyone believes. She was murdered. And I saw it all. I witnessed Woodward murder my mother and then I held her in my arms as she took her last breath. Woodward brutally killed her because he'd learned of her infidelity.

"As I was the only witness, naturally he wanted me dead as well, but he couldn't kill me too—it would have incurred too much suspicion. Just as he saw no way to have me imprisoned, so he did the next best thing. He threatened me into silence for several years until he finally found a reason to justify sending me away. After what happened between me and Adonis, he banished me to that convent and had me strictly cloistered, and no one questioned him."

"Why didn't you tell anyone about what happened?" Ares demanded to know.

"At first, because I was a frightened child and he threatened to pin her murder on me, and I believed him. I know now that, if he could have done such a thing, he would have. He would have had me sent to prison or watched me be sentenced to death without a second thought. He must not have seen a way to frame me, so the convent was the only way to ensure I would never reveal what happened. Yet had I been determined, eventually his threats would not have been enough to ensure my silence, especially once I grew older and was no longer a scared little girl. But by the time I was old enough and brave enough to say anything, I'd already made the decision that I would deal with him *personally*. And in the convent I knew it was only a matter of time before I could escape and do just that."

"So the fire—at the convent. You killed someone then dumped their body so that you could escape."

She glowered at Ares. "I am many things but I do not kill the innocent. Jarrod stole a body from the morgue and left it at the convent. He set the fire after I was gone."

"And what about the other fires—at your sister's place, Adonis' hotel, his home…"

"Serena started the one at her bordello." She smiled then. "And yes, you were right, Ares, to accuse me of setting the others. I was the one who set those."

"You planted a bomb in my penthouse? You nearly killed yourself in that fire." She heard the distress in Adonis' voice. She glanced at him—to do even that made her heart ache.

"It was necessary. I needed you to believe I was in danger."

"So the three of you are all involved in this—Serena, Jarrod and you."

She shook her head. "Serena's role is minimal. She set that fire because I *asked* her to and that was all she needed to know. She is my sister and, no matter what, we are loyal to one another. Serena knows nothing of Woodward's hand in the death of our mother. That is why he did not insist on having her sent to a convent. She was ignorant of all his sins and I want to keep it that way for as long as I can."

"Why? Why would you keep something like that from her?"

She studied Ares. He would not understand her reasoning. Few could. "Serena has a purity of heart that is rare. You could say she is a whore with a heart of gold."

"While you're the nun with a heart full of coal."

She smiled at Ares' statement. Some might see it that way. She was certainly not a virtuous woman free of sin. She may have lived the life of a nun, but she was not one. Not in thoughts or in deeds.

"And what is Jarrod's role in all of this?"

She shrugged. "He is Woodward's illegitimate son. I didn't even know about him until a few years ago. For the last three years, Serena has visited me at the convent at least four times a year. Since I could never leave and we are twins, she would take my place and I hers for a day or two. It was the only way I could get out. It was during one of those times that Jarrod visited Serena's brothel and revealed his identity to me. My father would have nothing to do with him. He'd left Jarrod's mother with no money and a child to raise. His mother ended up simply working herself to death to take care of him, while Woodward lived lavishly. And when his mother died, my father simply foisted Jarrod off on a couple who Woodward paid to raise him. Needless to say, Jarrod is as bitter as I."

"If that is the case, then how did Jarrod come to live at your father's home? Why would your father offer Jarrod a place in his home, but nothing else?"

"Blackmail. I told Jarrod what happened to my mother and he used it to blackmail Woodward into 'giving' Jarrod that home. Woodward hasn't lived there in over a year. I assume the maid told you otherwise, but, I assure you, Marcy works for my brother and is paid to tell you whatever he tells her to say."

"If what you say is true, and Jarrod blackmailed your father into ceding him the house, why not get your father to give him some of his money as well?"

"Jarrod tried to blackmail him for money, but he soon discovered my father can only be pushed so far. After two failed attempts upon his life, Jarrod did not push anymore and Woodward went into hiding after that."

"He went into hiding?" Ares' eyebrows peaked. "When? Why?"

"A little over a year ago. As to why and where he has gone, well, that is what I am trying to find out."

"But what has changed?" Ares demanded. "Why, after all these years, have you only just now decided to leave the convent to go in search of your father?"

Selena smiled, a smile that was as serene as it was cruel. That question was the easiest of them all. "I promised my mother as I watched her die that I would kill the man who did this to her. And I'm sure you know better than most that revenge never dies. When he disappeared, I knew it was time to act before I lost my chance forever."

"And Rutherford McGurie—you killed him too? Was his death part of your plan?"

"Not at all. I didn't kill him, and I can assure you it wasn't Jarrod, either."

"And how do you know that Jarrod wasn't involved?" asked Ares. "How well do you know this long lost brother of yours after all?"

"Admittedly, not as well as I know my sister, but, in the time I've known him, I've come to realise that Jarrod is loyal and he is meticulous about following the order of things. He did not kill Rutherford because *that* was not part of the plan. The plan was for Jarrod to help me get out of the convent and get Adonis and the rest of you to trust me long enough to believe I was in danger by setting those fires. In the meantime, he manipulated the transfer of money so you would be convinced it was the money Woodward was after."

"So your father is *not* after you," Adonis said flatly. She looked at him, holding his gaze longer than she'd dared to before. It was painful. His eyes were cold, devoid of any emotion as if he felt nothing.

She'd been ruthless in orchestrating this plan. She'd never imagined she'd still have feelings for him, or that he'd still have feelings for her. On both counts she'd been wrong and now her heart ached at the pain she glimpsed in his hooded eyes...pain she'd caused.

"No, Woodward is not after me. Quite the opposite. It is *me* who is after Woodward."

"And those rings? Your brother planted those as well?"

She returned her attention to Ares, her brow creased in contemplation. "Again, that was not part of our plan. I have no idea what those rings symbolise, and I was as surprised to see them as you."

"Then it would appear as if we have a mystery on our hands, now, don't we?" Ares said dryly. It was clear he did not believe her entirely, but that was his concern not hers. On that point, she was telling the truth.

She'd never seen those rings in her entire life, had no idea who had left them at the scene of those fires, or why. And she certainly did not grasp the point in killing Rutherford. He'd been such a minor player in this grand scheme. His death seemed almost pointless.

"So was the business of your mother's estate and her will a lie? Did you fake that too so that I would believe Woodward was after you and you were in danger?" Adonis' voice was whispery quiet and she looked to him again.

"Not at all. My mother's estate is very real."

"And you knew you could use it to draw your father out."

Adonis shoved a hand through his hair. "Then why send a note to me? Why threaten me when it's obvious you're not in danger, when you've planned all along to spring a trap for your father? Why did you need to gain the trust of me and my brothers? Why did you need us to believe you were in danger? Why did you need us at all?"

"I needed you to believe I was coming for you. I knew your sense of guilt would force you to at least give me an audience. I knew that if you believed I was in danger, that your sense of guilt would also force you to offer me your protection."

"And here I believed *I* was orchestrating your return to protect *you* from your father, when it was you pulling all of the strings. But I sense there is something else, something you're not telling. Why did you need me to offer my protection, when truly you *don't* need it at all?" Adonis pressed.

She sighed. Adonis could be unrelenting, but there was one last secret she could not reveal, one last component of her plan that still had yet to play out.

"Because, under your protection, I knew you would take me somewhere safe."

Adonis narrowed his eyes, and she was certain Ares did the same. They were shrewd men, astute. There was no doubt they recognised there was far more to her statement...and there was. When Adonis' gaze probed deep, straight to the heart of her, she stilled, his next words causing the blood in her veins to freeze over.

"Somewhere safe...or *here*?"

Somehow she managed to recover quickly. "What is the difference?"

"I don't know, Selena. You're the one coordinating this grand performance—you tell me."

Selena didn't. After that she didn't say another word. None of them did.

And after *that*, she found herself sitting atop the bed with one arm cuffed to the headboard, waiting for Ares and Adonis to decide what they would do with her next.

This was not part of her strategy, but even the best laid plans could go awry. Her fate now rested in the hands of the two men who stood on the other side of that door. If they made the wrong decision, it would alter everything she'd so carefully crafted, but no matter her fate, neither man could stop what she'd set out to do. This game was bigger than any of them and once set in motion, it would not be stopped until the final piece was played.

* * * *

Adonis stood before the closed door leading into his childhood bedroom. The woman beyond that door was not the woman he'd once known and loved. She was someone far different, far worse.

The woman he'd loved had been many things, but she would never have lied to him, manipulated or betrayed him. He'd offered his very soul to take Selena's pain away because of the guilt he still carried, because of the love he still felt. And she'd simply been using him…for sport, as a means to an end. In the end, Selena had proven to be just like all the others who sought his company—she used him as she took her pleasure for as long as he was useful.

"You cannot blame yourself," Ares said from behind him. "We were all manipulated by them."

And now Apollo and Eros were with Serena, presumably at a safe house, where neither of them could be contacted. They'd done as instructed and now there was no way to communicate with them, to convey to them that Serena could not be trusted. And, despite her sister's claims, it was very likely that Serena had her own role to play and her own agenda.

It was possible that Serena wasn't a threat, but they didn't know that. His brothers could be in danger and he was responsible. He'd placed their lives in danger for the love of a woman who'd betrayed him.

"You should go after them," Adonis said to his brother as he finally turned to face him. "You should find them. They no longer need to guard Serena since we now know she is not in danger."

"We don't know that. We don't know if any of us are yet safe."

That raised Adonis' eyebrows, but he remained silent, waiting for Ares to finish.

"Let's say we believe Selena and Jarrod. Let's say they are telling the truth about Rutherford McGurie and those rings. If they didn't kill him and plant those rings, then who did? And why?

"If it was just the matter of the rings I might be able to simply chalk this up as a hoax. But to kill a man and drop him from the sky onto your car is no hoax — it's a warning, a threat...a message. From whom, and *why* it was sent, now become our questions to answer."

"We cannot trust a word Selena says," Adonis protested. "Jarrod could have killed McGurie and he may now be coming for us —"

"I doubt that, or he would have killed me tonight. He had his gun trained on me. He could have easily shot me if he'd wanted."

Adonis frowned. His brother was a trained assassin — not easily distracted or bested. That Jarrod had pulled a gun on him and could have shot him told Adonis two things — either Ares was becoming rusty, which he doubted, or his attention had been preoccupied, which worried him. Only something truly disturbing could distract the focus of a man such as his brother.

"All right, so Jarrod and Selena do not want us dead, and neither does Serena. All the more reason to find Apollo and Eros and warn them."

"And leave you alone with *her?* And her brother on the loose? We still don't know her true motivations."

"You being here will not get us any closer to learning them." Adonis decided. He could get far more out of Selena if he was not under the careful scrutiny of his older brother. "Besides, you do not have to worry about me. I can handle Selena. And as for her brother... With the added security you've seen to, this place is more secure than a prison. Jarrod Gowen cannot get inside and Selena certainly cannot get out."

Ares was hesitant. He did not want to leave his brother alone with that viper. Selena was one to be feared. She possessed a duplicitous nature and the charisma of a chameleon. She could change at any moment, and you would trust that new version of her, just as easily as you had trusted the last. In one moment she was a deadly assassin, and yet Adonis had let her inside his home. The next moment, she was the tortured victim of the past, and yet Adonis had let her into his bed. Now she was the vengeful daughter of one of his enemies and still Adonis would not cast her out of his father's home and wash his hands of her. Instead he'd chained her to his bed, where he would keep her until she gave him the answers he sought. Ares had no doubt the information she provided would turn out to be useful, but at what cost to the soul of his brother?

Selena would become another version of herself again, and he feared Adonis would let that version of her into his heart where she would have the power to destroy him all over again, but worse this time.

"I see the look in your eyes, but you must trust me. To remain here, waiting for something to happen, doing nothing until it does, will only frustrate you. Especially when Apollo and Eros could be in danger. There is more to Selena's plan, I'm sure, and I will uncover it. In the meantime you must find our brothers and warn them."

Adonis was right. Ares acknowledged this with the stiff nod of his head. His brothers could be in danger from Serena, Jarrod Gowen, or an enemy who had yet to reveal himself. Apollo and Eros were as well trained as he, but it was hard to stop the enemy one did not see coming—one they thought they were protecting, that they thought they could trust.

"I see the wisdom of your plan," Ares said finally. "And I will go, but promise me this..."

Ares held his younger brother's stare, his gaze unwavering so that Adonis would grasp the totality of his words.

"Do not let your guard down with that woman. She is not to be trusted. You see that now. As you deal with her, remember that—as well as the fact that this all began because she threatened to kill you, and there is no evidence to suggest that that is still not her intent. "

* * * *

Ares departed from *Le Siège d'un Dieu* an hour later, just before dawn. Their brothers had deliberately set out to disappear and now it was Ares' duty to find them. If anyone could, it was Ares.

Long after his brother left, Adonis sat in the living room of his chambers still staring at the door to his bedroom, mulling over his brother's parting words.

'This all began because she threatened to kill you, and there is no evidence to suggest that that is still not her intent'.

Just hours ago, he'd made love to her and she'd whispered tender words in his ear, assurances that made him believe two people ravished by their pasts could heal one another.

He'd been wrong. He'd been a fool.

He crossed the room on stilted legs and opened the door, stepping quietly into his bedroom. Sunlight was just beginning to stream through the grey windows, delicately illuminating her sleeping figure.

Still wearing the robe she'd donned earlier, she slept awkwardly, one arm secured to the bed while she was slumped against the headboard. He touched her shoulder and roused her, her sooty black lashes fluttering over deep, round pools of topaz.

He retreated into the corner of the room while she fully awakened. He stood against the wall, his arms folded across his chest, his body obscured by the space where the sun could not reach.

It took a few seconds for her to come to, as she sat up straighter, her eyes searching for him in the darkness.

"I waited a long time for you to come back." Her voice was raspy, hoarse from sleep. "I guess I finally dozed off." Her lashes fluttered and she slid her tongue across her lips, until they glistened with moisture. He did not want to notice, he did not want to feel, but the clenching of his belly betrayed him.

"I am sorry, Adonis. I wanted to say that to you in private, beyond your brother's suspicious gaze."

"His gaze was suspicious because obviously there was much to be suspicious of."

"I never meant to hurt you. I hated that I had to lie to you and manipulate you but there was no other choice." She stopped abruptly, probably because she glimpsed the hardening of his expression.

"There is always a choice. Isn't that what you told me, Selena?"

A long silence stretched between them and if he listened carefully he would swear he could hear her heart pounding.

It was a long while before she spoke again. "I am truly sorry, Adonis. Truly. When we made lo—"

She did not finish the word when he emitted a low growl.

"The physical intimacy we shared. I did not fake that, not any of it. I truly did not expect to find myself in your arms, in your bed, but I could not resist you. I couldn't. I didn't want to say that in front of your brother, but I wanted you to know. Every response, every emotion, everything I said to you in those moments—that was all real."

"How nice of you, Selena, to stroke my ego." His smile was bitter. "I am happy to hear that you did not fake the orgasms I gave you. I would be an even richer man if I had a dollar for every time a woman praised me for the time well spent in my bed."

Her eyes flickered with pain and fury. "What we shared went beyond just the physical and you know it, just as you know that I am not every woman."

His laugh was harsh. "Believe me, I do not need further confirmation that you are not like *any* other woman."

Adonis leant away from the wall and crossed the room to the locked armoire in the other corner. He brandished a key and unlocked it, then flung the doors open. They slammed against the wall. The sound of the armoire's brass knobs ricocheting against the wood shattered the strained silence in the room.

She gasped as she stared into the bowels of the closet, seeing what he'd intended for her to see. Her fear was almost palpable. She feared what he would do, she feared the unknown.

"What you are is a snake, Selena. A liar and a rat. You manipulated me into placing the only family I have in danger so that you could have revenge against your father. I understand your need for revenge. What I cannot accept are your methods."

He found the object he was searching for and turned around, his palm curling around the stiff leather.

"You preyed upon my guilt, my feelings for you, and you used me. Had you left it at that I would not feel such rage, but that you brought my brothers into this is unforgivable."

"I am sorry about that, Adonis. That every one of your brothers would be dragged into this was neither my plan nor my intent and I will never forgive myself if anything happens to them."

He studied her. She seemed genuine, earnest, but he could not be certain that this was still not a part of her plan, the master game she still played.

"My father trained each of my brothers in the art of seduction, the art of lovemaking." As Adonis spoke he took a step towards the bed where she was still his prisoner. "Just as my father trained each of us in the art of weaponry and the art of war.

"We were trained to kill, just as we were trained to seduce, to inspire lust…to fuel and fulfil desires. We were chosen, each of us, not only because of our ability to master the lessons he taught, but also because of the unique skills which we already possessed, that were innate."

He stopped at the edge of the bed, on the side where she was cuffed.

"When we came to *Dieu*, we had names—normal ones like every other boy—and we went by those names for many years until after our mother died, until after we completed our training.

"Ares was named because he has always possessed a darkness that makes him capable of a type of violence that others might be haunted by, whereas he remains impervious. He was *Dieu's* chief assassin and executioner. Apollo earned his name because of his ability to hunt—to track anything and anyone. It is a shame that Apollo has disappeared with Eros because, now that we need to find them, Ares is only the next best at it. But for Apollo, finding things, people—that is as natural to him as breathing. It is because of his tracking abilities that *Dieu* made Apollo his chief spy and retriever."

He smiled then. "Eros' abilities are naturally more obvious. He is as skilled as any of us in weapons and the art of fighting, but he is a lover—a natural born charmer and seducer. Woman or man, if Apollo could not get close enough to a person to obtain information, Eros was sent in to obtain it with time well spent in the bed sheets. When Eros chooses to unleash the full powers of his charm, I have rarely seen anyone deny him. But he was mainly used to ensnare and disarm using the art of seduction. And that is why, while all of us are adept at seduction and were used for such purposes, *Dieu* chose Eros as the chief consort among us all."

"And you?" Selena asked, when he did not immediately continue. "Why were you so named?"

A smile curled his lips. He couldn't be certain if it was seductive or if it was cruel...but then again, if it was both, then that was the greatest irony of it all.

"I was the hardest for *Dieu* to name. I was beautiful, but not as beautiful as Eros, nor was I as natural at seduction. The same can be said for the art of war, and when it came to tracking. All of which I'm good at, but my brothers were still better. I was the last he named, but when *Dieu* discovered my strengths, he was very pleased. He often said he'd saved the best for last. And at one point he even admitted that I was his favourite."

With each word he spoke, he wrapped the length of the object he held within his grasp around his hand, his eyes never leaving her. Fear leapt in her gaze, wary and unfocused as it danced between his hand and his face.

He did not change his expression — knew it revealed nothing of his inner depths, his inner emotions.

"*Dieu* had a penchant for cruelty that apparently I shared, but not in the same way. I have always been fascinated with the dichotomy of pleasure and pain, and I have always been a master at delivering them both. I said that it was rare for people not to fall under Eros' spell, but some didn't. Eros' strength is seduction, but he does not have the temerity to push. If a lover did not furnish what he sought, he did not press further. And that was always where I came in.

"I would bestow upon that person unimaginable pain, but then I would take it away, their saviour, and offer them solace by bestowing upon them unimaginable pleasure. Secrets that people swore they would take to their grave, they parted with before I was done with them. And, unlike Eros, there was no one—man or woman—who did not provide me with what I sought."

Selena's eyes widened, her lips trembled, but still his face remained impassive. It was so natural for him to slip into this role again, as if sixteen years had not passed since he'd been called upon to force one to reveal the secrets they swore they never would.

"Wielding both pleasure and pain was my strength, and it was a gift, just as it was an art. *Dieu* possessed the same skill, but even he admitted that he was not as adept as I, nor had he seen anyone else that was. It was because of this I was his chief interrogator or torturer—the title is a matter of perspective, I guess.

"I was a master at torture, at dominance, at making anyone and everyone submit to me." A small grin tugged at the corner of his lips. It was fleeting. "You once called me a masochist. To hear the word associated with me, I thought ironic. Because I'm a natural sadist, Selena. I can withstand immeasurable pain, but wielding it, along with pleasure...that is my strength. That is my gift."

Chapter Eleven

Fear clawed its way inside Selena, and, once it lodged itself inside her belly, it would not relinquish its hold. It only grew, intensifying until it became evident to her that she only maintained her sanity, her courage, because deep down she still believed, no matter his words, that Adonis would never hurt her, not truly.

Yet, as her attention strayed to the flogger he twisted in his hand, she surmised that his version of hurt and hers were grossly inconsistent.

"Has anyone ever died under your" — she gulped — "ministrations?"

"Killing is Ares' duty, not mine."

His response did not answer her question, but she did not point that out. The knowledge that someone had suffered under his hand then died would not be comforting at this point.

She stared curiously at him when with his free hand, the one unburdened by the coiled leather, he reached out to untie her robe. She sucked in a breath when his hand gently pushed aside the slips of fabric. Heat fanned out across her chest. His fingers touched everywhere—a subtle caress of her breasts, testing the weight in his palm, teasing her stiffened nipples. It was shameful. This man sought to cause her pain, to torture her and yet her body still lusted after him, still craved him. He removed the robe from her body, though, with her bound arm, it hung limply from one side.

Almost as if he could glean her thoughts, he produced a key and unlocked her wrist. She grasped her aching wrist, massaging the stiff muscles in her arms as she glanced at him in question.

"I do not need you bound in this manner to do what I will do. There were many who I did not bind and they still yielded beneath my touch. Sometimes I simply commanded them to clasp their hands together, and they did it until I told them to stop."

"And what will you command me to do?"

"Anything I want, until you give me the information I seek. I will do many things to you this day, and the next, and the one after that until you have told me the truth and answered every one of my questions."

She had no doubt he would try, but she was equally determined to resist.

"There are some questions I will not answer because I cannot."

"You will answer every one of my questions, Selena."

"I will jeopardise everything if I give you the answers you seek," she continued as if he hadn't spoken.

His lips slashed into a cruel smile. "But I have not even begun. How do you know what questions I will ask? You never know. You may be able to answer all of them…"

"Or none of them."

His cruel smile did not waver. "You talk of jeopardising everything, and yet you risk the lives of me and my brothers?"

She could not argue that, so she didn't. Selena sat there atop his bed, her body entwined in the sheets that still carried his scent, that still wore the stains of their lovemaking from just hours ago.

Everything had changed between them.

And yet, nothing at all.

Fear and mistrust still lingered between them.

"Lie down on the bed, on your back, with your hands above your head and your palms gripping the bars of the headboard."

She could have resisted, but what would have been the point? An army of guards were posted at every exit…and that was if she managed to escape this room.

Ares was gone. She'd heard him depart earlier and before he'd left the threat and warning he'd issued had been clear — harm his brother and he would not hesitate to end her life in those most agonising of ways.

He'd left soon after that, so now it was just her and Adonis, alone in this house, alone in this room.

She lay down as ordered, her body stretched out, her hands on the headboard.

There was no point in resisting.

"Will you handcuff me again?"

"I see no need to at this point. As I told you, there are ways to force one's obedience so that bindings are completely unnecessary."

He began to unravel the leather from around his hand and she stared at the unwinding black material, entranced. It was because of her acute fascination with the leather flogger that it was not until he was fully nude that she realised he'd even removed his clothes.

She had not imagined torturing someone would require both parties to be nude, but she knew nothing of such matters so she remained quiet, staring at him, wondering what would happen next, what he would do.

She did not have long to wait.

"When it comes to this, I am adept at discerning a lie." His smile was wry. "Obviously, I am not so skilled at it elsewhere or I would have long been on to you. But, in these matters, I will know if you lie, so every question I ask of you, Selena, I suggest you answer truthfully."

"And if I don't?"

"I shall punish you."

Her attention flickered to the flogger for the hundredth time. "And if I refuse to answer?"

"I will punish you."

She pierced him with her gaze. He'd not yet brought the hard leather within an inch of her body, and already she panted.

"And if I answer truthfully?"

"Then I will pleasure you."

Despite herself, she shuddered.

"How will you be able to discern truths from lies?"

"I did this for many years. I have many ways, but the most obvious is by using your body."

Her brows arched. "My body? How so?"

"Just as your body betrayed your mind sixteen years ago and you surrendered to me, your body can betray your lips when they work to form the lie born of your mind."

She gasped at that, in shame and anger.

He would use her body against her...*again*. He would use her body to betray her. That was somehow fitting, for she'd betrayed him, then used his body.

"Why are you here, Selena?" Adonis asked, his whispered words breaking through her thoughts, his deep voice seductive against her ears. Even his voice was sexy, sensual.

She stared up at him. His face was stoic. She notched her chin higher. All those who'd come before her had surrendered, but she was not them.

She answered his question, but it was not the answer he sought. It was a lie and she paid for it.

When the braided leather struck her nipples and a bubble of pain burst in her chest, she writhed against the bed, closing her eyes.

She would not yield to him. She would not surrender...not *ever*.

* * * *

Adonis asked Selena the same question he'd posed hours earlier.

"Why are you here?"

Her lips trembled, her focus drifting between his face and the object in his hand. Sweat glistened across her naked body, like crystal gems sparkling in the desert sand.

She bit down on her lips, her eyes defiant, glazed with lust and tinged with pain.

He struck her again, across her breasts, lightly, and she closed her eyes, her head falling back on a long, soul stirring moan. She'd given up telling him lies several hours ago. Now she simply remained silent, quietly waiting for him to strike her again.

Angry red welts crisscrossed her chest and her belly and yet she did not yield. She did not surrender. His strikes were heavy enough for her to feel the sharp sting of pain, but just light enough to tease and taunt, to tempt her body with the other face of pain— pleasure. Selena's body vibrated with the dual sensations and yet she still remained defiant, belligerent in her silence.

Adonis would not say it, but her fortitude impressed him. Men far stronger than her had yielded beneath his leather ministrations within an hour or two. Women far more resilient than her had begged him to stop and soothe their pain with pleasure after ten or twenty lashes. That Selena was strong and resilient did not surprise him. That she was far stronger and more resilient than all the others, did. None had lasted for this long without crying out, without begging him to stop. None had refused to yield to him...except *her.*

By now she should have begged him to stop, begged him for the physical release he'd steadily nurtured within her. Yet she did not beg. She did not utter a word, not even a soft whimper of pain. Quite the opposite. Her body seemed to welcome the pain, relish it, as if the pleasure that her body craved came second to her desire for pain.

He bit back a grim smile. He'd called her a masochist.

He now considered the truth of such a statement and decided that she probably was. He wondered if she even knew it, if she understood that about herself. Did she feel shame or revulsion because of her nature? Was she repulsed by it? Or did she embrace it?

He wondered.

He set aside the flogger. She looked curiously between him and the object of her torture, but still she remained silent and did not question him.

When he began stroking his swelling cock as he stood nude before her, she still did not question him.

It was only when he approached the bed and settled between her parted thighs that she asked on a breathless gasp, "Wh-what are you doing?"

His lips curled into a smile as cold and as cruel as he knew himself to be — this side of him which she'd awakened with her betrayal. He did not answer her as he hooked her legs over his arms and held her spread before him.

Moisture glistened on the folds of her sex, and a small puddle had gathered beneath her where her juices had trickled from her body to stain the bed.

His smile did not waver.

A masochist indeed.

She'd orgasmed. He hadn't fully realised it until now, though he'd suspected she had when her perfumed scent hovered in the air between them. She did well in hiding her arousal, the full extent of her pleasure, but now that he knew — now that she *knew* he knew — she realised she was in danger.

He should have sensed this earlier when he'd suspected her nature. That was his fault, his mistake. One he would correct, starting now.

A true masochist found pleasure in pain, which was why she had not surrendered. He'd never encountered a true masochist...until her.

Selena would not yield to pain, because she thrived upon pain. Just as those with masochistic tendencies could even endure being denied pleasure, where he would bring them to the brink of climax and then retreat. The same was true of Selena, for whom the denial of her orgasm would not force her surrender.

Unlike those with masochistic proclivities, who could simply endure being deprived of release, with Selena — a true masochist — her body would go so far as to welcome the physical deprivation and accept it as pain.

Adonis now understood what would crumble her resolve, what would force her to yield to him, to completely surrender. It was pleasure that was her weakness — true pleasure, unending pleasure. And he had the power to give her that as well.

The first swipe of his tongue against the lips of her cunt was not gentle, not teasing. He was relentless as he breached her, spearing her with his tongue, dragging hoarse needy moans from her lips and a gush of wet warmth from her pussy.

Selena twisted and writhed beneath him, her thighs trembling. She gasped at the pleasure roiling through her body, assaulting her like waves crashing violently against jagged rocks. Adonis was unrelenting as he devoured her pussy like a man starving. She knew what he was about and she fought to resist, until she was a powerless, boneless heap spread before him, helpless and quaking.

When she could not stand it any longer, she did something she'd not done in the entire time he'd struck her with his leather flogger. She released her hold on the headboard of the bed to grasp his head and push him away. But he would not be denied, nor deterred from his ultimate goal.

Adonis held fast between her thighs, his lips nibbling her clit before taking it fully within his mouth and sucking hard. A lightning bolt of heat and desire sizzled through her, from her core, along her spine until it exploded behind her closed eyelids.

Her sheath filled with the juices of her pleasure and he swallowed them hungrily, deeply, his tongue probing her cunt, searching for more until she gave it to him. He wrung her body of climax after climax until she swore she had nothing left to give, and then he wrenched yet another from her.

He wanted to know why she was there, and she'd refused to tell him. The pain had been excruciating, unending, but she'd taken it within her body, accepting the stinging whips. She hadn't cried out, not once. After a while, she'd stopped speaking altogether. The pain had been pure agony, but it had not been unbearable. Quite the opposite. After an hour, a warmth had spread throughout her, inflaming her until she welcomed every leather strike against her tender skin. She'd been forced to bite her lip so that he would not notice the slight flush of her skin, the hitch in her breath as she came one time after another. Selena would never have dreamed her body would welcome pain as pleasure, but it had.

She could have endured if he'd continued to strike her, indeed for many more hours. She was certain he could have drawn blood and she still would not have surrendered. But this? This was far worse. It was unbearable, and already she could feel her resolve beginning to crumble.

Adonis did not stop. He was determined in his ministrations, his attentiveness to her body, her needs. An hour later, after what felt like hundreds of orgasms, even as sweat poured from their bodies, he remained between her spread thighs, feasting upon her cunt, sucking the tiny nub at her opening, his tongue spearing her hole as he dragged another orgasm from her and lapped up her juices.

She had lasted several hours beneath his flogger, but barely one against his lips before she was tearing at his hair and crying out.

"Please stop," she gasped, her chest heaving. "Stop," she cried as she exploded against his lips again.

He lifted his head, his face stained with her juices as they glistened from his smirking lips.

The bastard.

"Why are you here, Selena?" he demanded for the hundredth time.

She pinched her lips together, refusing to answer.

He shoved two fingers inside her, his eyes never leaving her.

"Why are you here?"

She closed her eyes, desperately struggling to shut him out. She could ignore the image of his smirking face, which she no longer saw, but the pumping of his fingers inside her, she could not.

He repeated his question, his voice harsher as he buried two fingers, then three inside her. She clawed at his wrist, his forearm. He only speared her faster, harder, deeper.

"Adonis, please," she cried, tears leaking from her eyes. She hated herself, she hated him. She'd sworn she wouldn't beg.

Her pleas fell upon deaf ears. A fourth finger found its way inside her, pummelling her cunt, stretching her.

"Answer my question. Tell me what I want to know."

She shook her head back and forth against the pillow, her eyes still clenched shut. Tears slipped down her cheeks, staining the bed as they fell from her chin.

She refused to tell him, she couldn't... But when he curved his fingers, brushing against the roof of her tunnel, against the rough patch of skin nestled there, the very place that brought her indescribable pleasure, she could no longer deny him.

Her orgasm rocketed through her at the same time she said on a rush, "I'm here to kill my father."

"I know that already, Selena. There is more to it than that."

"But that is the truth," she screamed in pleasure, in frustration.

Her frustration evidently fuelled his because he cursed violently. "Why are you here, Selena?" he shouted.

Her eyes flew open, clashing with his murderous expression. "I already told you," she hurled back. "And that is the truth."

"But not all of it."

No, it wasn't, but she could not reveal any more than she already had, or she risked ruining the plan she'd so carefully constructed. For hours she'd endured and suffered his relentless torture, until, finally, she'd yielded. It shamed her, humiliated her that this man would be the only person to ever witness her at her weakest, at her most vulnerable.

With Adonis' fingers still inside her, still thrusting, and on the brink of yet another climax, she finally broke and began to sob.

"I can't tell you any more. I just can't."

Adonis swore harshly as his entire body seized up. He'd broken enough people to know when one had hit that point, and Selena had passed hers.

She covered her face and sobbed into her hands.

It shattered him.

The rawness of her tears, her crumbling resolve, her helplessness—to know he'd broken her, cleaved his heart from his chest and he cursed again.

What happened after that shocked him as much as it must have shocked her.

In all his years, he'd never done this.

In all his years, he'd never caved.

But her tears pierced him. Her weakened spirit crippled him.

Withdrawing his fingers from her sheath, he covered her body with his. Grasping her wrists, he pulled her hands from her face. Her lids snapped open, her gaze clashing with his. The look in her eyes laid waste to whatever resolve he still possessed.

He kissed her tear-stained cheeks, then claimed her lips at the same time as he claimed her body.

He swallowed up her startled gasp as he plunged inside her then drove deeper. She embraced him, enveloping his thrusting length with her sheath, as she wound her arms around him and clasped her legs behind his back.

He'd never done this. Not once had he been driven to repair the damage he'd inflicted. Not once had his body been driven to the brink of desire by an object of his punishment.

Her pain had not touched him.

It was her pleasure.

It fuelled his, nurtured it...ignited it until he'd practically trembled with the need to take her. Her sobs had shattered the last vestiges of his resolve, had snapped the tenuous thread of control he'd still possessed.

Five thrusts. He may have shoved his cock inside her five times before he erupted, and splintered apart in her arms.

He buried his shaft inside her on a harsh grunt and came so hard, his eyes rolled to the back of head and his toes curled. Adonis spurted inside her until he filled her up, until he was boneless and weak. Then he collapsed atop of her in a heap, panting, still nestled inside her.

When he finally found the strength to pull out of her, Adonis lifted his body and braced himself with his arms, but he stilled when his eyes met hers, nearly swallowing his heart in his throat. Tears still glistened on her lashes as she raised her hand to cup his cheek. She dragged his head down, and he let himself be ensnared by her, his eyes closing shut. When their lips met, she kissed him deeply and passionately, but it was the tenderness with which she held him to her, with which she cradled him close, that caused his heart to stutter.

He hated himself because of his weakness for this one woman. He hated himself because he still loved her, deeply, desperately. He hated *her* because she had the power to make him realise this.

She must have sensed the change in him because she drew back from him, her eyes watching him closely. He wrenched away from her when her gaze began to probe him, searching deeper. Trained to detach himself from his emotions, he slammed up a wall between them, his expression once again inscrutable.

She could not be trusted. No matter his feelings for Selena, he could not do what he'd just done ever again. He could not let her see that she still possessed power over him, that she still had the power to control him.

That he was still vulnerable to her.

He rolled off her and stood. He found the handcuffs that Ares had used to tether her to the bed and he once again put them on her, slipping one end around her wrist and the other around the rail along the head of the bed.

"I need to use the bathroom and bathe myself."

"You can do so after I've showered," he replied, his back to her as he stalked across the room and entered the bathroom, slamming the door behind him, shutting her out.

He could not forget himself. No matter his feelings for her, he could not allow himself to see her as anything but what she was — the enemy.

That she'd staunchly refused to tell him the truth, that she'd put his brothers in danger, made her his enemy.

That he still did not know the depths of her purpose made her dangerous.

That she was still his weakness and he did not know her true motivations made her deadly.

He could not afford to forget that.

Adonis showered quickly and returned to his bedroom where she waited atop the bed, naked and impatient.

He released her from the cuffs and watched as she entered the bathroom, but when she moved to close the door, he stopped it with his hand and the swift shake of his head.

She frowned. "There are no windows in your bathroom, and the only doors are this one and another that leads inside the linen closet. Where do you think I will go?"

"If you tell me why you are here, the *real* reason, then I may be inclined to trust you enough to close this door."

Silence was her only response, along with the thinning of her lips into a taut line.

He did not release the door, and she was forced to suffer the mild embarrassment of him being able to hear every sound she made as she relieved herself.

At the sound of running water, Adonis left his position near the door and crossed the room where he replaced the towel slung around his hips with a pair of black silk pyjama pants he found in his dresser. One to sleep naked, he'd not worn such things since he'd abandoned his father's home, so the feel of the soft fabric against his legs dredged up memories long forgotten. But as quickly as they came in one moment, he firmly pushed them aside in the next.

With his memories once again in the past, he returned to the present, and it was the absence of sound that struck him.

He was inside the bathroom within three strides, expecting to find it empty and a hole somewhere in the floor or ceiling where Selena had managed to crawl through. He drew up short when he found her — her head resting against the marble tub, her body beautifully naked beneath the crystal clear water.

"You're bathing." The words came out before he could stop them.

Her eyes flickered open. "Yes."

She would not understand. She had no way of knowing how deep some of the scars were that he still carried.

"Would you like to join me?" Her words as well as her expression were guileless, innocent, not ones of seduction.

She lifted her hand and reached for him. "Come. Join me." The gesture was a touchingly intimate one.

He recoiled, before he could stop himself.

Her hand dropped, plunging into the water once again. Disappointment flickered in her eyes, but she buried it, so quickly he would have sworn it had never been there.

He'd hurt her. His rejection had hurt her.

He turned to leave. He did not wish to hurt her, at least not in that way, but hurt and pain embodied the nature of their relationship.

"You do not like to bathe, do you?"

Her words froze him into place.

"Showers are quicker."

"But that is not why you take them."

He turned to face her, his eyes empty. "No, it isn't."

"Will you tell me?" He followed the erotic journey of the sponge in her hand as it lathered her skin with soap and water. "Will you tell me why you prefer to take showers? Why you do not like to bathe?"

He was entranced by the water sluicing and sliding across her copper skin. It was a long while before his gaze found its way to her face, and, when it did, the compassion he saw in her eyes levelled him.

He'd not told anyone this, not even his brothers.

"Of the four of us, Eros and I were the most highly sought-after consorts. Whether it was truly skill, or our appearance…or both… I do not know. But we were successful at pleasing others, though Eros was the best." She watched him intently as he spoke, her eyes full of compassion.

"Eros prefers women," he continued. "But he still enjoys bedding men. I never did. At first I was repulsed by it until I simply came to accept what I was forced to do. Pleasure is a strange thing. It does not care about the source, as long as it is satiated. My body came to accept this. My mind never did."

He glanced at the gilded shower head above her. "*Dieu* must have had this installed after I left." He returned his attention to her. "I would spend hours, days even, pleasing an endless string of men, and then I would return here and bathe in that tub until my skin was red, until it was raw, as if I could somehow erase what I had done, what had been done to me.

"I may have cleansed my body, but my mind, my soul... Some things you can never erase. I stopped taking baths the moment I left this place. And the thought of taking one ever again turns my stomach."

She remained silent for a long time, staring at him, studying him, until he thought she would never speak.

But then she said the unexpected, the last words he'd ever thought to hear.

"Thank you."

"For what?"

"For loving me enough to bare your soul to me." Her words stilled him, even as they sliced him open.

"I do not love you, Selena." That was a lie. She knew it. He knew it. And he knew that she knew, but his revelation had left him raw. Her statement of his love now left him bare. His battered emotions simply could not take any more.

"You have not trusted me since the moment I entered your hotel room. You do not trust me now. And yet, you tell me something so intimate, so revealing..."

Her voice trailed off. He did not utter a sound. The only noise to be heard in the room was of the water sloshing against the tub as she continued to bathe.

"I do not love you, Selena," he repeated, as if saying the words would somehow make them true.

"I know what it is like to love someone and hate yourself because you do. To hate them for making you love them when you wish you didn't, when you wish you could do anything but. I know what it is like to not trust them, and yet open yourself to them so fully because you can do nothing less, because your heart will not allow anything less. I know what it is like to love a man who hates me, who does not trust me, who would rather see himself dead than admit he loves me. I know what it feels like to be tortured by love, to be tortured by my love for you, but it doesn't make what I feel for you any less true, any less real."

"You do not love me, Selena." His voice was firm, resolute. His insides quivered.

"How I wish that were true," she whispered, her smile sorrowful.

"I do not love you."

Her solemn smile did not falter. "I imagine you wish that were true as well."

Chapter Twelve

In his anger, Adonis had stormed out of the bathroom and slammed the door shut. Now alone, she was free to bathe undisturbed, but she could no longer find peace, so she climbed out of the tub and dried herself.

She would never know what demon had possessed her, what devil had driven her to say the things she'd just said. Every word was true—even the ones he'd steadfastly denied. Yet, she did not fully grasp why they'd flown from her lips so effortlessly, and without warning to even her. She'd not known what she was saying until she'd said it, and when she had, she'd wanted to snatch the words back, but it was already too late.

Adonis was not ready to hear of her love for him or to be confronted by his love for her. But the desolate look in his eyes, his tortured expression when he'd revealed that something as simple as bathing caused him pain, that the thought of him doing it ever again made him sick... She'd been powerless beneath his shadowed gaze, full of sins and darkness from his past. Maybe that was it—the look in his eyes that had hollowed her out. Or maybe it was simply what he'd said. He'd revealed an intimacy, one that had cost a piece of his soul…and she'd not known what else to say except 'thank you'. When he'd asked *'for what?'* she'd had no choice but to tell him the truth. It did not matter if he was ready to hear it or not—it *was* the truth.

Selena pushed open the door quietly, her steps hesitant as she entered the bedroom. The light of the moon spilled through the window, casting Adonis in a silvery halo. He stood before the window, staring out into the void, seeing nothing. She knew this because his eyes were vacant, hollow…empty.

She treaded softly over to him. Instinct told her to give him a wide berth. He was raw emotionally. Yet, her heart demanded that she push him until he admitted what they both knew. Her heart told her to be prepared to console, to soothe his wounds, because his own heart would not give up such secrets without a bloody fight.

And a bloody fight is exactly what she got.

He felt her presence, knew she stood just off to the side of him, that if she reached out she could touch him. So when she did, he should have expected it. What *she* did not expect, however, was his fury, his undeniable rage.

"Do not touch me, Selena."

She did not heed his warning. Instead, she was emboldened by it as she pressed both palms to his back and began to caress the uneven flesh of his scars.

"I cannot help but touch you," she whispered, her heart hammering inside her at her boldness. This was a dangerous game she played with him. He could hurt her if he truly wished to, and, right now, she knew he did. "I cannot help but touch you, Adonis, when you are in pain, when you are hurting. My heart will not allow me to stand here watching you suffer while I do nothing."

He tried to pull away from her, but he was trapped between her body and the window pane. He whirled around, nearly throwing her off balance.

His hand closed around her neck, his grip firm. Real terror shot through her, and for a moment she worried he would do her harm, until something flickered in his eyes and he relaxed his hold on her, though he did not remove his hand.

"You're afraid of me," he said. "Just now, you thought I would kill you. I *should* kill you."

"But you won't, because you can't. And we both know why."

Dark fury flashed across his face. "I do not love you, Selena!" he shouted. She wondered if he thought yelling it would finally convince *him* of the soundness of his statement. Or maybe he thought it would convince *her*. But if he thought he could convince *both* of them, then he was foolish.

She should have left him alone.

She should have remained silent.

She didn't... She couldn't.

"Denying it will not change it." Her eyes softened. He looked so lost, so desperate. "Believe me. I know all about trying to deny my love for you." She touched his hand that still held her neck, lightly teasing her fingers across his flesh. "But it doesn't work—you know that, just as I do."

"Why are you here, Selena?" he gritted out.

"To kill my father, to have my revenge, but also to take away your pain, to love you enough for the both of us, to love you enough to heal you."

If anything, her words only made him angrier. In the span of a heartbeat, he stripped her of her robe and dragged her across the room to push her down atop the bed. She fell face first, her hands splayed across the rumpled sheets.

She whipped her head around to see him kicking off his pyjamas and then he was atop her, his cock nudging the swells of her ass, his chest to her back.

"You're a liar, Selena. You do not love me."

"I do."

"After what I did to you, you could never love me."

She reached around to cup his chin. Her hand barely settled against his face before he flung it away. "It was not your fault," she said, swallowing her disappointment. "I always knew that."

"And yet you used my sense of guilt. You used my shame to manipulate me, knowing how deeply it hurt me to know how I'd hurt you." She swallowed her remorse at what she'd done, what she'd been forced to do. "That is not love, Selena."

"I know," she whispered brokenly. "But I love you, Adonis. I will hate myself for the rest of my life for doing what I had to do to you, but there was no other way. I had no other choice—"

"There is always a choice," he said harshly. "Is that not right, Selena?"

She couldn't respond. Her throat was choked with emotion. She'd betrayed him, lied to him, and manipulated him for her own selfish purposes. He was right...that was not love.

"I love you, Adonis," she said weakly.

"You do not know what love is."

"Then show me," she demanded. "Do to my body whatever it is you must and I will take it—I will accept it just to prove to you I love you. Give me your pain, your pleasure, whatever it is you desire, whatever it is you need to believe my love for you is real."

"Would you take my cock inside your ass, while I fucked you with a dildo? Would you accept clamps on your nipples, my flogger against your backside? Would you welcome my semen all over your body, anywhere I chose to spurt it?"

She did not hesitate. "I would suffer every humiliation. I would endure any pain if it will prove to you my feelings are genuine."

He scrutinised her. "That is because you're a perversion of nature — sick and depraved. More so than even me."

She gasped in shock, his harsh insult stunning her into silence.

"I can endure a great deal of pain, Selena, I even enjoy it well enough, but not as much as I enjoy causing pain, and not as much as I enjoy experiencing and giving pleasure. I am a dominant sadist, with masochistic traits. That I enjoy pleasure, both giving and receiving it, just means that, despite my tendencies, I experience desire as most others do. But not you, Selena. You know what I discovered as I tortured your body?"

He waited as if expecting a response, so finally she shook her head. She did not know what he'd discovered at all.

"You, Selena, enjoy giving and receiving pleasure, which, like me, means you are capable of normal desire. But that part of you, that part of you that craves pleasure and the need to give it is only a *small* part of you. The other part of you is what defines the essence of your desires."

"And what part is that?" she asked softly, when he did not appear as if he would finish.

"The part that is wholly masochistic."

Masochistic? She was already shaking her head in denial.

"You are a masochist, Selena, the likes of which I've never witnessed before. You are a dominant masochistic, with no sadistic traits. That is why you could not cause me pain when you sodomised me — that is why you demanded I experience pleasure. No part of you is capable of causing another sexual pain. And yet, your pleasure is found in pain. You could exist wholly on sexual pain and your body would find greater satisfaction than if I pleasured you all day."

"That is not true," she vehemently denied. She did not crave pain.

Yet...she had no experience in things like this. Adonis had been her one and only lover. But if what he said was true then that would make her a —

"Freak," Adonis said the word as if he'd read her mind. "A freak, a deviant, a pervert — yes, Selena, you are all of those things."

She looked away before he could glimpse the moisture in her eyes. She had no experience in sexual matters and now Adonis, who had unending experience, had told her she was a perversion of nature. It hurt.

"There is no reason to be cruel just because you don't want to hear that I love you."

"Is that what I'm being? I thought I was being honest...like you."

She whirled around to stare at him again. He was mocking her.

Her gaze bore into him, determined and defiant. "Very well, I am a masochist and I love you. Is that honest enough?"

His jaw tightened. "You do not love me."

"Prove it. Use my body, however you see fit. Do whatever you must to me, but I promise you I will take it all because I love you."

"Not because you love me—because you enjoy it, because that is your nature. There is nothing I can do to you that you *won't* enjoy."

"And does that not make you wonder? Does that not make you question, why you can touch me however you see fit, and I still experience pleasure beneath your touch when for sixteen years I shunned the touch of *any* other?"

She knew her words shook him, because he drew back in surprise.

"I don't think I'm a masochist at all. I think my body simply craves you, as it always has, as it always will. And we both know why."

She was insistent, but Adonis was resolute. His lips thinned.

"You do not love me, Selena. And I do not love you."

She believed nothing from his lips, which is why his denial did not cause her pain.

"Then prove it. Your cock is at the gate of my anus, already dripping with cum. If you do not love me then release me and walk away."

Their gazes locked, and he began to withdraw, but she reached behind him, her nails digging into the firm muscles of his taut ass.

Holding him firmly, she reared back, impaling herself on his cock until the head slipped inside.

They gasped in union, their bodies trembling.

She pushed his cock deeper inside her as she taunted him, "Walk away from me, Adonis. Leave this bed, the heat of my body, the solace I offer you with my flesh. If you do not love me then stop what I am doing. If you believe that I do not love you, then walk away from me now."

His golden gaze smouldered with anger, with desire and desperation.

He fed her another inch of his cock, one hand gripping her hip, the other draped across her chest, holding her securely. "I hate you."

She moaned as he slipped deeper into her. "You love me, as I love you," she whispered when he was lodged all the way inside her ass. Her hands gripped the bed sheets and her head lolled forward, the pain unbearable, the pleasure even more so.

He buried his face within the crook of her neck, ploughing inside her on hard, slow strokes, stretching her rectum, forging a path that was as wide as it was deep.

Her body accepted him—her untried passage that had never been used this way and had not been prepared for the invasion. The pain mingled with pleasure, yet the pleasure overrode the pain. She gasped as heat flared inside her, uncoiling, straining to reach the far corners of her body until every inch of her vibrated with wanton desire, with warmth and need.

She gasped when she realised what was happening to her.

Adonis was right. *She* was right.

When her body experienced pain, it took it and turned it into pleasure. Maybe she was a masochist, or maybe it was that her body simply recognised Adonis, and this was how it responded to him.

Maybe it was both.

She gasped again, this time all pleasure, as he went deeper than he'd ever gone before. He filled her, stretched her, opened her to the full assault of his body.

"Adonis," she called his name on a tortured, broken cry.

"It hurts, doesn't it?" he whispered against her neck, his breath warming her sweat-slick skin, tickling the sensitive shell of her ear.

"Yes," she rasped.

"And yet you want more."

She could not deny it. "Yes."

His arm that was draped around her chest slipped lower until his hand was nestled between the lips of her pussy, his fingers stroking the hot tight button of her pleasure.

"Lay flat against the bed and I shall give you more."

She did not hesitate, and a soft, languorous moan rolled out from her, when she flattened against the bed, sending his cock tunnelling even deeper and trapping his hand against her clit.

Pain shot up her spine as he pummelled her, pounding into her.

Tremors of pleasure quaked within her belly as he stroked her.

She buried her face in the pillow, muffling her cries, muting her screams. Her hands clenched the bed until her knuckles turned red.

Adonis stopped.

"Lift your head," he commanded harshly. "I would hear every sound you make."

Her head snapped up, and she looked at him from over her shoulder. His eyes blazed with sexual heat and an intensity of need she'd never glimpsed before.

He loved her. He still hated that he did, but, with his body's betrayal of his mind, there was no denying it. Even as he refused to say the words, his eyes radiated his deeper emotions so strongly and purely.

"I love you," she whispered plainly.

A small frown slipped across his face. "You love what I do to you, to your body. That is all."

"I love you," she repeated, but his only response was his lips pressing tightly together. He surged into her on a violent thrust, drawing an agonising moan from her lips. She swivelled her head around and clutched the sheets tighter. The pain racking her entire body meant she couldn't speak for seconds until she could gather her breath. That had been his intent, to silence her, but at least he no longer outright denied her claims.

His strokes changed then as he rocked inside her, pulling the thick, bulbous head of his cock all the way from her body, only to slam himself fully within her. She reached behind her body, her hand pressing against his hips, her nails digging into his flesh to stop him...to urge him on.

"You want this, Selena, so take it. Take all of it," he commanded giving it to her harder than he ever had before.

His whispered words against her ear ignited the slow churn of heat inside her and wetness pooled from her cunt, staining the bed sheets. He stroked the hard, little bud of her clitoris, pumping and thrusting his shaft into her on deep, hard strokes until she was breathless and shaking.

Her passage burned and throbbed as he penetrated her, but she did not cry out for him to stop. It was the opposite. The dual sensations of pleasure riding the rough edge of pain unravelled her until she was pulsing and panting beneath him, begging him to fuck her, not to stop.

"Oh, I won't stop, Selena. You don't want me to stop, do you?"

She shook her head. "No."

"Then give me your ass," he breathed. "Open wider for me so that I can get even deeper."

"I-I can't."

"Yes, you can." He stopped powering inside her long enough to take her hands and splay them across the cheeks of her ass. He released her hands to grip her shoulder with one hand and to plunge the other back inside her pussy, now stroking her clit furiously, while she kept her hands where he'd placed them and spread herself wide so that she was open fully to him. "That's it. Take my cock all the way inside you, all the way to the back of your tunnel."

This would hurt in the morning...would hurt within minutes after he was done. It hurt now, but she didn't care. Selena had never felt so full, had never been stretched so completely but she welcomed it, as she took him deeper, all the way inside her.

His skin slapped against hers, the heavy sac between his legs pressing against her with each thrust. His hand between her thighs rubbed her clit, stroking and pinching it until her pussy poured forth hot, sticky wetness as she cried out in climax and splintered apart beneath him.

Pleasure stormed through her body, racking her with endless waves of desire. The tremors that powered through her caused her pussy to clench and the dark, tight tunnel of her ass to vibrate with slight tremors. Her muscles squeezing him were his undoing and he cursed in surprise, in mid-thrust as if he hadn't been expecting to come.

His curse was lewd, and the hand gripping her shoulder tightened. Adonis held her beneath him, imprisoned by the weight of his body as he pumped his seed inside her. He pulled his ruddy cock from her and continued to spurt, jacking his flesh with one hand as he sprayed her ass with the last of his semen, with the final evidence of his pleasure.

When he'd wrung every last bit of his release from his flesh, he collapsed beside her, and she stared at him as he stared at the ceiling. He did not want to look at her, nor did he want to admit what had happened between them—his loss of control, his weakness for her...his admission of his love by the very fact that he'd fucked her.

He would not look at her or admit the truth...and she would not force him.

She rested her palm across his chest and closed her eyes. When he covered her hand with his, she smiled.

* * * *

Adonis awoke the next morning at dawn, surprised that it *was* the next morning. He'd fallen asleep at dusk and had slept for almost twelve hours. He hadn't slept that long in... He could not even remember the last time he'd slept more than a few hours.

A voice whispered in the back of mind, a nagging voice he'd been trying to ignore for days now.

Selena gives you peace.

Selena gives you solace.

Selena gives you love.

The last statement pierced him at the very depths of his soul. He did not want her peace, her solace, her love. He wanted none of it. But especially not her love. As if he could run away from what brewed inside his head, he tried to shoot up off the bed, a violent curse ripping from his lips to singe the air when he found he couldn't.

He stared at his offending arm that would not budge.

Then he stared across the room, his gaze crashing into to the very object of his thoughts, and the one he knew to be responsible for his current predicament.

"Release me, Selena."

She stepped from the shadows that still clung to the room. Even in the faint light he was still able to notice two things—the firm shake of her head and the knife she held in her hand.

"You must have been tired. You have been asleep for many hours. You did not even stir when I handcuffed you, or when I slipped from your chambers to borrow a knife from the kitchen."

As she spoke, she crossed the room—her footsteps delicate, her naked body on display, framed by the golden haze of the waking sun. She was beautiful—as beautiful as she was dangerous, treacherous...deadly.

"If Ares is right, then I should have killed you while you were naked, cuffed and asleep." She trailed the sharp tip of the knife across his bare chest and he sucked in a breath when she nicked one nipple then the other.

"If Ares is right then I would kill you now."

"Go ahead and do it. That is obviously why you're here—for revenge, for retribution—"

"But not from you." She set the knife on the table beside his head.

"Why are you here, Selena?"

"To kill my father."

When she deigned to answer his question, the one he'd posed over and over again, *that* was her only response. That and nothing else. She was the equivalent of an automaton, he decided as he fought to squelch his exasperation with her. "Is your father in my bedchambers, then?" he asked dryly, sarcasm being what he always resorted to when he was frustrated, and she'd frustrated him well beyond his endurance.

She shrugged. "I don't know."

His eyebrows lifted at her odd response and he stared at her curiously before his gaze darted around the room. "Take a look around. Does it look like he is here?"

"No. It would appear that your room holds only you and me."

"In that case, if you've come to kill your father, and your father is not here, then why are *you* still here?"

His question was met with silence, and, chained as he was, he was in no position to question her further. Adonis sighed.

"Well, while you wait to kill your father, what do you plan to do in the meantime?"

Her eyes brightened. "It would seem that I am enjoying you, though that was never my intent."

He could not believe the oddity of her statements, but he would not stop now. This was the most she'd discussed of her *plan* since Ares had exposed her. "Don't you think enjoying me is somewhat counterproductive? If your plan is to kill your father, and it is obvious your father isn't here, then shouldn't you be out *looking* for him instead of wasting your time with me?"

Something shifted in her eyes, and he knew this was the last question she would answer. "I am not wasting my time. I know where my father is."

Her odd words struck him because he'd remembered hearing her clearly say that her father had disappeared and she did not know *where* he was. "So where is he then?"

Her mouth flattened into a tight line. Her expression revealed this line of questioning had met its end, so he pursued another. "Why did you handcuff me to the bed?"

"To prove to you that I am not here to kill you, to show you that I mean you no harm, that if I wanted you dead, I could have ended your life hours ago."

"Just because you're not here to kill me, does not mean that your presence will not cause me harm, even if you don't intend for it to. Your presence has already caused me harm." He thought of the feelings of guilt she'd aroused. She'd awakened feelings he'd buried but had never forgotten. They'd torn him apart inside for years. He'd been tormented by them, only to have her walk back into his life and reveal she'd always known the truth and she'd forgiven him years ago. She'd meant no harm, but she'd caused it nonetheless.

"Trust is earned, Selena, and you've not proven yourself trustworthy." He gestured with his head to the knife. "After everything you've done, the lies, the deceit—I am inclined to believe you staged this just to engender my trust, to get me to let my guard down. And then..."

"And then *what*?"

He'd stopped because he had no idea what she planned to do next. "I don't know." He shrugged. "And then you will do what you've really come here to do."

"I've already told you, I've come here to kill my father."

"An impossibility at this point."

The small frown across her face told him she was annoyed with him, but within seconds her dark expression gave way to sparkling eyes.

"I would prefer to change the subject—"

"I bet you would. It must be difficult keeping up with all the lies."

Her smile dimmed, but it did not disappear. "I will not be deterred by your surly disposition. I had a reason for cuffing you."

That raised his brows. "And what was that?"

Her cheeks bloomed with splotches of red and despite himself he could feel his body responding to her wanton innocence. "I wanted to explore you, to do things I've only read about in magazines and books that were forbidden within the convent."

He peered at Selena, his expression watchful. Her statement reminded him of a question he'd had for her ever since Ares had revealed her deception. "You told Ares that you and Serena would trade places from time to time." When she nodded, he continued, "Did you not take advantage of your time spent inside a brothel to"—he searched for the right words—"explore your desires?"

She shook her head. "I considered it, but, while I knew what you'd done to me had not been your fault, it was a long time before I understood my inner longings. What you said yesterday, about me being masochistic, resonated with me. It seems to explain everything. When you first took me, you caused me pain, but it was the pain that made me beg, made me burn with pleasure. My sexual fantasies have always involved a man hurting me, causing me pain. I didn't understand that, and I was ashamed because of it. I wanted to experience other men, but I could barely understand the needs of my own body. In the end, I was always too afraid."

Adonis was surprised by the sharp pang of jealousy, even more so when it stole his breath. She'd wanted to experience other men. She'd even fantasised about it. The beast inside him began to retreat when he remembered that, while she may have *wanted* other men and thought of them, she'd only ever been with *him*.

"What happened to your back?"

Her question jarred him as violently as a quake trembling through his body. "Excuse me?"

"It is obvious you were whipped, then burned. I would like to know what happened."

Her words were softly spoken. His were harsh. "That is none of your business."

She reared back, her expression unreadable. "I am sorry. You asked me a question of a private nature. I thought I could do the same."

"There are some questions that go beyond a private nature. Some questions can never be answered, so they should never be asked."

The light in her eyes dimmed. "I said I was sorry," she offered quietly.

Her apology did not appease him, even though he knew it was her nature to probe, that the intimacy they'd shared emboldened her to ask such questions.

"I am also sorry that your father hurt you, that others hurt you and took away your ability to love...to trust."

"I love my brothers. I trust them."

"But *they* are not a woman."

His lips twisted into a sardonic smile. "According to you, I love you."

"But you do not trust me—"

"And whose fault is that?"

"Just as you do not love me in the way a man should," she continued as if he hadn't spoken. "You only love me because you have no choice, because you can't seem to stop."

The compassion in her eyes and the love that shimmered in their depths speared him. He desperately wanted to look away, but he couldn't. "What do you know of love?" he bit out, anger his only defence when he felt her beginning to expose him.

"Admittedly, I do not know much." She touched him, her soft palm against the rough, masculine skin of his legs, his thighs, his rippled abdomen, his jutting cock. She touched him – all of him, all over him. "But I do know of how I want to be loved. How I want to love you."

"And how is that?" The words came out on a desperate, raspy groan before he could stop them.

She straddled his hips, her cunt already wet, the juices slipping across his stomach. She continued to touch him, her hand caressing his chest, his shoulders, the coarse hairs along his unshaven jaw.

"I want to love you with tenderness, with compassion, and I want to be loved the same way in return."

His free hand found its way to her bare thigh, her backside. He trailed his hand across her middle then lightly cupped her breast. "And what of passion?" he breathed out, his voice unsteady from a question he did not wish to ask, but for the answer he needed to know. "Do you want to be loved with passion as well?"

Her eyes were already glazed with lust, and, for the briefest second, he imagined what it would be like to wake up beside this woman — this passionate, sensual, sexual woman — every morning, and fall asleep with her in his arms every night. He imagined making love to this strong, resilient woman who dared to love him, filling her with his cock, planting his seed inside her womb and giving her his children. His gut clenched, his heart stuttered, his breath slipped from his chest. It was terrifying. It was comforting.

"Yes, I want passion as well," she replied.

"For how long?"

"Forever, for a lifetime, for an eternity."

Her eyes blazed with every emotion she sought and each emotion she offered. He could not resist her.

"Come here."

She looked at him, puzzled. "Come where?"

"Come here so that I may kiss your pussy."

Her eyes widened. "But then you will not be able to breathe."

A chuckle bubbled out of him. "Did you not just say you wanted to be loved with passion? That is my intent, Selena. To love you with passion."

"But I-I've never —"

"Ridden a man's face?" He'd forgotten how innocent she could be at times. He bit back a small smile. Of course she'd not ridden a man's face because she'd never been atop his.

"I know," was all he said, but still she hesitated, sceptical. She truly thought she would suffocate him.

"You cannot hurt me," he assured.

She inched forward, but stopped just beneath his chin. He took his free hand, palmed her ass and pressed her the rest of the way until her cunt was against his mouth, her juices wetting his chin.

Her moan was as heady and intoxicating as the perfumed musk of her sex. She tasted sweet and he licked her folds, plunging his tongue between them, inside her.

He pierced her cunt—her hot, tight hole—curving his tongue until it scraped against the roof of her sheath, until he was tickling the most pleasurable spot inside her pussy.

She moaned above him, her hips lightly rocking so that she could grind her cunt against his face. Every feathered sigh was a delight, every soft cry a treasure. To love Selena was a beautiful thing, to be loved by her even more so. What they shared was ill-fated—their past, present...even their future conspired against them—but in the time they had, Adonis wanted to love her with passion. He wanted to love her with his body, because he would never—*could* never—admit to loving her with words.

Prickly heat needled its way down his back along his spine. His cock, hard and heavy, sought release, and he trailed his hand across the length of his body and pumped his shaft in time to the bouncing of her buttocks atop his face.

She rode him with an undulating, lazy rhythm, building his desire and hers. He'd closed his eyes to savour every stilted breath, to delight in the scent of her hovering in the air. He opened his eyes and glanced up. Her head was thrown back, her lips parted as she fondled her breasts—massaging them, plucking at her tight nipples harder than was necessary, but with just the right pressure to satisfy her baser needs.

In her unbridled desire, she was as beautiful as she was wanton, and he loved her with passion...with tenderness. His lips hungrily seized upon her hot nub and he sucked gently, then harder and harder still until she flooded his mouth with a rush of liquid warmth, trembling above him.

Her hips moved in earnest, her cunt bouncing against his face. He plunged his tongue inside her, lapping at her juices, teasing her with the tip before probing inside her again. She quivered above him and he knew she was close. He tightened his fist around his cock and jacked himself harder, faster. When he felt her jerk against him, then release a splintering scream, he relaxed his jaw, working his mouth furiously to swallow every drop, to fill himself with her essence.

Adonis drank from her pussy until she was spent. He expected her to collapse against him and gather her breath but she didn't. She wove her way down his body, and, with deft movements, she pushed aside his pumping hand and swallowed his dick in a single gulp.

"Selena…" He grunted her name, his eyes clenching shut, his hips surging off the bed so that he pushed himself all the way to the back of her throat. She took him there, then she took him deeper. His free hand found its way into the tangled mass of her hair, and he guided her mouth up and down his shaft until his rod was glistening wet and he was trembling with the effort to restrain himself. He wanted to last a while longer, to savour the pleasure of her sucking him off, but she must have sensed his strained need. She snapped his control when she shoved her finger into his puckered anus and found that soft, spongy space that caused him to erupt on a violent curse.

He thrust up off the bed, and she held his hips, her face buried in his groin, her nose tickling his pubic hair. Adonis came on a long, harsh groan, his seed jetting out of him into her mouth and down her throat.

Like he'd done just moments before, she relaxed her jaw and swallowed every drop.

He was soft and flaccid by the time she released him, a boneless heap by the time she unlocked the cuff from around his wrist. He did not move for a long while. He simply lay there atop the bed, staring up at the crown moulding that ran along the ceiling.

"Am I still a prisoner here?"

Adonis frowned through his euphoria. "Why do you ask?"

"I would just like to know if I can leave, and, if I can't, then where can I go inside this place."

He sat up then and rolled out of the bed. "No, you cannot leave. As far as where you can go inside this home, there are places that are off limits, but most are not. Cassius can show you around wherever you would like to go."

"Cassius? Your bodyguard from the hotel?"

He stared at her. "Do you know him?"

"Only from the other night. You called him by name."

He relaxed. He'd never been a jealous man until her...and *only* with her, it would seem.

"Yes, well, Cassius will know where you can go, and where you cannot."

"When will I be able to leave?"

He was halfway across the room to the bathroom when he stopped. "When my brothers and I deem so."

"You cannot keep me here forever."

He sighed. "Believe me, Selena, we do not intend to." With that, he closed the bathroom door, shutting her out if only for the half hour it would take him to shower and change.

* * * *

When he left his bedroom, he found her in the sitting area, sipping tea and reading the newspaper.

She looked up when he walked in.

"Where are you going?"

"I have an errand to run."

He nodded then at the tea and paper in her hand.

"Cassius," she said, answering his questioning gaze. "I told him of my desire to tour the house. He seemed amenable."

Adonis frowned. "If Cassius tells you a section is off limits, then do not press to go where you do not belong."

Her brows arched. "What are you hiding in an old home that has been empty for a year?"

"Selena…"

"I am simply bored, Adonis, trapped in this house with nothing to do, and now you will be gone for the day. What do you expect me to do?"

She had a point, but he knew Selena—her curious mind, her probing nature. She would wander, and she would find things that she wouldn't want to know. Things about him. Things about her.

"I would have you promise me, but I know you will only do what you wish. I will be sure Cassius has strict orders to not be swayed by you, but I warn you—do not go where you do not belong."

"Or what?"

"Some secrets are never meant to see the light of day. Understand that and respect it."

He didn't know if his words had fallen upon deaf ears or if she'd truly heard him. He didn't question her either, nor did he stay to find out. Selena was headstrong and determined. He could tell her no, and she would just do it anyway. Just as he could place an army of men before her, and she would still find a way around them.

All he could do was hope that Selena heeded his words—there were some secrets so heinous, so depraved, that they would destroy all if they were ever exposed. The secrets locked in his father's home could destroy many—the two of them included. He hoped she believed him.

He truly hoped she did not go where she did not belong.

Chapter Thirteen

As the proprietor of the western district, Adonis believed in encouraging the arts along with fashion. *La Maison d'Adonis* had represented a departure from such pursuits, but the establishment had been born out of his desire to create a place of beauty and luxury, fashioned out of the imaginations of the artists who lived and worked within his domain.

Every room had been carefully conceived and constructed — not one detail had escaped his notice, not a single decision had been made without his input. That was why, upon entering *La Maison d'Adonis*, every patron was greeted by an intricate tapestry of painted images along the ceiling of lovers entwined. The same was true for the mural splashed across an entire wall within the lobby that depicted a man and a woman bathing naked in a serene garden.

Everywhere one looked, there were images of lovers and sculptures of the nude form. His vision for *La Maison d'Adonis* had been to create a place of beauty that inspired the imagination and nurtured feelings of love and lust. And he'd succeeded in doing just that.

Adonis made his way through the lobby of his hotel, cordially greeting his staff and the guests as he passed by. He was not there to entertain a business associate nor was this a social call. He had a purpose, but he also had a statement to make. Whatever the rumours circulating—of the fires, of someone threatening his brothers and their dynasty—Adonis wanted to send a clear message that he was very much alive, well, and still engaged in his business pursuits.

He walked past the guest elevators and punched in the code to enter a small room. A single elevator greeted him, and he punched in another code, waiting patiently until the metal doors slid open. After climbing to the top floor, the elevator opened again and he stepped into his penthouse.

The place was as he'd left it, the only difference being the fumes that greeted him. Adonis walked into his bedroom, which had been transformed into an inferno just days ago. Already, the room appeared as it had been before—eggshell walls had been plastered then painted. The dark wood furniture had all been replaced. It was as if nothing had happened.

Adonis stalked over to his closet, pushed aside his clothing then opened the safe nestled deep into the wall. He'd come back there to retrieve four items, and he pulled them from the safe and closed the door.

Captured inside a small black velvet pouch were four rings—*the* four rings—one for each fire…for each brother. Before the fire in his penthouse, Ares had turned the rings over to him and he'd placed them in his safe. He'd come back to retrieve them.

Selena claimed she hadn't left the rings and that Jarrod had not either. Adonis opened the pouch and pulled out one ring to study it. Diamonds sparkled in the platinum band, identical to the one *Dieu* had once owned. She'd said she'd had nothing to do with it, and Adonis was inclined to believe her. How would she have known?

How would she have known of the symbolic meaning of such an object? Known of the hellish memories that seeing this ring again had dredged up for each and every one of his brothers...and for him?

No, Selena would not know what these rings meant to him and to his brothers. But the rings had been left by someone, and Adonis wanted to know who...and to what end?

The sound of something clicking drew his attention and Adonis looked up. He hurriedly closed the closet door and moved to leave the room, but halted in the next instant.

Every single muscle in his body corded hard and tight with tension then fear, as ice solidified within the wall of his chest. He stood before the mirror in his room, the mirror that spanned the entire wall. His gaze clashed with a pair of reflected eyes. Violet eyes...familiar eyes...

Eyes that he'd not stared into for over a year, and, before that, sixteen years.

He heard the bullet explode from the gun just moments before he felt it whiz past his cheek and slam into the mirror, shattering the glass.

Adonis twisted around at the same time he crouched low, expecting to find a gun pointed at him and a man he'd thought long dead holding it...

There was nothing behind him but a single window, framed by draperies. The window had been left cracked open and Adonis stood to close it, staring out of it, but he found nothing. No trace of the man who'd just wielded a gun and shot at him.

He looked at the hole in the centre of the mirror. *Someone* had taken a shot at him, someone had been in this room.

Someone with eyes the identical colour of his father and who looked exactly like *Dieu*.

Adonis gathered up the pouch he'd dropped when he'd ducked. He checked inside again to find all four rings still there. This time, as he left the room and rode the elevator down, he was careful…cautious. His eyes were wary as they darted around the lobby, searching for a man with violet eyes, searching for a ghost.

He left *La Maison d'Adonis* behind him as he slid into his car and made the short drive to a shop he'd visited a few times before.

He was still on edge when he entered the place, even more so when he left some fifteen minutes later. Adonis pulled out his cell phone and dialled Ares, but was not surprised when he got his brother's voicemail. With Ares tracking his brothers and Serena, he would be careful to stay off his phone and off the grid in the event that he himself was being tracked.

Adonis had little doubt that Ares was being watched, just as *he* was. He was certain his brothers Apollo and Eros were also being followed. The fear he'd managed to stifle ratcheted up a notch at the idea that Apollo and Eros were being tracked by an enemy they'd thought long dead—a ghost of a man.

Adonis left a brief message for Ares, most of it cryptic, but his brother would have no trouble understanding. When he received the message, Ares had strict instructions to immediately give him a call.

His brothers needed to know what they were facing, although Adonis was not certain himself. He glanced down at the velvet pouch glaring at him from the passenger seat, as if its very presence could harm him.

He'd stopped to have the rings appraised—not for value, but for authenticity—and what he'd discovered had not been the news he'd desired, although deep down he'd expected it.

Adonis had thought the rings were fakes...but he'd been wrong. He'd thought the rings were recent replicas—another incorrect assumption. The diamonds were from Sierra Leone, the platinum South Africa. Those mines had been shut down over twenty years ago. The rings were not fakes or replicas. Adonis had asked the appraiser if it was possible the rings could have been made recently from material stored somewhere safe for all these decades. Unlikely, he'd been told.

Something forged out of preserved material would sparkle brilliantly and reflect the light in such a way that indicated it was newly made. Despite their pristine condition, the rings wore the signs of age.

Adonis pressed down on the accelerator and gunned the engine, picking up speed as he travelled back to his father's home. With the recent events over the past days, he'd not thought to check *Dieu's* safe, but that would be the first thing he did when he returned. It would not change anything whether he found his father's ring tucked inside that safe or if he found it gone. He simply wished to know if it was there. Maybe it would provide a clue, maybe it wouldn't.

Either way, it did not matter. Someone had shot at him, presumably to end his life. Someone wanted him dead, and he knew neither why nor to what end. The only thing he did know was that he'd stared into the eyes of a ghost who'd come back to haunt him and his brothers because of the secret they shared. The secret that bound them, that ensured the bond between them was stronger than birth, stronger than blood.

* * * *

After Adonis left, Selena showered and dressed and then went in search of Cassius, but she didn't have to look for long. As soon as she opened the door to the sitting room, she found him.

He stood just outside the door, guarding it like a bouncer would guard the entrance to a popular nightclub. His face was fearsome, his expression was intense. The beauty she'd glimpsed that night in another hallway not too long ago was still there, only harsher...harder.

"I am sorry about having to disarm you the other night," she said, acknowledging that his dark expression had to do with who she was and what she'd done.

He nodded, but said nothing else.

"You must understand, I had no other choice. I needed to get to Adonis, and I knew you would not simply let me past."

Again he silently nodded.

"I was hoping you would escort me on a tour of the estate." When he moved to nod again, her temper flared.

"Won't you say something? I cannot believe you're still upset about that night."

He frowned. "You've already apologised for that."

"Then why do you insist on remaining silent?"

His gaze darted about, as if searching for something that was not there.

"What is it?" she demanded when he still hesitated.

"My boss suggested that I not speak with you."

"Adonis?" Her eyes rounded when he nodded. "Why?"

"He said you are manipulative and that to speak with you will endear me to you until I come to trust you, but that I should not trust you."

Adonis' warning—*not to go where she did not belong.*

She frowned. Of course he would warn Cassius not to fall prey to her, not to be manipulated into letting her see something she was not supposed to see or letting her talk him into taking her somewhere for just a minute...

Her frown gave way to a smile. Adonis knew her inner workings far too well. Everything Adonis had told Cassius was true.

Now that she knew Cassius' position, she was forced to change her own. She would not be able to charm him as she'd hoped, which meant she would have to ditch him.

"Adonis is overly concerned," she said finally.

"I have never known him to be wrong."

She bit her lip to keep the scowl from her face. "Very well then, shall we go take a look around now?"

He nodded but, before he left his post, he locked the door to Adonis' chambers. They walked down the hallway and actually made it to the next floor before she was tempted to speak.

"How long have you been in Adonis' employ?"

Her question was met with silence, which elicited a sigh from her. "Look, I have no desire to return to an empty room so I plan to be on this tour for quite a while. If you choose to remain silent, this entire experience will be that much more painful for the both of us." She looked at him. "Or you can choose to be reasonable instead, and use your judgement when speaking with me, so this does not become unbearable."

He was quiet for so long that she decided Adonis had hired nothing but machines as guards, who followed every order to the letter. She would have found it impressive, except that she'd simply gone from a silent and empty room, to a silent and empty home with a big, burly mannequin—who wanted to play mute—as her companion.

When he spoke, the abrupt end to the silence was so startling that she nearly tripped over her feet.

"I have worked for Adonis for five years now."

"And do you enjoy what you do?"

He glanced at her. "I do. His expectations are high, and he demands this of all who work for him and at all times. But he demands the same from himself, and everyone who works for him would say he is a fair man."

There was little doubt in her mind that every word Cassius spoke was true. Adonis was a man who expected near perfection, if not perfection entirely, because that was what he expected of himself. *Dieu* had drilled that into each of his sons. She knew that much from their courtship years ago. Yet, she also knew Adonis to be fair, just, and compassionate in how he treated people.

"How did you come to know Adonis?"

This was what she desired more than anything—to get a glimpse of the man from one who was close to him. To see Adonis as others saw him.

"We met as boys, working for his father. When I left *Dieu's* employ, I sought Adonis out. Many of those who guard him used to work with him. We trust him with our lives."

"As he must trust you with his."

She listened to what the man beside her did not say—yet conveyed with his gestures and the emotion in his voice. Cassius spoke of Adonis with admiration, with unswerving loyalty. To inspire such devotion, for men to be willing to die for him, said more to her than words ever could and told her what she already knew — Adonis was a man of honour and of principle. She knew this as surely as she knew she breathed.

Dieu had raised him to pretend as if he was perfect, but to always remember that he was flawed. Adonis did not see himself as a man worthy of loyalty…or as a man worthy of *love*. Whatever he'd been when *Dieu* had plucked him from the grimy streets, and whatever he'd become after, had convinced Adonis he was still that same boy — a boy who'd grown into a man believing himself still undeserving of love.

They turned a corner and Selena looked up at Cassius to ask, "Where are we going?"

He stopped all of a sudden. "You did not specify a place so I was simply wandering the halls."

She took a moment to consider where she wanted to go. "Will you show me the bordello below?"

Cassius stiffened, his eyes flashing grey and hard as stone. She already knew without asking, but did anyway. "You worked there as well?"

He nodded. "I did."

And his memories remained as unpleasant as Adonis'. She longed to see the rooms again, but Cassius was already uneasy in her presence. She did not wish to make her companion any more uncomfortable than was necessary.

"What of *Dieu's* chambers then, instead of the bedrooms below?"

"The master's wing is off limits," Cassius replied with a stiff shake of his head.

She'd expected as much, but pressed anyway. "Well, can I at least visit that floor and walk the hallways?"

"I'm afraid not. The doors leading to his wing are locked. Even I do not have that key. Only his sons."

Disappointment filled her. She'd not expected that Adonis would let her wander through *Dieu's* apartments, but she'd never expected that the entire wing would be locked.

"Where do you suggest I go then?" she questioned Cassius.

"Back to your chambers?"

She was not amused by his attempt at a joke and her swift glare erased the hint of a smile from his lips.

"What of Rosalina—*Dieu's* deceased wife? Are her chambers off limits as well?"

"Her private chambers are, but not her study."

Selena smiled at that. Rosalina's study, *any* study, was bound to have a book or two. If she learned nothing of value in her tour of the woman's study, at least she could entertain herself later with something to read.

"Excellent. I would love to visit Rosalina's study."

And so that was where Cassius took her, up three flights of stairs and through the winding maze of the vast estate, until she found herself in a wing on the opposite side of the home.

With Cassius by her side, she walked down a long corridor, her footsteps muffled by her slippers. Soft, warm light flickered from the wall sconces, illuminating their path, but, even with the spill of light, the hallway remained dark and oppressive as shadows stretched out from every corner. This hallway, the absence of light and rich colour, was so unlike the one leading into Rosalina's private quarters that Selena knew the woman must have either shared the study with her husband or it had once been *Dieu's* before they'd married.

They passed two doors as they walked down the corridor, and Selena learned those were the other entrances to the study. She did not understand why a simple study needed three entrances, until Cassius stopped at the third and final door and unlocked it.

She realised instantly why the study had more than one entrance, because it was not a study at all. The room took up one side of an entire floor. To call it a study was a gross insult to the room she now stood inside. It was a library — a vast one, full of books. The only objects inside the room that lent themselves to a study were the Queen Anne chair and large cherry oak desk in the centre.

Cassius flipped a switch, plunging the entire space into a sea of light. Before she'd been confined to the convent and the reading of purely religious texts, Selena had been an avid reader of many genres and authors. She walked along the shelves in awe. At first she was struck by the classic works of Hobbes and Locke, the Brontë sisters and the eclectic writing of Whitman — all of which appeared to be first editions. She delicately trailed her fingers across the leather bindings, afraid to do even that.

She was so engrossed in studying the collection before her that she momentarily forgot herself, forgot Cassius, but mainly she forgot that she had not set out to tour the house because she was simply bored and eager to explore. Selena had left her room for a purpose.

For over a year, she'd plotted Woodward's death. She'd had Jarrod study his habits, his routine, until he'd disappeared. Her father's trail had grown cold after that, except for one seemingly minute clue that had led her here, to *this* house.

It had taken Jarrod some time and had cost them both a great deal of money to obtain the original floor plan to this estate, but, upon doing so, Selena had studied it, almost daily, until she knew every secret passage, every hidden entryway.

The floor plan she'd studied had not done justice to this room, however, and certainly not to the collection contained within, but she was certain the information was accurate. Selena knew every idiosyncrasy this estate possessed, probably better than Adonis himself.

She glanced over at Cassius, who was now perusing a row of books. He'd watched her like a hawk at first but had gradually begun to relax. She took advantage of his inattention and inched her way into the far north-eastern corner of the room. If Cassius were to look up, he would think she was simply engaged in the titles at the end of the shelves. Selena's expression was far too intense, however, to say she was simply studying a row of books.

There was a small gap between the wall and the bookshelf, just big enough for her hand, a woman's hand. She slid it into the space and felt around until her fingers brushed a tiny knob of cool metal. She gave Cassius one last glance to be sure he was still looking in the other direction.

He was.

She tugged on the handle, gently at first, but when it did not budge she pulled harder, then harder still. She was about to give up until she pulled at the same time she twisted her hand to the right.

There was a soft click as the bookshelf pushed away from the wall. Whether he heard the noise or glimpsed the flash of movement, Cassius looked up abruptly, but he was too late.

He called her name, but she had already slipped into the small crack and was pulling the bookshelf closed with a firm, hard slam.

Cassius' voice was muffled in the chamber, but, from all the banging he was doing, she was certain he was cursing her violently. She did not wait to find out. If Cassius searched long enough he would discover the knob. She did not have much time.

Selena walked quickly, her heart thumping erratically in her chest as she navigated the tunnel that wove its way through the entire estate. The darkness was heavy, stifling. Without a flashlight or candle, she was virtually blind. Her eyes struggled to adjust to the dearth of light, but, even after they did, she was forced to make her way through the corridor slowly, with one hand on the brick wall as a guide.

She remembered enough from the floor plan to know where she was going—she simply could not see her way. The noise of something creeping across the floor made her heart pound harder. She imagined it was probably a rat—the passageway presumably had not been used in over a year. Selena decided it would not be wise to chance it. She knew what lurked in these tunnels, in the empty corridors of the haunted estate, so she pulled the gun from between her breasts—the tiny revolver she'd kept hidden, even after Ares had searched her, just before he'd locked her to the bed. After the brothers had left her tethered there, she'd quickly removed the gun and hidden it inside Adonis' bedside table, where it had remained until he'd gone.

Ares should have let Adonis do it...search her, that was. He would not have been afraid to look under her shirt and between the valley of her breasts, but Adonis had not even wanted to look at her, let alone touch her.

The gun was steady in her hand as she crept forward. She turned a corner, then another until she heard the distinct sound of heavy footsteps. A shadow hovered a distance away from her, and she froze. Whoever created the silhouette against the stone walls did not see her and the shadow flickered then disappeared, leaving Selena to wonder if the shadow had belonged to Cassius, who was presumably still searching for her. Or was the owner someone else? She eased forward slowly, searching, listening, but the only sounds she heard were the ones she made.

She turned another corner, steadily making her way to her ultimate destination, yet when she barrelled into a solid, immovable object she knew her journey had come to an end. A hand clamped around her arm and an ear-splintering scream flew from her lips. She dropped her gun in the commotion, though she did not realise it at first. Selena was still screaming when a light flickered on, illuminating the person who held her. Her screams died in her throat.

"Cassius?"

He looked furious and he did not say a word as he dragged her through the dark maze until they were once again in Rosalina's study. With one hand still clamped around her arm, he slammed the bookcase firmly until the lever locked into place with a deafening click.

What came after was no surprise. She was dragged unceremoniously back to the other side of the estate and deposited in Adonis' chambers without another word from Cassius.

"Will you tell Adonis?"

Her question was met with the door slamming in her face.

She imagined that would be the first thing he did — relaying to Adonis the details of her little adventure. Which meant any future tours of the estate were out of the question. And she doubted Cassius would be inclined to speak to her again. After all, he'd been forewarned. She was 'manipulative and not to be trusted'…her escapade had proven that.

Selena flopped down on the bed and waited for the storm that would come when Adonis returned home. She was less concerned about Adonis' reaction, however. She was more furious with herself than anything else. She'd wasted an ideal opportunity. Adonis would trust her even less now, and he certainly would not let her out of his sight again.

She cursed herself as she began to sift through her remaining options. It was unlikely she would get another chance like the one she'd just had, which left her with only one viable option that was as dangerous as it was foolish. She'd hoped it would not come to that, but she had no other choice.

She'd been wrong when she'd told Adonis there was always a choice.

Sometimes there wasn't. Sometimes there was only one path to choose.

Chapter Fourteen

Getting shot at would be a bad day for anyone. Adonis could not have imagined a day such as his could get any worse, but then he returned to his father's home that afternoon to discover he was mistaken.

Upon returning, the first thing he did was investigate his father's safe, only to find that the ring that he'd watched Ares place inside the safe after they'd buried *Dieu* was gone. Ares was still not answering his phone, which meant that Adonis could not inform him of what he'd learned about the authenticity of the rings, nor could he find out if Ares had taken *Dieu's* from his safe. He was fairly certain Ares had not removed it, because that was something none of his brothers would do without informing one another. Which meant someone besides them *had* taken it—someone who knew the code to the safe and knew the intricacies of his father's estate. Adonis had thought only his father and his brothers would be privy to such information, but he was starting to suspect there was another.

He slammed the door to his bedroom, an almost malicious smile curling his lips when Selena shot up from the bed, her eyes wide. She stared at him in surprise, which soon gave way to comprehension when she glimpsed the expression upon his face.

"You spoke with Cassius," she said, and he was happy to see she did not resort to pretence. They were well past that point.

"I did."

"I know how this must look but I assure you it is not as it appears."

One brow quirked. "And how do you think it appears to me?"

"As it has always appeared—that I am lying, that I cannot be trusted."

"Well, are you lying? *Can* you be trusted?"

The look she shot him sent chills down his spine it was so intense. "No matter what you think, I would never do anything to harm you—to put you or your brothers in danger. I admit that I have been less than truthful, but you can trust that I would die before I ever caused harm to come to you."

Her words as well as the conviction behind them surprised him, but he was not moved. "You set fire to my hotel, then to my home. I could have been killed saving you." His gaze slammed into her. "You have already harmed me, Selena."

She could not argue that and so she didn't. She looked away, unable to bear the weight of his stare.

"Why were you in the hidden passageway this afternoon?"

She looked at him. "I cannot answer that," she said quietly.

Maybe it was the events of the day, or the events of the entire week that weighed upon him, but in that moment he snapped.

He instantly plucked her from the bed and held her by her arms, her feet dangling in the air.

"Tell me what you know, Selena!" He shook her. "Tell me why you're here!" Adonis shouted, his face within inches of hers. When she did not speak, when she simply stared down at him with rounded eyes, his anger redoubled. "I was shot at today and something has been stolen from my father's safe. If I find out you or your brother had anything to do with any of it, I will kill you both myself."

He released her then, setting her away from him as if she disgusted him. And in that moment she did.

She had dragged him into this game of deceit and intrigue that she was intent upon playing and he was tired of it. Whether she'd had anything to do with the shooting did not matter. If she could not trust him with her secrets, then he could not trust her and, because of that, she was dangerous to him. Tomorrow he would have Cassius remove her from his father's home.

No one was after her as he'd first believed. She was not in danger. She'd never been. The only reason why he'd allowed her to stay this long, and against the strong wishes of Ares, was because he'd arrogantly believed he could break her, that he could wring the truth from her. And when he couldn't force it from her, he'd believed she would trust him enough to simply *tell* him the truth. But he hadn't broken her, and she would never volunteer the information he sought. He accepted that now, just as he was forced to accept that he could not allow her to continue to prey upon his sense of guilt and manipulate him further, to use him any more than she already had.

Adonis turned away from her and moved to leave.

"I obtained the architectural plans to this estate. That is how I know of all the hidden passageways. When you found me the other night looking at Rosalina's portrait, I was actually looking for one of the entrances."

He stopped, his back facing her, but he did not turn around nor did he speak.

"I know nothing about a safe and I have stolen nothing from you. That is the truth. Just as you know deep down I would *never ever* shoot at you, nor would I have anyone do such a thing. Jarrod simply wants the inheritance he believes my father owes him, and I simply want Woodward dead. Shooting you, hurting you, or stealing from you is not a part of our plan."

He whipped around to face her, his eyes glittering with anger. "And what *is* part of your plan?"

When she bore down on her bottom lip with her teeth, he gathered she would not tell him anything different from what she already had. It was all just as well. Tomorrow he would send her away and he would be rid of her and all of her lies. She could keep all the secrets she wanted then.

He started to leave again, only to be frozen in place by her next words.

"I believe your father's home holds a clue to the whereabouts of Woodward and the reason behind his disappearance."

He faced her in puzzlement. "That makes no sense. Why would you believe such a thing?"

She eased her way towards him. "When it comes to your father and mine, there are no coincidences. I believe we established that with the portrait of your mother. It is no coincidence that your father died around the same time Woodward disappeared. It is no coincidence that our mothers share similar names, identical appearances."

He shook his head. "I agree there are no coincidences. But what does any of that have to do with the connection between your father's disappearance and this house?"

"By themselves nothing, but, given the special relationship our fathers shared, I became convinced *Dieu's* death prompted Woodward's disappearance and that this house holds the answers to where he has gone and why."

The circumstances of *Dieu's* death did not trouble him. He knew for a certainty Woodward had *nothing* to do with his father's death. Adonis' eyes narrowed. It was her other statement that sparked his unease.

"What special relationship are you referring to?"

"Come now, Adonis. You do not have to protect me any longer. I know they engaged in business dealings together, but, more than that, I know they were also lovers. "

His eyes rounded. "How did you —?"

"Find out?" She shrugged. "When I was fourteen, I overheard them arguing. It was a lover's quarrel. I knew. Just as I'm sure my mother did as well. It was some years later when I finally told Serena."

Her eyes softened as she studied him, a gentle smile curving her lips. "That was why you didn't want me poking around. You were afraid of what I would discover."

He nodded. He was afraid of the many things she could uncover within these walls, and that was certainly one of them.

"Do not worry about the other secrets within this house," she said as if reading his mind like an open book. "I did not come here for secrets. I came here to find a clue as to Woodward's whereabouts, but thus far I have found nothing."

"And I doubt you ever will. Secrets are what my father's home is best at keeping, secrets that could destroy many lives. But useful information it has never seemed to produce."

She shrugged. "Maybe you are right. Maybe you are not."

"Unfortunately, you will never know." Her eyebrows arched at his statement. "I have asked Cassius to take you home tomorrow," he said in answer to her puzzled frown.

She seemed to want to argue, but she simply nodded, saying only, "I see."

"It is for the best." Adonis did not know why he felt compelled to explain himself, but the expression on her face seemed to warrant it. If he did not know any better, he would think he'd hurt her, but he knew better.

This time when he turned away from her, he left his room. Selena had her own agenda, and he had his. It was safer for the both of them if they simply parted ways. It was for the best...or at least he would keep telling himself that until he believed it.

* * * *

Selena would never have imagined the loss of Adonis again would feel this way. She'd never imagined her father would have the power to come between them yet again, but the absence of Adonis from her bed had made her night sleepless, the sheets cold.

He had slept in the sitting room, on the couch, so that he would not be forced to sleep beside her, so that he could not be seduced by her and tempted to touch her. She knew well the inner musings of the man who now dressed in the other room. She knew the inner workings of Adonis probably better than she knew her own.

Within the hour, Cassius would come for her and take her home.

Home — wherever that was. She no longer had a home. She could not return to the convent. She supposed she would have to stay with Jarrod, but the house he lived in was her father's, and that space dredged up memories she'd prefer to leave buried in the past. Maybe when she left she would simply stay at a hotel. She did not know.

What she did know was that Adonis was kicking her out and sending her away. He believed her a liar, unworthy of his trust, and so she could not remain in his presence any longer.

Selena had failed. She had not found the information she'd sought. She was no closer to discovering Woodward's whereabouts than she had been a week ago, a month ago, a year ago.

She had failed.

She looked up when Adonis walked in dressed for the day. She'd failed him too. For a brief moment, a stolen moment, they had rediscovered what it was like to love again. Had she closed her eyes and allowed herself to dream, she could have almost imagined there were still enough feelings between them, enough passion there between them that they could somehow escape their pasts and love each other again. Selena knew such a thing was an impossibility. Too much time had passed, too many lies had been told. They were two very different people now. She was not the girl she'd once been, the girl he'd once loved. There was no denying the passion they still shared, the emotions that burned inside them, but their lives had taken them too far apart.

"Cassius will be here to escort you home within an hour."

She nodded. "And will you be here then?"

"No. I have an errand to run."

"I see."

He hovered in the doorway, and she stood there entranced by his golden gaze.

It was obvious they both wanted to say more, but they were either too stubborn or too afraid to part their lips. In the end they both said nothing, except goodbye.

"Thank you for offering your protection and allowing me to stay here," Selena added when Adonis turned away.

He stopped to look at her. "You're welcome." With that he left the bedroom, and there was only the sound of the door to his outer chambers closing.

Adonis walked out of his childhood bedroom, then out of his father's home. He got into his car and sped away from *Dieu's* estate as if the devil himself tailed him. He drove as fast as he could, and, if it had been in his power to do so, he would have put as much distance between himself and the woman whose face had haunted him for sixteen years.

Selena.

There was no denying that he still loved her, still wanted her, but she was not the woman he'd once known. She was not the woman he'd fallen in love with. And yet, his heart did not seem to care. Adonis did not wish for her to go, just as he did not wish to send her away. But it was foolish to pretend they had a future together. For a few stolen moments, he'd believed they could put their pasts to rest, but that had been the musings of a foolish man.

Even if she had not lied to him and betrayed him, even if he could trust her—he could not ignore the time that had separated them. Their lives had taken them too far apart. She had changed. And he was not the man he'd once been—he was worse. Time had hardened him, had irrevocably changed him. He'd been damaged then destroyed in those years. He no longer possessed the power to love another intimately, to trust them with his heart.

He'd resigned himself to such a fate long ago, and he'd been foolish to think he could ever experience happiness again. Such things were no longer possible for a man who'd seen what he'd seen, who'd done what he'd done. Love and happiness did not belong in the life of a man such as he.

Adonis pulled his car to a stop along the sidewalk and piled out of his vehicle. Ares had sent him a note by messenger, letting him know a package awaited him at the depot. The note had not told him what was inside, and Ares was still not answering his phone. He imagined Ares could no longer use his phone for fear of being tracked, so Adonis suspected the package would provide a clue as to where his brother was, where all of them were. Or at least that is what Adonis hoped.

He was still uneasy from yesterday's shooting, and that he had lost contact with his brothers did not improve his feelings of disquiet.

The depot was a small, nondescript building on the fringes of the border between his district and Ares'. He pushed open the door to find the place empty, which was usually the case. With the courier service, people only sent packages to the depot that were either too large for the courier or when one wanted such a transaction to remain discreet. The depot was known to be lax in verifying the identities of either the sender or receiver. As long as the transaction was paid for, the staff did not care. Such was the reason why the owner barely glanced at Adonis after he handed the man his tracking number and in turn was given a small brown package the size of a shoe box.

Adonis studied the package in his hand as he returned to his car. There was no address from the sender, no name either. He opened the trunk of his car and placed it inside. He would open the package when he returned home, and, coward that he was, he would only return home once Selena was gone.

Adonis glanced at his watch. He still had a little over half an hour. He continued down the sidewalk, his eyes alert. Still wary from yesterday, he did not think it wise to remain out in the open where so many strangers milled about. So he made his way into a nearby cafe where he ordered a cup of coffee before taking a seat at a table facing the door.

Twenty minutes later, he was still seated at that same table when he heard what could only be described as a rumble of thunder, followed by a wave of flames and fire. The explosion shook every building on the street, setting off several car alarms. Adonis was out of his chair and standing on the sidewalk within an instant.

The entire street was immersed in complete chaos as people shouted all around him, and debris floated in the air. Adonis was immune to it all as he stared down the sidewalk into the distance. What he saw made his blood run cold as his heart sputtered to a halt within his chest.

His sleek silver car, which had been parked on the corner at the other end of the street, was gone. In its place was a hollow, charred skeleton of a vehicle with flames still dancing all over it.

* * * *

Selena had come to Adonis with nothing, and so she had nothing to pack, nothing to take with her when she left.

It took her only a few minutes to shower and dress, and when she was done, she prepared to make her way into the sitting room. She would wait there until Cassius arrived to escort her from the premises. Selena was just turning the knob to the bedroom door when she heard two male voices. They were shouting, their words muffled. She opened the door at the same time as a shot rang out, followed by a distinct thud.

Selena froze in the doorway between the sitting room and bed chambers. Cassius lay prostrate in the centre of the room, his beautiful eyes open in surprise, staring up at nothing. Blood trickled from his mouth and spurted from a gaping hole in his chest.

A flash of silver drew her attention from the fallen man's still form and she gasped when her gaze collided with cold, jade green eyes. Familiar green eyes.

"Father." She said the word as if it was a slur, a curse. From his expression, the venom in her voice was not lost on him.

Woodward Gowen had once been a handsome man, with auburn hair and sparkling eyes. Now he was a shadow of a man, his once muscled frame now hunched with age and his lustrous hair shock white and thinning. His strong, firm hands were now covered with spots of age and his face was sallow and sunken in. Selena was not fooled by his weakened appearance, though. The silver gun pointed at her chest would not allow such a thing, just as his cutting eyes reminded her that the man before her may have aged, but he was just as cruel and sinister as he'd always been. More than foolish, she would be stupid to believe her father would not hesitate to pull that trigger and burn a hole through her chest.

In that moment, as inconvenient as it was, Selena remembered she *had* come to Adonis with something—her gun...which she'd dropped the night before in the tunnel. How she wished she still had it now, tucked within the valley of her breasts.

"Daughter," Woodward replied, with the same animosity dripping from his voice. "You have been busy, I see."

She glared at him. "Apparently not busy enough or you would be dead."

"I guess it is unfortunate for you that I am very much alive and will remain so." His eyes burned with malice. "The same cannot be said for you, however."

He marched over to her, the gun still aimed at her chest.

"Into the bedroom," he ordered, and she turned around, her hands in the air, very much aware that her father had a gun pointed at her back.

Once inside the bedroom, Woodward closed the door. She watched in awe when he reached behind the armoire in the corner. There was a soft click, then a whining creak as the wall separated from itself to reveal a set of steps leading into a passageway.

She had not been aware of an entrance into the tunnel from Adonis' bedroom. It had not been on the plans she'd studied. She wondered if Adonis knew of the door. She suspected that he did.

Woodward gestured for her to go ahead of him, so Selena found herself walking down the stairs, deeper into the bowels of the estate. She noticed her father did not close the door behind him, but she did not question him. Hopefully he'd forgotten, although she doubted that was the case. For whatever reason, he did not think anyone would follow after him, which filled her with a grave sense of unease.

Selena felt as if she'd walked for hours although it could not have been more than a few minutes. As she led the way, the only words spoken were from Woodward as he barked out directions through the dark corridor. Eventually the tunnel came to an end and she found herself inside a large room. What she saw took her breath away. It was decorated in the same fashion as the rooms in the bordello — white walls, a king-sized bed draped in white dominating the entire space. Even the furnishings were white. In one corner was a small desk, with a tiny computer atop it that was the size of her two hands. In another corner there appeared to be a small bathroom. It reminded her of a water closet from centuries past. Though no tub, there was a small basin and a toilet, tucked behind a divider.

Selena looked at her father with eyes that, no doubt, reflected her dark, menacing thoughts of the man before her. "I always knew you were here. I knew you would return here when I put a price upon your head."

His smile was cold. "I was not surprised when you arrived. I knew all along you would track me here."

"You always sought your lover out when you were in trouble. I knew, despite his death, you would return to his home." Her eyes narrowed. "You have been here watching us, haven't you?" All along she'd felt another presence, as if foreign eyes shadowed her. She'd suspected it was Woodward, but she'd never been able to determine if it was indeed his presence she'd felt, or simply her wild imagination.

He nodded in answer to her question. "So you have found me, Selena. You and that bastard brother of yours. Too bad it has all been for nothing.

"As soon as your lover returns, he will give me what I want and then I will kill you both. By the time anyone discovers your bodies down here, you won't even be recognisable."

She cringed at the image he painted.

"When I am done with you, I will take care of your brother next. He has caused more trouble than you and your sister put together. The greedy bastard almost wiped me out, but I will see that he gets what he deserves."

"Do not harm him!" she shouted. "He only wants what is rightfully his. You provided him with nothing. Your own son and you did not give him a penny."

"Jarrod knows why I did not provide for him. He knows why he will never see a cent of *my* money." He lifted the gun higher. "But Jarrod's situation should not concern you. Your only concern should be how long it will take before Adonis returns and I decide to kill you both."

He gestured with the barrel of his gun for her to sit down on the bed and she did, even as she raked him with her malevolent gaze.

She'd known all along that Woodward was here. That was why she had needed to gain entrance into this house. *Dieu's* home was virtually impenetrable, except by his sons...and apparently by his former lover as well.

Step by step she'd followed the plan she'd laid out to the letter. Go to Adonis under the pretence of revenge, prey upon his sense of guilt, then create a threat so that out of his deep-seeded guilt he would feel obligated to protect her. Adonis would *never* have taken her to his father's home unless this was the *only* place he believed she would be safe. And she'd made sure that it was.

Once inside, she'd taken advantage of her time alone to explore the tunnels, that was, until Ares had learned the truth. Obviously, that had not been a part of her plan. Just as she had never expected her feelings for Adonis to resurface, and that her feelings for him would lead her to regret using him, manipulating him, lying to him.

She would now have to add another regret to that list. She had hoped to find Woodward and kill him before he could find her and do the same. But he *had* found her, and with her misstep she'd put Adonis in danger.

As she heard heavy footsteps along the corridor, growing louder as they drew closer, she realised it had been complete stupidity on her part to believe she could involve Adonis without him being swept up in her entire plot.

Selena stared between the silver gun and the darkness leading into the tunnel, watching...waiting. Her heart pumped violently, her breath caught in her chest when she saw him. Pure golden beauty.

Adonis.

He was not a god, he was a man. A mortal man who could die just as easily as she.

And she would never forgive herself if something happened to him, if he lost his life because of her foolish plan and her desperate need for revenge.

Chapter Fifteen

After the explosion, Adonis had not returned to his car or waited for the authorities. In the commotion, he'd slipped around the corner and hailed a cab to his father's estate. The drive there had been short, passing without notice. It had taken him longer to make his way from the foyer, up the stairs and into his chambers.

As soon as he'd entered the house, he'd sensed something was amiss. Whether intuition or foreboding, he was cautious as he crept upstairs to his private chambers. He'd smelt the copper scent of blood from the other end of the hallway, so Adonis was not entirely surprised to find Cassius' body in the centre of his sitting room.

The fear clogging his throat was pushed aside by a stronger emotion. Adonis stooped down beside his friend and closed his eyes. He had loved Cassius as a brother, just as he'd loved the other men he'd taken into his employ as his guards. But Cassius was special. Many years ago, when *Dieu* had confined Adonis to solitude for some unmemorable transgression, it had been Cassius who, along with his brothers, had smuggled food to him when Adonis would have starved. When *Dieu* had found out, he'd beaten all of them, including Cassius. Adonis had never forgiven himself for that, just as he'd never forgotten what Cassius had done for him.

He felt the sting of tears. And this was how he'd repaid his friend, by causing his death.

Adonis left Cassius to enter his bedroom, and he was struck by two things as soon as he stood within the room—the entrance leading into the tunnels beneath the estate was open and Selena was gone.

He'd never imagined her to be capable of murder, but Cassius' body and the open door suggested otherwise. What had happened? Had Cassius discovered something he wasn't supposed to? Had she refused to leave when Cassius arrived to take her away?

Adonis did not know and he did not care. He flung open the door to his closet, pushed aside his clothes and opened the safe nestled in the back of the wall. Pulling the small handgun from its resting place, he slipped it into the waistband of his trousers.

He'd told Selena he would kill her himself if he discovered she was part of a more sinister plan than the one she'd innocently conveyed to him. It was apparent that Selena was far more dangerous and deadly than he'd first believed, just as it was apparent she was not the girl he'd once known.

As he entered the tunnel, plunging himself into darkness, he mourned Cassius as he mourned the girl he'd loved, and what he would have to do.

The tunnels were a vast network beneath the estate that created a maze to those who entered. Adonis knew every winding pathway as intimately as he knew every line across his palm. He did not know where Selena was, but he could have closed his eyes and still found her.

He was not as good a tracker as Apollo, but he knew Selena's scent, the smell of her perfumed skin. Adonis followed the winding trail of jasmine and vanilla until the darkness faded from the tunnel and he approached light.

As he drew closer to the room where her scent came to an end, he concluded that he was a fool for not figuring this out sooner, for not realising she would eventually come here.

Palming the gun in his hand, he crept closer, his steps quiet, not knowing what to expect. He should have known she would find her way there, to the place where their fathers had rendezvoused, to the place where he'd given his body and sacrificed his soul to protect his love for her.

That was the irony. She would die—and, with her, his love for her—in the very room in which he'd bartered his body and soul to spare her life because he'd loved her more than he'd loved himself. He still did. Which was why he knew that when he was done, he would be forced to turn the gun upon himself. What was left of his soul would not survive this final act.

With his weapon trained in front of him, Adonis stepped from the shadows into the open room, expecting to greet Selena and the barrel of her loaded gun. What he found was Selena sitting atop a bed, her eyes wide with terror, and shaking her head as if warning him away. He turned in the direction to where her attention kept straying, and then he did greet the barrel of a loaded gun, but, instead of Selena's, his eyes met those of the only man—besides

Dieu—who'd haunted his nightmares ever since that night in this very room, sixteen years ago.

"Greetings, Adonis." Woodward jerked the gun in the air, gesturing for Adonis to hand over his weapon and take a seat beside Selena. He hesitated.

"Turn over your gun now, or I will shoot her before you can take your next breath." Adonis did not hesitate this time. He gave Woodward his gun then sat down next to Selena.

"This is oddly nostalgic, don't you think?" Woodward crooned. "You and I together in this room and once again you are sacrificing yourself for *her*."

The mocking tone in Woodward's voice chilled him. The older man's gloating expression ignited the rage Adonis thought he'd buried years ago. Selena stared at him, but he could not meet her eyes or answer the questions he knew brewed within them.

Woodward knew of his shame because he'd been the cause of Adonis' humiliation. There were secrets contained within this house, this room even, that he'd hoped Selena would never learn, that would destroy whatever feelings she'd once harboured for him. He'd tried to shield her, then he'd tried to protect himself, but the look in Woodward's eyes revealed to Adonis that her father would take great pleasure in destroying him again, in ruining him before the woman he loved, and there would be nothing he could do to stop him.

He would kill Woodward. He did not yet know how, now that the deranged man had a gun for each of them, but he vowed to rip him to pieces, limb by limb for what would come next.

"Now that you are here, we can finally begin," Woodward said to Adonis.

"Leave him out of this," Selena demanded. "This is between you and me."

The guns jerked in Woodward's hands. "This is actually not just between you and me, daughter." Woodward held him with his gaze. "Would you like to tell Selena just how intricately *you* are entwined with the both of us?"

Adonis' jaw began to hurt his teeth were clenched so tight. "What do you want, Woodward?" he managed to bite out.

"I want what is rightfully mine. What your father promised me. I want your inheritance."

Adonis knew it was because Woodward was broke. He'd actually run out of money over a year ago. Between his gambling debts, the money he spent on whores and booze, and one business misadventure after another—it had all finally caught up to him.

"My inheritance in exchange for what?"

"In exchange for nothing." His eyes were dead. "As soon as you give me the passwords to your accounts, I will kill you both."

"And if I don't?"

"I will still kill you both," Woodward replied. "And with you dead and out of the way, I will simply find them myself, unencumbered by your presence."

"You won't get very far on your own. As soon as my brothers catch up to you, they will kill you, and you'll never see a dime of my money."

Woodward's cruel eyes glinted with insanity. "You assume your brothers are even still alive. Have you heard from them lately?"

Adonis was off the bed and halfway across the room before Woodward got off the shot that burrowed into the wall behind Adonis, halting him where he stood.

"Come one step closer and I will kill you!" he shouted.

"Adonis, please," Selena cried, but he barely heard her above his thundering heartbeat.

"What have you done to my brothers?" "I've done nothing."

Adonis' eyes narrowed. "Someone shot at me yesterday then planted an explosive in my car —"

Selena gasped, but he did not spare her a glance.

"You know who is stalking me, stalking my brothers. You know who is trying to kill us, don't you?"

"And, one by one, they will pick you off until all of you are dead. Now sit down before I decide to shoot you for that little stunt you just pulled."

Once again, Adonis sat down beside Selena.

"Your password, Adonis."

"Wait," Selena interjected. "Take mine. You can have the inheritance mother left to me and Serena."

Woodward turned his attention to her. "Why do you think you're even here, Selena?" His laugh was maniacal, the laugh of one who'd lost all sense of reason. "It is only because of your inheritance that you are even still alive." He glanced at Adonis. "And because I knew your lover would need an incentive." Woodward turned both guns on Selena. "Give me your password now, or watch her die beside you."

Selena protested, but Adonis shook his head. "It is just money."

He gave Woodward the information he'd come there for, and Adonis noted that Selena's father was forced to set one gun aside in order to type the information into his computer. Adonis' attention oscillated between the weapon in Woodward's hand and the weapon that was not.

"And now you, daughter," Woodward said when he'd completed the transaction.

Selena was more reluctant, but then Woodward pointed the gun at Adonis, and soon she too was rattling off numbers.

"How touching to know that true love never dies," he mocked, and closed his computer once the transactions from their accounts were complete.

"I wonder how true your love would be for one another if you both knew the truth."

Selena looked at him, but Adonis kept his glare trained on Woodward. This is what her father had truly brought them there for. Stealing their inheritances was simply a necessity, a basic means to an end, but what Selena's father took pure pleasure in was inflicting pain.

Like *Dieu*, Woodward thrived on cruelty, relished the destruction of innocence and purity. He could not simply steal their inheritances and kill them both. It was not enough for him. He had to kill the love they shared as well. He had to torture their souls before the added insult of taking their lives.

"My daughter looks at you as if she is puzzled." He tsked. "But you do not seem puzzled at all. How could you be? You already know the truth, don't you Adonis? And yet, you have kept your true love ignorant. How bereft of you."

"What is he talking about?" Selena whispered to him.

"Tell her. Tell her the truth."

"You tell her," Adonis gritted out. "Since you seem so eager for us all to know the truth, then tell her what you and my father did to me, tell her what the both of you forced me to do."

Adonis' entire body trembled with shame, with rage. He'd buried these memories so deep within his subconscious that he'd grown numb to the pain, to the humiliation, but both emotions now engulfed him, overwhelming him until it was as if he was drowning. Every breath clawed through his burning chest.

The touch of her hand against his arm snared his attention and he found himself staring into fathomless topaz eyes that implored him to tell her the truth. He carefully removed her hand and moved away. Selena would not want to be near him once she learned the truth, once she discovered who he truly was.

Selena felt the emotional loss of Adonis long before he pulled away from her. He was shutting her out, erecting a wall between them in order to shield himself from her, and soon he would burrow deep inside himself to a place where no one could touch him — not even her. *Especially* not her.

She glared at her father. "What did you do to him?"

Her father's smile was as cruel as it was sinister. It made her stomach turn, and she suspected what he said next would make her want to vomit where she sat.

"The question is not what I did to him, but what *he* did to me — for me — and then what I had him do to you.

"Adonis was always my favourite. I was sad to let him go, but, then *Dieu* approached him with an offer. Adonis agreed to *Dieu's* terms, but on one condition — that *Dieu* would never make him pleasure another man again."

Selena gasped as she stared between Adonis and her father, but Adonis would not look at her. He kept his eyes fixed straight ahead.

"Did he tell you I was his first? I paid handsomely for that pleasure, but it turned out to be such a waste. He cried the entire time."

Selena could not take her focus off Adonis even if she wanted to. He refused to look at her, and when she reached for him he flinched, forcing her to lay her hand in her lap. In that moment, he was neither god, nor man, but a boy who'd been used and manipulated by the very man who'd taken him in and sworn to protect him.

A sob welled up inside her. It was no wonder that he'd felt so betrayed by her. She too had used and manipulated him, the woman who had claimed to love him.

"You're a monster." She hurled the insult at her father. "I'm ashamed I share your blood, let alone your name."

"Blood?" He laughed. "You still do not know, do you?" Woodward's eyes hardened then. "Well, then, I won't tell you."

Selena looked at him in confusion, but nothing upon his face revealed the meaning of his cryptic words, and he did not make any attempt to elaborate.

"You have always been so self-righteous. That is why I'm not surprised you took to the convent while your sister became the whore. But do not be so quick to judge, Selena. Ask Adonis what he promised to do if his father agreed not to force another man upon him."

Selena looked at Adonis, but he still would not look back at her. She focused on Woodward instead. It seemed he was the only one willing to divulge the secrets of their shared pasts.

"You think Adonis is noble, that I forced him to take you, to ruin you. I didn't force him to do a thing. Long before that night I asked *Dieu* to send a young man who could seduce you into loving him, who could seduce you into trusting him. It was Adonis who volunteered to be that man, in exchange for *Dieu's* promise to him. That night was simply the culmination of months of contrived courtship. How do you think you were able to see a man such as Adonis? How do you think it was that I allowed you, a respectable woman of means, to be courted by a man with his reputation unless I wanted you to fall for him—and you fell hard. Even I was surprised at how skilled he was in convincing you of his sincerity."

Selena did not try to look at Adonis this time. She could barely even look at her father as a sea of tears pricked her eyes. She'd always wondered why her father had not protested her relationship with Adonis, even though she'd been very discreet. Some things, however, could not be kept secret forever, and yet when Woodward had learned of Adonis, he had not been upset at all. She should have suspected something then, but she'd been young and in love. It wasn't until years later that she'd begun to question Adonis' true intentions.

Almost as soon as that thought filled the space within her consciousness, she remembered what she'd done to him just days ago, what he'd begged her to do to him so that she could mend the scars upon her heart for his actions sixteen years ago. She knew then, if Adonis had not loved her, he would not have allowed her to do the things she'd done to his body. Even years of guilt did not warrant such a sacrifice.

"You understand now that he never loved you, that he used you to purchase his freedom. I thought Adonis did brilliantly, until the final stage of the plan—when he failed to kill you. But he still used you to free himself from this life. Just as he promised to have nothing to do with you ever again—"

"Only because you threatened to kill her, you bastard. I would never have turned my back on her if you hadn't threatened her life."

Woodward's gaze narrowed on Adonis and he shook his head. "If you had simply killed her you would have spared yourself so much pain. If you'd done as we'd all agreed, I would never have had to hurt you. I hated what I had to do to you, but you had to be taught a lesson. We had an agreement and you disobeyed me, and shamed your father."

Adonis glared at Woodward, his amber eyes full of hatred.

"That was where you and my father made the mistake. You thought you could control me, that you could make me do whatever you wanted me to do, simply by telling me to."

Selena grew nervous when Adonis stood up. She called his name, her hand tugging on his sleeve, as she looked between her father and the man beside her. Woodward's finger pulsed on the trigger.

"Adonis, please sit down."

He ignored her.

"Your mistake was believing that your interests were mine, that I did not have my own agenda, just as I have my own agenda now."

Before Selena could stop him, Adonis launched himself across the room, slamming her father into the wall at his back, but Adonis was not quick enough. He was not faster than the bullet that Woodward got off that lodged itself in his chest.

"Run, Selena, run now!" Adonis shouted as he clutched his chest, blood spilling across his fingers.

Selena didn't run away, which was why Woodward was able to shoot at her. The bullet grazed her shoulder, but it did not stop her.

She slammed into her father while he still struggled with Adonis. Caught off guard, Woodward stumbled back, dropping the gun as he fought to steady himself. The gun skidded across the room. She felt Adonis slump to the floor beside her.

Woodward looked between the both of them, then at the gun that was now several paces away. He must have calculated his odds, because he twisted around and raced out of the room through the tunnel.

She was across the room within seconds, but she was not fast enough as she grabbed the gun and raced after him, shooting into the darkness.

She started after him. She was even several feet into the darkness before she came to a halt.

She'd spent years plotting her revenge and spent this past year putting it into action. If she let Woodward get away now, she knew he would take the money he'd stolen from them and disappear. He would get away with everything he'd done.

Her desperate desire for revenge—for what he'd done to her, to her mother, to Adonis—warred with the needs of her heart.

Her chest tightened and ached, her insides trembled as she turned around and returned to Adonis' side. She could not leave him there to die. His eyes were closed, his breathing shallow, but he was still alive.

She fumbled around in his pockets, searching for the phone she knew he always carried on him. When she found it, she dialled the authorities. Her memory was not perfect, but somehow she managed to direct them to where she was with only a couple of mishaps.

When they found her, Adonis was still unconscious, but he was also still alive...for now.

She did not miss the grave expressions of the two medics who attended to him and pulled him from the tunnel, just as she was all too aware of the growing amount of blood that continued to flow like a river from his chest.

Chapter Sixteen

Dead.

Adonis wished he was when he first awoke to a searing pain in his chest and his brother's fearsome expression. He tried to sit up but grimaced when a sharp pang of agony shot through him, piercing and swift.

"I wouldn't do that if I were you."

He glared at Ares who simply smirked while he pushed a button that lifted the bed beneath Adonis until he was sitting up.

The change in position caused his chest to ache, but he forced himself to ignore it, even as his breathing was strained and ragged.

"What happened?" Adonis looked around. Grey walls, sterile floors, and the acrid smell of bleach and stale urine. He was in a hospital.

His gaze found her at the same moment he remembered what must have brought him there.

Woodward.

The tunnel.

He'd watched Selena run after her father.

He'd thought he'd die down there.

"I take it you remember now," Ares said, obviously glimpsing the comprehension dawning in his eyes.

Adonis nodded. "How long have I been out?"

"Just two days. The bullet went clean through. You didn't even need surgery. They only kept you sedated so that your body could begin healing itself before you started moving around."

"How did you find out I'd been shot? I've been calling you for the last few days, but you never answered."

"And you know why," Ares replied quietly. "But apparently that didn't matter to Selena. She called me practically every five minutes. I even turned off the phone but that did not stop her. She flooded me with messages until my voicemail was full. When I finally checked them, I realised why she'd been so adamant. I came back immediately. I only just arrived an hour ago."

"Any news on Apollo and Eros?"

"No, and, now that you're awake and I know you're all right, I plan to resume looking for them in the morning."

Adonis heard what Ares did not say—what Ares would probably never say because he did not want to upset him in his current condition, but Adonis knew his brother far too well. He was worried for Eros and Apollo. They should not have been out of touch for this long and he feared for them. Adonis shared his brother's fear, especially after what had happened to him over the past few days. Selena and her sister were not the real target—they'd never been. One ring for each brother—the message was clear, the threat even clearer. Someone was still out there—hunting them, haunting them—which meant none of them were safe.

"Did you check all of your messages?" Adonis asked him, wondering if he'd received the messages he'd left Ares, even the most recent one about the car bomb.

Ares nodded, and Adonis did not miss the unease swirling in his dark gaze. "I got every one of them," he answered. "And that is why I plan to leave at dawn."

He did not elaborate, and Adonis did not need him to. "I wish I could go with you," he said, finally earning a small smile from Ares.

"In your feeble state? You would only slow me down."

Adonis laughed at that then regretted it when his chest began to throb. Ares squeezed his shoulder. "I am going to get some coffee." He glanced at Selena, who still huddled in the corner. When Ares spoke again, his voice was so faint only Adonis could hear what he said.

"I always knew that one was dangerous. I had a feeling she would get you killed." Ares' smile turned warm. "What I never imagined was that her feelings for you were genuine. But they are."

Ares walked out of the hospital room then, and, with a quiet thud, closed the door behind him, leaving Adonis alone with Selena.

She was hesitant as she inched her way over to him. She seemed nervous. He stared at her, drowning in her warm topaz eyes, wondering what it was she saw when she looked at him.

Was she repulsed by him? By what she knew her father had done to him, by what he'd done to her father? Or were her feelings far worse than revulsion. Did she hate him for using her as a means to escape his life? He'd been so self-righteous in his condemnation of her manipulation of him, but neither of them were innocent…certainly not him.

"How are you feeling?" she asked lightly, her fingers gentle as they pushed a wisp of hair from his brow.

"I have felt better, I can assure you."

She smiled and a long, awkward silence stretched between them before she said, "You almost got yourself killed with that foolish stunt."

"You almost got yourself killed with that stubborn nature of yours. I told you to run."

"I would never leave you," she said quietly, vehemently.

He'd thought she had, and as he'd closed his eyes and prepared to die in that room beneath his father's estate, he had not blamed her.

He knew what it was like to be consumed by revenge, what it was like to have it within your grasp.

"Why did you come back? Why didn't you go after him?"

"I never left. It was as I just told you, I would never leave you, Adonis, alone and dying on a floor. *Never.*"

The door opened and she drew away from him when a nurse entered the room. The woman clad in white checked his vitals and gave him some more medicine for the pain. She was gone within minutes, but her presence had shattered the fragile moment between them, and, soon after, Ares returned.

"Now that you are awake, I should go," she said. She stood there for several seconds as if waiting for him to say something.

"Thank you for saving my life," was all that came to mind. The look in her eyes told him those were not the words she'd waited to hear.

Ares glared at him, and, if he'd had the strength to shrug, Adonis would have. *What?*

"Wait, Selena. I will walk you out," Ares offered as he followed after her.

The look his brother shot him just before he stalked out of the room was clear. Ares thought he was an idiot. Adonis frowned. What had he done wrong?

Selena left Adonis's room feeling like a fool. She'd told him she'd loved him so many times over these past days. She'd revealed the feelings of her heart because she'd naively believed he felt the same way — that he simply needed to feel secure enough in her love to say the words back.

No more lies stood between them, no more deceit. He should have felt free to tell her that he loved her in return. Unless he didn't. Unless he couldn't.

"My brother is an idiot."

Selena yelped in surprise as she whirled around. She'd forgotten all about Ares. Her frown was grim as she turned back around and headed towards the elevator.

"He is not an idiot. He has simply been through a great deal."

"He has no idea that you need to hear him say the words. He believes you already know his heart."

Her gaze snapped to his face. She did not know how he'd seemingly guessed her thoughts, but she did not pretend his words were less than true.

"Have you considered that he simply does not love me? That he can't?" Her voice choked up, not because she did not have Adonis' love, but because of what she had to say next. "Did you know what my father did to him?" When he nodded, she felt the tears she'd held back since she'd learned the truth spill down her cheeks. "He was just a boy in desperate need of love."

"I know."

"How could he possibly look at me and not see my father when he does? How could he possibly love me when every time he is with me he is reminded of a past he longs to forget?"

"You look nothing like your father, Selena."

She glared at him through her tears. "Is that your idea of a joke? If so, it is not funny at all."

"It is simply the truth. When Adonis looks at you, he sees only the woman he hurt and then lost. When Adonis thinks of loving you, I know it is the past that gets in the way, but not the one you think. Adonis does not believe himself worthy of your love and so he will not ask for it. Adonis does not believe himself deserving of happiness so he will not hope for it. If you want my brother's love, you will simply have to be brave enough to demand it, but it will not be easy."

She looked up at him through tearful eyes. "What do you suggest I do?"

"Show him that you will not take your love away, by simply being there for him. Show him that he can trust you with his heart."

Ares caressed her cheek in a gesture that was oddly endearing, and in the manner that one would comfort a sister. Surprisingly, she found solace in the touch of a man who'd glared at her with hate in his eyes just days ago.

"I must leave again tomorrow to continue searching for your sister and my brothers. I ask that you would stay with him."

"You do not have to ask such a thing. Of course I will stay with him, but are you sure he wants my company?"

Ares smiled as he let his hand fall back to his side. "He would never admit it, but he does. Remember what I said, Selena. He will not simply admit to loving you out of fear that you will reject him, so you will have to demand it of him. And from the sounds coming from his bedroom before I left, I am sure you have it in you to get him to admit to anything your heart desires."

* * * *

Adonis was back at his home and asleep in his bed when his brother left the next morning, but he was fully alert when *she* arrived.

He'd felt her presence in his home the moment she'd entered.

His lungs had burned with the scent of her the moment she'd walked into his bedroom. He'd hoped she'd come, but he truly did not know if he would ever see her again when she walked out of his hospital room.

"I suspected my brother was up to something when he followed after you yesterday. What did he say to convince you to come back and nurse me to health?"

Warm golden rays of the dawning day embraced her as she left the shadows of the doorway and walked into the centre of the room.

She wore a simple white dress that fell to her ankles and hugged her curves seductively, while her unbound hair hung in gentle waves, caressing her shoulders and slipping down her back. She was beautiful in the morning sun and he almost could not breathe as she captured his gaze and held it.

"Ares said nothing to convince me. He simply asked me to stay with you and so I told him I would."

He did not know why her words disappointed him, or maybe he did. He wanted to hear that she'd returned because she loved him, because she could not stay away, not because his brother had asked her to babysit him until he was back to full strength.

"I am sorry he wasted your time, Selena. I do not need a nurse. I can get around on my own and the doctor said I should be nearly recovered by the end of the week."

"I know the bullet went clear through and hit nothing. You were very lucky, the damage was minimal." She walked over to the window and spread the draperies wider, allowing in more sunlight. "And I am glad to hear you do not need a nurse." She turned to face him. "Because you do not have one."

When he frowned in confusion, she smiled.

"I am here because you need me, Adonis, just as I need you." Her voice was soft, quiet. "There is nowhere else I'd rather be. I told you I would never leave you, Adonis, and I meant it."

He could not speak. The emotion in her eyes stole his voice. He wanted to believe her, wanted to trust her, but how many had he believed, trusted and loved, only to be abandoned and hurt? His parents, Rosalina, *Dieu…*

"Before we begin our day I think we should get you cleaned up." She strolled over to the bathroom. "Do you need help standing or walking?"

He shook his head as he planted his feet on the floor and stood. She disappeared into the bathroom when she saw for herself that he did not need her help walking. It took him a little longer than usual because he was still sore, but he made it to the adjoining bathroom. She'd left the door slightly ajar so he pushed it open then froze where he stood.

He turned to leave, but she easily brushed past him to close the door and lock it.

He growled out her name in warning.

"You do not want to fight me, Adonis, not in your current state."

His expression hardened, his heart ricocheted violently in his chest.

She began to remove her dress, then her high heels, and his heartbeat quickened for an entirely different reason.

Even as lust waged a war with his anger, he could not simply set the latter emotion aside.

He glared at her, then at the water filling up the tub, then back at her.

"You know how I feel about this. I told you so that you would understand, not so that you would use it against me."

Her eyes were soft, her palm against his chest gentle. He jerked away from her, but she was persistent. She would not let him retreat from her touch, not even when his back was pressed against the door.

"I do not know of all the people who have hurt you, but I have an idea. You loved them and then they took their love away and hurt you." She placed her other hand against his chest. "I will not take my love away, Adonis. And I swear on my life that I would die before I ever intentionally hurt you."

He tried to set her away from him, but she would not budge.

"I know you love me, but you will not say it. You will never say it until you face the demons of your past."

"I do not need therapy, Selena."

"You do, but lucky for you I am neither a nurse nor a therapist."

He was not amused by her coy retort or the twinkle in her eyes. He tried to push her away again, but, like before, she held fast, clinging to him.

"I want to make new memories for you, to chase away the old, just as you did for me."

When she looked at him like that, with soft eyes, and spoke to him with soft words, he was powerless against her. He was weak.

"You have asked what happened to my back many times." Her body tensed against his. "The night I ruined you, the night I refused to take your life, I returned to my chambers and bathed. I scrubbed my skin, desperately trying to erase what I'd done to you from my mind. In my bathtub is where your father found me. And then he took me to that same room beneath my father's house where he tortured me. He alternated between whipping me and using me for several hours. When he grew tired of one perversion, he would take up the other, until even that wasn't enough, and he began torturing me with flame and wax from a candle."

Her sob and the tears streaming down her face caused his gut to clench, but he refused to stop. Now that he'd begun he could not seem to stop. "My brothers found me and they threatened him until he was forced to release me. It took me weeks to heal physically. I thought my own father would at least be upset with him for ruining my value as one of his whores. Instead, my father was upset with *me* for not doing as I'd been instructed. My back had barely healed before *Dieu* beat me, for good measure, I suppose. I knew then I had to leave but he would not let me go without the one promise that I was never to contact you again, that I would never have anything to do with you again or you would die—a promise

Woodward was well aware of. I thought it strange that promising to never see you again would be the *one* thing to secure my freedom, but I kept it and gained my freedom. After my father died, I wanted to come to you but hesitated because of Woodward and my fear of what he would do to you if I broke my promise. I now realise our fathers wanted to keep us apart because it simply pleased them to know we were both in pain."

He stared down at her upturned face, expectant and full of hope. He did not want to disappoint her, but he had no choice.

"What I did to you that night I never forgot, just as I never forgot what was done to me—none of it. So do you understand now, Selena, why I cannot get into that tub?"

Something as simple as bathing and he could not do it. He could not sit down with her and pretend that every bitter memory of being wrenched from his bath and slowly abused and violated for an entire night did not resurface just from looking at the water sloshing back and forth.

She reached down to turn the knobs, shutting the water off. The tub appeared to have been filled to a fourth of its capacity. If he got in and sat down, the water would barely reach the sides of his thighs. It certainly would never cover him.

"When you took baths before, did anyone bathe you?"

He shook his head.

"Did they lather your skin in soap and rinse you with care?"

His throat tightened. "No."

"Did they straddle you and ride your cock while you held their hips?"

"Selena—"

"Did they, Adonis?"

"No."

"I cannot force you to get into this tub. I can only promise you that, if you do, I will give you new memories to replace the old." She stepped into the basin, the water just above her ankles.

Her eyes sparkled with lust as she sat down in the water, and with merriment when she parted her legs to drape one over the rim of the bath.

"Would you get in and sit between my thighs and let me wash you?"

He hesitated. Years of pain and bitter memories could not be erased in a moment, a day...even a lifetime.

She waited patiently, not prodding him further, not pushing.

He glanced down at her naked body, glistening wet and spread before him, then at the water roiling back and forth. There were maybe two inches of water in the basin.

He looked at her again and swallowed the knot in his throat.

Her eyes were patient, gentle and full of love. She reached out her hand. Droplets of water splashed to the floor. He took her fingers in his.

He'd vowed never to do this again.

He placed one foot into the tub, then the other. Once inside, he crouched down between her thighs and leant back until her breasts were flat against his back. She wrapped her arms around his chest and locked her legs around his hips.

For the first time in a long time, he felt safe, secure...loved.

Selena's hands were gentle as she ran the sponge across his back, his arms. She touched his scars with delicate fingers, tracing the ridges as soap trickled across his flesh. His body was tense against hers, vibrating with corded energy as if he would bolt at any moment.

But he didn't.

He gradually relaxed against her, settling deeper within the cave of her body.

"Do you remember the first time we met?" she asked, running the sponge across his back.

He turned. His golden mane was now a honey brown as it clung to his shoulders, dripping with water.

"I remember. It was at the Winter Cotillion." She could almost hear the smile in his voice when he spoke. "You were not to be introduced that year, but I still thought you were the most beautiful sight in the room."

She grinned at that. "Besides my twin sister, of course."

"No." His gaze was direct. "There was a fire in your eyes, a boldness in the way you carried yourself that intrigued me. An innocence to your mature beauty that appealed to me. But it was the sadness, the loneliness that I glimpsed which drew me to you and compelled me to ask you to dance."

"I thought it was your father, along with mine, who forced you to seek me out?"

His smile was faint. "No one needed to force me to fall for you, Selena."

He turned to face forward again, for which she was grateful. She did not want him to see the disappointment in her eyes. He had easily fallen for her—*that*, he would readily admit—but not that he'd fallen *in love* with her.

"Do you know what intrigued me the most about you?" she asked him.

He tilted his head, so she could see the side of his face, but he did not turn fully around.

"When you introduced yourself, I demanded to know your real name, but you refused. Until then, no one had ever told me *no*."

"*That* was what intrigued you the most?" He seemed surprised.

"Yes. Are you disappointed?"

"No, it's just that..." He hesitated and her brow puckered.

"What is it?"

Adonis shrugged. "Most have said it was my beauty that attracted them, or my handsomeness. My physique, perhaps. And several have been so bold as to acknowledge it was my reputation, but none have ever said it was my stubbornness."

"Would you rather I said those things?" she questioned, out of curiosity more than anything. His defiance had attracted her—she could not change what was true.

"No. I was simply surprised."

"Why?"

He leant back all the way so that his head rested against her shoulder. She cocked her head to stare down into his upturned face.

"I guess I was surprised that even back then you saw who I truly was, and not what you were supposed to see."

"And what was that? What was I supposed to see?"

"A man with the face of a god...but you have always seen only the man."

Adonis.

The man, the god.

He was just a man—with the same needs as any other, the same yearnings, the same weaknesses, the same desires.

Adonis.

He was just a man.

He spoke softly, and she leaned closer to hear the faint words when he repeated them.

She looked at him in bewilderment. "I do not under—"

"You wanted to know the name I was born with."

He closed his eyes, his head still resting against her shoulder and her heart did a tiny stutter.

"What would you prefer to be called? I mean, when we're alone like this." Her cheeks heated in embarrassment at the words she'd spoken without thinking. She'd just assumed they'd be alone like this again—that there would be many more times...

His eyes snapped open and she waited, her breath stilling.

"Adonis."

She exhaled. "Even though Adonis is not your real name and with it comes the weight of so many painful memories?"

"The boy I was before I became Adonis is long dead. He does not exist anymore." He closed his eyes again. "It is simply enough that you know who he was, who I once was. That you will mourn for a boy who died long ago, when no one else will."

She closed her eyes and willed herself not to cry even as the tears burned the back of her throat. He was right.

She did mourn for the boy who'd died years ago, whose death no one knew of but her.

But she also mourned for the man who'd been born, the man she now held, who'd died many deaths. The man who everyone thought a god.

Adonis.

A god he was not. Just a man with the same needs, the same yearnings, the same weaknesses and desires as any another man.

She trailed a series of kisses along the back of his neck and across his shoulders, until his skin warmed beneath her lips. He tilted his head at the same time as she dipped hers, and their lips met in a gentle, searching kiss. Their breath mingled, as intertwined as their bodies, and she clung to him, enveloping him within the circle of her thighs, her arms.

His tongue probed, then forged deep, filling her...branding her. She moaned into his mouth, desperately wanting him to take her body as deeply and fully as he now claimed her mouth.

She pulled back, gently separating their lips. He looked at her curiously when she stood. His eyes darkened with lust, with fervent desire, when she stepped from the tub only to climb back in to straddle his hips, with her back facing him.

She settled in his lap, her bottom nuzzling the engorged length of his cock that continued to thicken against her. He held her hips, his fingers digging into her flesh.

She turned and held his gaze, her eyes trained on him as she slowly lowered herself onto him, sinking onto his cock inch by inch.

Her muscles tightened around him as desire warmed her core, causing him to ease further inside her slick, tight tunnel. A deep, sexual hunger stirred in her belly, the pulsing, pounding rhythm of pleasure and need filling her and warming her. She gasped when she rocked against him, taking him to the hilt until he was buried deep and tight inside her wet passage.

He groaned—a harsh, soul-stirring sound that made her stomach clench and her toes curl. Her body began to move as if it had its own mind and its own desires. She yielded to her body's demands as she engulfed his cock, up and down, shallow and deep.

Adonis held her firmly, jerking her on his length at the same time as she impaled herself atop him. They moved in unison, their bodies a harmonious blending of lust and desire, their sighs of pleasure weaving together, filling up every space within the room.

He held her writhing, pumping body to him as he slowly slid his palm along her belly to cup the mound of her breast. She drew in a sharp breath when he tugged on her nipple, sending bolts of pleasure sizzling and slicing through her until she was panting, dripping with sweat that beaded across her body, mingling with the droplets of water that also clung to her skin.

Adonis' breath suddenly became shallow and she looked at him again from over her shoulder, her gaze caressing him. His eyes were hooded, drowsy with lust. The longing in their depths called to her, fuelled her until she was riding his cock wildly, heedless of the water sloshing, of the creaking of the tub, of the soreness that would surely creep inside her body by morning.

All that mattered was his pleasure.

And hers.

Their eyes met, and a jolt of energy arced between them, scorching them both. She was powerless to stop what came next and she didn't want to. Her lips parted, but no sound came out, not a word as her muscles clenched around him, then her cunt flooded with juice, drenching him until he was coated with her desire.

She shuddered violently, coming on a long, endless wave of pleasure. He joined her in her bliss with a hoarse shout of pleasure as he poured himself into her, holding her locked to him, her body imprisoned within his grasp.

He called her name and on a breathless moan he shattered her heart with the only words that could break her apart and then mend her back together again.

Tears clogged her throat as he healed her with his trust…his love.

When he was spent, his body weary, his gaze captured hers and she lost herself in the warmth of his eyes, the closeness of his body.

His arms tugged her to him, and with his soft member still inside her she rested against his chest, letting him wrap his strong arms around her, as she'd done with him just moments ago.

She burrowed deeper into his embrace, listening to the beating of his heart, the steady rhythm of his breathing.

With one hand, he pushed aside her wet hair and kissed her neck, then called her name, and the words that she'd feared would be locked inside him for eternity flowed effortlessly from him again.

I love you…

"I love you too," she whispered, closing her eyes, and, for the first time in a long time, she felt safe, secure and loved—because she knew that she was. And now the man she'd loved forever—and always would—knew the same.

About the Author

Nadia Aidan lives, works and writes on the West Coast in the United States. Under her real name, Nadia holds a PhD in Political Science and Public Policy and by day she works as an Assistant Professor.

She writes across all genres, from historical, to fantasy/sci-fi to contemporary. In addition to writing erotic romances Nadia enjoys reading other authors, playing flag football, studying muay thai, working out, listening to music, scuba diving, and target shooting.

Her other interests include collecting Top Cow comics, especially Witchblade and Tomb Raider. She loves professional football and soccer. Her favorite teams are the Washington Redskins and Manchester United, respectively.

Nadia loves watching, reading about, and writing about strong, assertive heroines which is why she is an enduring fan of Fight Girls, Xena, Buffy, American Gladiators—New and Old, and La Femme Nikita!

Nadia also loves interacting with people so feel free to visit her at http://www.nadiaaidan.com for more information about her and her new releases.

Nadia Aidan loves to hear from readers. You can find her contact information, website details and author profile page at http://www.total-e-bound.com.

Total-E-Bound Publishing

www.total-e-bound.com

Take a look at our exciting range of literagasmic™
erotic romance titles and discover pure quality
at Total-E-Bound.